SKYBOUND

LOU IOVINO

For my parents

PART I

1

LUMINESCENT STARCHES SLOWLY DRIFTED to the bottom of the cell membranes like tiny bits of white plastic in a snow globe. The laws of gravitropism held fast even in the microgravity of the space station. And no matter how Yanez Prescott twisted or turned her subject, doing her best to confound it, the tomato plant from New Jersey circling hundreds of miles above its native soil always figured out which way was up and which way was down, its roots determined to seek out the darkness of the Earth and its shoots ever rising toward the sun. Just as nature had intended since the very beginning of it all.

Yanez rubbed her watery eyes and forced herself to take one last look through the dual eyepieces of the Light Microscopy Module. She'd been at it a long time, but in a few weeks, she'd be rotating off the station, and she was behind on her experiments. Every day was critical, especially when splitting time with Anatoly and his zero-gravity combustion project. Both of them were in a race against the clock, and neither winning.

"Root cap sample twelve positive for graviresponse," she said into the terminal's microphone, getting the words out just before a jaw-cracking yawn.

Every square inch of the Destiny Module was optimized to

hold as much scientific equipment as possible. This made the trips between workstations pretty short, but Yanez still loved gliding back and forth, if only to remind herself of where she was and what she was doing and the specialness of it all. She pushed off gently to maximize the float time, closed her eyes, and let herself drift in the early morning silence, sleep a wolf at the door of her consciousness. Luckily, her aim was true and she bumped into the Glovebox just as she started to drift off.

Yanez pushed back to an arm's length and slid her right foot into the metal floor anchor at the base of the clear plastic chamber. Black latex gloves hung from the two openings on the front of the box like socks from a shower rod. It took her several tries to align her fingers with the inside-out tips of the gloves' five slots, but with a great deal of effort and a few curses aimed at everyone from Charles Darwin, the first person to postulate the role of gravity on plant growth, to NASA, for making her run the damn botany experiments in addition to all her other duties as mission leader, she managed to get everything just right and push one hand and then the other through the airtight openings.

Inside the box, the tomato plant was clamped horizontally, its stem just beginning to reach upward.

"No fooling you, huh, pal?"

Yanez twisted open the jaws of the device holding the root ball. She let the plant float as she reset the angle, little clumps of dirt breaking loose from the mesh-covered ball and orbiting the dark green leaves and tiny budding tomatoes. The plant kissed the side of the Glovebox, its stem gently bending then recoiling, spinning it off on a new course. Yanez swiveled the apparatus to its new angle, one that would set the roots above the main stem but would predictably yield the same results as the previous dozen angles, and prepared to lock experiment number 13 into place.

The digital display indicated it was 02:30 CST—only a few hours before Houston would get going. Once she secured the plant she'd have to grab a few hours in her rack. Their last data transfer had stalled, and mission control was hot to send up procedures for an OS patch. This would lead to hours of reboots and troubleshooting, as it always did, and she'd wilt under control's scrutiny if she didn't get some sleep first.

Inside the chamber, the little plant ricocheted off the back wall and slowly angled toward Yanez's waiting hand. But just as it grazed her latex fingertips, it shot upward and smacked against the top of the chamber. The station shuddered, groaned, and popped. Equipment snapped loose. The sudden jolt knocked her foot out of the floor anchor and sent her spinning, along with anything not buckled down or tied in place. She flailed and floated, eventually coming to a halt against the opposite wall when her chin caught the corner of a payload rack. She used a mooring strap to pull herself upright, and paused to listen to the receding clamor.

The echoes faded and silence returned. But it was a different silence. A thick and unctuous one, sticky with anticipation and fear. Yanez's pulse pounded in her ears. Beads of blood from her lacerated chin floated in the air. Then the red emergency lights flared to life and Susan's voice rang out over the intercom.

"Commander, do you copy?"

Yanez kicked off the wall and floated back toward the microscopy unit, pushing a thick spiral-bound manual and coil of copper tubing out of her way. She grabbed a handrail alongside the monitor and keyed the mic.

"Susan, are you okay?"

"What the hell's going on?"

"I don't know," Yanez said as she worked to pull up station status on the computer. "Stand by."

She squinted at the screen, confused by the readout. Alarms had been triggered in every module, and two of the solar panels were off their angles, but there was no sign of rapid decompression anywhere, which was the only thing that could have caused that sort of sudden movement.

"It wasn't a bolide strike," she said. "A solar flare doesn't make any sense. That would have never—"

"Oh my God!" Susan shrieked. "That's impossible!"

"What's happening?"

"Yanez, I need you! Please come!"

"Susan, slow down," Yanez said, trying to mask the anxiety in her voice. "Tell me where you are."

"Zvezda. I'm in Zvezda."

Yanez kicked off the terminal and shot toward the open hatch leading to the main body of the station. She left a red trail of blood in the air as she propelled herself through the nodes connecting the Destiny Lab to the Zvezda Service Module, which was on the extreme end of the Russian section of the ISS. Emergency lights swirled around her as she swam through a sea of detritus—books and magazines, tools and wiring, a computer tablet and a baseball, all hanging in the zero gravity of the wounded station.

A sharp clang rang out ahead of her as she flung herself through the hatch leading into the Multipurpose Lab. On the opposite side, Anatoly was striking the handle to the Zvezda Module with a wrench.

"Is she okay?" Yanez asked between Anatoly's strikes.

"She stopped talking."

"What does that mean?"

"It means we need to open this fucking hatch," he said, letting the wrench float away and leaning his weight into the handle.

Yanez moved next to him and grabbed the handle's other end. Bracing themselves, they twisted in unison. The sound of metal grinding inside the damaged mechanism set their teeth on edge, but after a few heaves they managed to throw the bolt, and the door popped open.

Food pouches and clothes drifted everywhere inside the module. A floating puddle of liquid morphed into different shapes. Susan sat underneath it all, beneath the galley table, her arms and legs wrapped around the center support, muttering to herself, seemingly unaware that Anatoly and Yanez were there.

"Are you hurt?" Yanez called out as she shot across the space between them. She used the galley table to slow down and then swung herself under it to Susan. "I'm here," she said, gently touching the woman's arm to break her trance.

Susan flinched, and then recognition dawned in her eyes. She clawed at Yanez's arm to draw her in closer, as if desperate for her boss to make everything right again.

"Tell me what's happening," Yanez said. She used the same neutral tone of voice she used when asking for Susan's shift reports, hoping it'd get her crewmate talking.

"It's over," Susan said.

"What's over?"

"The sheer force of it."

"Of what?"

"Everything's gone. All of it."

Yanez shook her head. "Susan, I don't understand what you're saying. Start from the beginning. What happened?"

But before Susan could answer, Anatoly Semenov, as stoic and solid a cosmonaut as was ever manufactured in the Russian space program, screamed.

Yanez spun around and pushed off too hard from the table, colliding with Anatoly, which had the merciful effect of stopping his horrendous cries. She turned to face him and saw only pure animal terror in his eyes, froth collecting in the corners of his mouth, spittle dotting his beard. She couldn't reconcile the terrified man before her with the man she'd journeyed to space with eight months ago, the one she'd come to rely on for his reason and rationality.

She couldn't make sense of any of it.

Until she turned and looked through the window.

2

THOUSANDS of tiny red dots zipped and zoomed above the world like electrons around a blue-and-white marbled nucleus. The ones closest to the planet circled quickly, the ones farther out more slowly. But if you stared at them long enough, all the little dots combined and created a solid, glowing band encircling the globe, a halo of light that shielded the Earth and all of its people from the darkness beyond.

"This is the way we like it," Noel Williams said, pointing to the image projected on the white wall behind her. "Everything has its place up there and we work hard down here to make sure it stays that way."

The group of local high schoolers watched the blur of thousands of satellites.

"How can you tell if it's right?" asked one of the students at the front of the pack, his head tilted to the side, struggling to find order in the chaos. "Everything is moving around so fast and all over the place."

"It seems that way. But it's actually all very orderly," Noel said, walking from the front of the room to where the students had gathered at the central console. "Let me show you."

The kids moved aside so she could take her seat at the

computer terminal. She pulled the keyboard toward her and switched the display to show a large constellation of geostationary satellites over North America.

"We know that the shape of the Earth's equator, gravitational pressures from the sun and moon, and other factors impact satellite positioning. But we can compensate for these things. Does anyone know how?"

The silence was predictable. A few kids giggled. Most just looked at one another, waiting to see who would be dorky enough to say something. Then a small voice answered from a step or two off to the side.

"What was that?" Noel asked, waving the girl over.

Everything about the teen seemed old, from her army-green backpack to her jeans and black canvas sneakers, all of it faded from use and years as opposed to fashion. She hesitated, twisting one of her many braids and silently pleading to be allowed to stay put with sharp, expressive eyes that probably spent far too much time aimed at the floor. But when Noel didn't relent, the girl finally sighed and stepped forward.

"Umm, engines or thrusters," she said. "Some sort of propulsion, probably?"

"Precisely. Ion thrusters, to be exact."

Noel leaned back in her chair, folded her legs, and weaved her fingers together behind her head.

"It's called orbital stationkeeping. Right here from this terminal, we can track satellite drift and make adjustments as needed to keep everything in order." She rocked back and forth, creating a metronomic squeak. "Pretty awesome, huh?"

A couple of the kids gave genuine nods of approval. They were the ones she'd talk to at the end of the field trip about summer internships. Their teacher, Ms. Collins, who was in her first year and hoping to impress both the kids and Noel, tried really hard to spur engagement from the others, but no dice.

"Okay, it's not really *that* cool, I guess," Noel said after a beat. "But it's one of the primary functions of this military facility. And if we didn't do it, you wouldn't be able to message each other fifty times an hour or binge YouTube."

She stood up and rested her hand on the thruster girl's thin shoulder. "Aster," she said, reading the sticker on the girl's gray t-shirt. "Wanna have some fun?"

"Sure, why not," Aster said, as if trying on cool and confident for a fleeting moment and squirming at the ill-fitting nature of it. Noel relinquished control of the chair to the awkward teen and gave her a don't-worry-it-gets-better smile.

Noel opened the daily logbook that was resting next to the screen and read out a set of coordinates as she strode back to the front of the room. Aster punched in the numbers, and the display changed to a depiction of twelve satellites, tightly organized in three rows of four within a green, glowing rhombus.

"This cluster of communications satellites handles television, cell phone, and internet traffic for most of the midwestern United States. We recently discovered that one of them is off by almost a half degree," Noel said, pointing to the declination readout next to the bottom-right red dot.

"Does that really make a difference?" asked Ms. Collins. "A half degree?"

"Absolutely," Noel said. "Any change, even a tiny one, is unacceptable."

She coached Aster through a quick set of commands, which the teen dutifully executed. When she was finished, a dialogue box appeared in the upper left of the display, asking for confirmation of the orbital maneuver that would adjust the rogue satellite's position.

The group tightened around Aster, who was struggling to contain her grin. Noel wondered what was more exciting for her, the telemetry instrumentation in front of her or the boys hanging on her shoulders to see the screen.

"Aster, you're about to move an object that's flying twenty-two thousand miles above our heads. Are you ready?" Noel asked.

"Ready," Aster said, her index finger poised above the enter key.

"Go for it."

Aster pressed the button, and the dialogue box disappeared. The misaligned satellite's initial declination of -0.42 degrees began to decrease, the numbers steadily climbing toward zero. The display refreshed every few seconds, showing the glowing red dot slowly rejoining its partners in the rhomboid constellation. It was all going very smoothly, exactly as designed. And then the satellite reached -0.06 degrees, and it wasn't anymore or ever again.

A thunderous, metallic clap exploded through the air. The enormity of it displaced all thought, like a child's rubber boots throwing water from a puddle after a mighty leap. Everyone in the control room was enveloped in sound that bounced from ceiling to floor to wall and back again. They were frozen, transfixed, short-circuited.

And then the building heaved and rolled.

People were tossed in all directions. The power snuffed out. Screams and cries filled the air as the echo from the massive boom slowly faded away.

Then came the silence.

No one moved in the darkness, trapped in a cold fear. Noel shouted for everyone to stay where they were until the base's emergency systems kicked in. An agonizing minute later, they did.

"I didn't do anything, I swear," Aster said, untangling herself from the chair. "I did exactly what you told me to do."

Noel made her way to the center console and gave Aster a quick once-over, finding only a few scrapes. Clouds of dust billowed down from holes in the ceiling and mixed with the red emergency lighting, making it hard to determine where all of the kids were in the room.

"Is anyone hurt?" Noel yelled.

"Ms. Collins is gushing blood!" said one of the kids from the back.

Noel and Aster ran to where a few kids were gathered around their unconscious teacher, one of them holding a wad of tissues to the woman's forehead. Noel knelt down and slowly lifted the boy's hand away, revealing a deep gash that was pulsing blood. She lowered the kid's hand to the wound once more and put some pressure on the back of it, encouraging him to do the same.

"You're doing a good job," she said to the ashen student with tears in his eyes as he watched his teacher's blood spill out over his knuckles. "Just keep up that pressure."

The rest of the class pushed in tight to get a look.

"I think she's going to be okay," Noel said, making eye contact with as many kids as she could. "Is everyone else all right?"

They all nodded. A few held each other.

"Hey, look," Aster said, pointing toward the front of the room, which was still illuminated by the projector. It had been knocked out of alignment, its image now crooked on the cracked and crumbling wall, and glowing lines of startup code had appeared. A system reboot. When the sequence ended, the satellite constellation returned.

But what the system showed was an impossibility.

The satellites were drifting beyond the green rhombus that had been their home ever since they were launched fourteen years earlier.

Noel stared in disbelief, expecting the computer to recalculate their locations and return the skies to normal. But her disbelief soon turned to a growing fear. For with each display interval, the satellites drifted farther away from their appointed places in the universe.

3

DUST motes shimmered and glowed as they caught the sunlight streaming through the tiny diamond pattern of the confessional screen. They danced and swirled to the perfect four-four meter of "Morning Purples All the Sky" as played by Theresa Donnelly, the freckled teen and fourth-generation Franklinite with boatloads of musical promise according to all who heard her play at Franklin High's Spring and Christmas recitals or the 8:00 a.m. and 9:30 a.m. services on Sundays. A bright future that one, for sure.

But it was a Thursday. And like every Thursday since he'd taken over St. Anne's from Father Morgan—who had decided to flee the Colorado cold and retire to Boca Raton after thirty-five years of service to the faithful of Franklin—Father Michael Williams listened to Theresa practice and waited for those who needed to unburden themselves by confessing their transgressions to God.

And like every Thursday, no one came.

It hadn't been an easy transition. The town loved Father Morgan. He'd baptized many of them, and then many of their children too. Hell, he'd baptized Michael himself. Everyone missed him.

Michael knew that. He understood it. Which was why, last

Christmas, his first Christmas as head priest, he'd tried to make a statement. A bright line to indicate that a new era had begun. He could never be Father Morgan, couldn't hope to be; he could only be Father Williams.

Father Morgan had always approached Christmas the same way. He would preach about the Christmas Miracle, the twinkling lights, the wise men and the star in the sky. Very traditional. So Michael thought that the best way to establish himself as Franklin's new spiritual leader was to be . . . provocative. Instead of limiting his sermons to Mary and Joseph and the Savior born, he spoke to the full house at St. Anne's about other celebrations, too —like Chanukah and Kwanza, even Festivus. It was a message of change, a larger worldview. It was hip. Funny. It was a new way of looking at faith and the gospel. An opportunity for them all to begin anew and with a new perspective.

Except . . . it didn't go well.

The people wanted talk of lights and stars. They wanted the little wee baby in the manger and Bing Crosby in their hearts. They didn't want to hear about the world, about other celebrations. They didn't want to explore new definitions or challenge their thinking. They didn't want change, period. Franklin liked what it liked. Change . . . that was for other folks.

Theresa was nearing her finish. The organ soared to the exact same heights as last week and the week before that, and Michael knew the appointed time for forgiveness was almost gone. But then he heard footsteps.

He grabbed his stole, quickly kissed it, and draped it over his shoulders in preparation. His anticipation rose as the confessional door opposite his chamber opened and the penitent sat down with a heavy thud. Surely a person so weighty in disposition must be carrying an equally heavy burden.

Then the telltale click-flick of a Zippo, and Michael's excitement evaporated.

"Bless me, Father, for I have sinned. It has been four weeks since my last confession."

"Seven," Michael said.

"Okay fine. Seven. Don't bust my balls."

The filter end of a cigarette poked through the screen. Michael grabbed it, settled back against the wall of the confessional, and took a long drag.

"I gotta get out of this town, Father. It's gonna kill me."

"Have you prayed for guidance, my son?"

"Don't give me that God-will-show-you-the-way shit, Mike. I mean it this time."

Michael took another long drag and then pushed the cigarette back through the screen.

"I've heard this song from you before. Shit or get off the pot already."

"Thanks for the stellar advice, Father Williams. You're a true spiritual guide."

"There's a plan for all of us, Jimmy. Even a dumbass like you." Michael waved away the wisps of smoke on his side. "Now, about that confession?"

"Too much booze. An awful lot of cussing. Some porn. You know, the usual."

With the air somewhat clear on his side and maybe a little bit on Jimmy's side too, Michael stepped out of the confessional. Jimmy followed with the butt clenched in his teeth, adjusting his holster.

"What's my penance?"

"Coffee and pie. You're buying."

Red, blue, green, and gold ribbons of light streamed from the stained glass above the altar and painted the church's original oak buttresses, blackened by the fire of 1937 but still solid to the core. When they reached the center aisle, Michael bowed to the altar and made the sign of the cross. Jimmy averted his eyes from the light show, perhaps because of its brilliance, perhaps because Theresa's playing punctuated what some might take as divinity or providence—or, at the very least, something pretty special happening with the sun.

"We're going across to the Biscuit," Michael yelled above the organ. "Lock up when you're through."

"Sure thing, Father Williams," Theresa said, switching from near dirge to *vivacissimo* and then back again as she watched them walk down the aisle and exit.

"That girl's a strange one."

"She's just very dedicated to her art," Michael said as they crossed the street to the Crispy Biscuit Diner.

"Never saw a sixteen-year-old spend that much time in church on purpose."

"Wish others around here would. Be nice to boost the take in the collection plate. We need that roof before winter."

The street was quiet. The regular line-up of municipal trucks and local contractors was parked outside the diner. Most everyone else in town worked at the nearby airbase or at the big distribution center in Colorado Springs.

The bell above the door dinged their arrival. Michael and Jimmy both said their hellos and then slid into their regular booth. Rose smiled and gave them a just-a-minute nod without breaking stride.

Rose was as much a fixture here as the leather booths and the black-and-white checkered floor. Ever since he was a kid, Michael's family had been having lunch at the diner every Sunday after church. And every Sunday Rose would give him an extra pickle with his sandwich. Even now, despite his having graduated from grilled cheeses to more adult staples like the Reuben or turkey club, the extra pickle was always there.

Michael watched Rose move about the diner, checking on all of her regulars, filling coffee mugs, trading smiles, pecking old friends from Franklin High on their stubbly cheeks, getting caught up on the gossip, and spreading it around in equal measure. Her orange-and-red sunbeam hair was a tempest atop her head and second in vibrancy only to her fire-engine-red heels, impractical in their design but a perfect calling card for Rose. This was her *Swan Lake*, and she was its prima ballerina.

"You boys up to no good?" she asked as she flipped over their mugs and filled them with coffee.

"Yes, ma'am," Jimmy said, lifting his mug in a little toast to her.

"Bruce make the banana today?" Michael asked.

"No, sweetie. Bananas were still too damn green. We got peach, though," she said, nodding enthusiastically, vouching for the pie's merits as an equally delicious option to the banana, which everyone knew was a lie.

"That sounds great. And make it a big one. Jimmy's buying."

Rose scribbled the order on her pad and had just turned to go when the concussive wave of a sound like lightning striking iron crashed through the diner. The noise rippled all around, so loud that afterwards many of them would swear they'd felt it on their skin and tasted it in their mouths. The building shuddered and jumped. The Biscuit's patrons let out a collective shriek. Plates, cups, ketchup bottles, and silverware clattered to the ground. People tumbled from their booths or flew from their cushioned perches at the counter, leaving streaks of blood and burgers in their wake. Even the great glass pie case rattled right off the counter, dumping fresh blueberry, rhubarb, and strawberry delights all over Edith McKenzie, reuniting the pastries with their distant cousins that had made Edith's lap so generous a landing zone.

The boom faded slowly, and the building settled. People scurried beneath tables and toward the corners of the diner, looking for any sort of shelter, not knowing whether the trouble, whatever it had been, was past.

Rose stepped over broken plates and menus to the window facing the street. A few people outside the diner were crouched on the sidewalk, shielding their heads, and a car had jumped the curb just down the street, which now featured a deep crevice up its center. She scanned left and right, searching for what might have caused all hell to break loose, but saw nothing.

Then she looked up.

"My God! What is *that*?"

Michael ran over, and she pointed up at the sky, the same big bright sky he'd lived underneath his whole life. The same sky he'd look to for answers and inspiration in good times and in bad. He'd always found so much peace and majesty in the Colorado heavens. But today, and for all the rest of his days, all he found were questions.

4

"SEE FOR YOURSELF," Anatoly said.

His momentary lapse of reason was behind him and the analytical and evidence-based prowess that made him and his entire family some of Russia's premier scientific thinkers was once again front and center.

"The Earth's crust appears to be completely intact and the atmosphere is clean. What other evidence do you need?"

"I know, but it doesn't make any sense," said Susan. She was trying to access the tracking and data relay network through one of the computer terminals. "Think of the rotational forces alone. Stopping it that fast would be like ripping the peel off an orange."

"That's enough," said Yanez, cutting off the speculation. "What's our location?"

Susan checked her watch. "We should be coming up on Ecuador in a few minutes."

"Have you been able to get anyone on the ground? Canaveral, or maybe Indra?"

"I can't even connect to the network. Maybe our main antenna was damaged?"

"Can you run diagnostics from here?"

"On it," said Susan, pecking away at the keyboard.

Yanez turned to Anatoly, who was already in motion, having anticipated her directive. He floated toward one of the other terminals that hadn't been knocked offline during the convulsions that ripped through the station.

"Scan for anomalies or energy signatures," she said, happy to have her rock back. "Look for anything outside norms for the last forty-eight to seventy-two hours. And make sure to include Earth-side and surrounding territory data. I want to see the whole picture."

Yanez floated over to the nadir window. A thick layer of clouds the color of cotton candy stretched across the sky below.

"I've never been to South America," she said, hoping to lighten the mood a bit while her crew worked. "I always wanted to go. See a soccer game in Brazil or hike in the Andes."

"Why didn't you?" Susan asked.

"Got the flight bug and joined the navy. But I almost went the summer after high school. A friend of mine was an exchange student. Her family ran a hotel right on the beach in Montevideo and they were looking for help."

Just then the clouds cleared down below and all Yanez saw was the deep blue of the Pacific.

"I thought you said we were coming up on Ecuador."

"Should be over it right now," Susan said.

Yanez stared down at the ocean, running the numbers in her head even though Susan was always spot on. At just under sixteen full rotations a day, it was pretty easy to know where they were at any given time. She did the math, and that's when it hit her like a thunderbolt. Her sharp intake of breath got the attention of both crewmates.

"Commander, what's wrong?" Susan asked.

"Did you run the diagnostics?"

"They're almost done."

"And?"

The progress bar filled and the results popped onto Susan's screen. She leaned in closer, trying to make sense of the readout.

"It says the antenna is operating within normal parameters."

Yanez immediately kicked off the wall and shot straight out of the module. Anatoly and Susan exchanged worried glances, then followed her.

Yanez propelled herself through the ISS, pulling on everything within arm's reach, anything that could get her to the Unity Module faster. By the time she arrived, she was moving so fast she tweaked her shoulder when she grabbed the edge of the main global positioning and satellite control rack. She winced as she pulled herself in front of the screen and got to work.

"What's happening here?" Anatoly asked when he and Susan caught up to her a minute later. But Yanez was consumed with swiping and typing and muttering.

Her crew floated up behind her and watched, afraid to interrupt, like waking a sleepwalker. Finally, Susan risked it and put a hand on her boss's shoulder.

"Yanez, what are you looking for?"

Before Yanez could answer, the screen switched from lines of scrolling code to a planetary display, including a depiction of the ISS's orbit.

"Is our heading off?" Anatoly asked. "Should I start plotting a correction?"

"We can't correct for what's happening," Yanez said, pushing away from the display.

"Has the orbital decay accelerated?" Anatoly asked, immediately taking up Yanez's spot at the rack, ready to fire the thrusters or blow a seal to re-establish them at 360 kilometers above the planet, anything necessary to get them back to where they were supposed to be.

Yanez put a hand on his arm. "Susan wasn't able to reach the relay network because the satellites aren't there anymore," she said.

"What do you mean?" Susan asked. "What happened to them?"

"Same thing that's happening to us."

The look in Anatoly's eyes told Yanez that he understood. But Susan was still confused, her eyes darting back and forth between her two crewmates.

"We're not falling toward Earth," Yanez explained. "We're flying off into space."

5

NOEL'S FINGERS flew over the keyboard. She made the data appear on the wall as bar charts, pivot tables, and 3D graphs. But no matter how they were displayed, the data always said the same thing.

All of Earth's satellites had broken free of their orbits and were accelerating away from the planet.

"What's happening, Ms. Williams?"

Noel looked up at Aster, who kept her distance a few steps away. Behind her, the rest of the teens were still gathered around their unconscious teacher. Once separated by cool and uncool, popular and not, nerd and burnout, at that moment they were united by one thing: terror. And their wide eyes all looked to Noel for help.

"Not sure yet. But we'll figure it out," she said, loud enough so everyone could hear, then shrugged in a fashion she hoped showed a lack of concern.

"I can't get a signal," one of the girls said, holding up her phone for Noel to see. Others confirmed the same.

Noel glanced at the latest projection on the wall—a scatterplot bisected by a sharp, upward-bending trendline indicating the speed at which the untethered satellites were fleeing Earth's grasp. With a great deal of effort, she averted her gaze, stood up from the terminal, took Aster's clammy hand, and rejoined the kids gathered around Ms. Collins.

Kneeling down, she peeked underneath the shirt they'd wrapped around the teacher's head to slow the bleeding. The wound still oozed, but more slowly than before. Ms. Collins's eyes fluttered when Noel cinched the shirt down again, but they didn't open.

"You typically don't want to move someone who has a head injury," Noel said. "But I think she's going to be okay, and I'd rather not stay here. So we're going to go to the base's emergency rally point. Okay?"

The kids all nodded vigorously, anxious to get out of the building.

"You three," she said, pointing to the nearest boys, including the shirtless jock who had sacrificed his Foo Fighters concert swag to serve as Ms. Collins's bandage. "Let's pick her up."

Ms. Collins was slight and no more than five feet tall, so the teens were able to hoist her off the ground with ease. She let out a small groan when they lifted her, but then fell silent again. Noel did a quick headcount to confirm she had them all, and then led the group out of the control room.

The underground corridors of the satellite operations center had been lined with large paintings of the Colorado landscape and early black-and-white portraits of Peterson Air Base as it was being built in the 1950s. Not a single one of these decorations had survived the ordeal. The jagged shards of glass and splintered frames had mixed with broken ceiling tiles and chunks of drywall to create a dangerous path to the north stairwell. Dust continued to spill from the exposed ceiling, the cascade illuminated in emergency-light red.

Noel looked back at the teens. "Show me your feet," she said. "Who has sturdy shoes?"

The confused teens held up legs for Noel's inspection. She moved through the group and chose a few of the kids who were wearing heavy, protective boots.

"You're up front with me," she said. "We need to clear a path for everyone else."

"I can help too," said Aster.

"Not this time," Noel said, pointing at Aster's beat-up sneakers. "Your feet would be cut to ribbons by the time we got out of here."

The kids at the front used their boots to brush aside the broken glass and worked together to move larger impediments. The going was slow but steady, and soon they were turning the corner to the stairwell that would get them to the lobby.

But there they stopped short. Sparks flew from a fluorescent light fixture that swung back and forth dangerously close to a growing pool of water from a fountain lying on its side. Spray arched through the air and dribbled off the exit sign above the stairwell door. There was no way Noel was taking a bunch of kids through such an obvious electrocution hazard.

She put on a calm face, ignoring the images of the escaping satellites replaying on a loop in her head, and turned back to the group. "We can't go this way," she said. "But that's okay. We'll just take the south stairs."

She checked on Ms. Collins and the three boys carrying her, who confirmed they were doing fine. She could tell they were scared though, as were all the rest of the kids, so she made sure to touch a shoulder or squeeze a hand as she moved through the pack.

They backtracked past the control room and took the opposite corridor. The debris along this route was worse, and as Noel and the others shoved aside the rubble, several of the students had coughing fits from the decades of dust and aerosolized plaster that filled the air. This was a much older section of the building.

"Breathe through your shirts if you can," Noel yelled to the kids, pulling her own shirt up over her nose and mouth. "We're almost there."

The emergency lights were out here, so they were forced to navigate the final stretch by the glow of cell phones. They reached the south stairwell, only to encounter yet another obstacle. There was a jagged fissure in the wall above the exit, bending the door frame. As a result, the door was jammed within it, and wouldn't open.

"It's all right," Noel said as the sniffling started. "We can make this work."

She waved forward the shirtless jock, who handed off Ms. Collins, and another kid with Popeye forearms. "See if you can get your fingers underneath and lift while I turn the handle," she said.

The kids squirmed their fingers under the door and managed to lift it an inch or so, but not enough for the latch to disengage, no matter how hard Noel twisted the handle.

"How about we wedge something under it and use it as a lever?" said the jock.

"Umm, no. Wait a second," Aster said. She threw her backpack down, unzipped the main compartment, and started rooting through it.

"You got a car jack in there?" the jock asked.

Aster ignored him and kept rooting around, eventually fishing out a pair of Fiskars.

"When I say go, lift," she said, putting the pointed end of the scissors on the bottom of the door's upper hinge pin. "Ready?"

The boys got back in position.

"Go!"

They lifted the door again while Aster gave the bottom end of the scissors a whack with the palm of her hand. The hinge pin moved upward just a bit.

"Again! Go!"

After a few more attempts, the hinge had popped up enough for Noel to twist it free. Then they repeated the process on the bottom hinge pin. When it too was freed, it took only a hard, sharp yank to remove the door from its frame. They set it aside, gaining access to the stairwell.

"Good thinking," Noel said to a beaming Aster, offering her a fist bump. "Almost makes up for you breaking outer space."

The kids once again arranged themselves behind Noel and her newly christened deputy, and they headed up the stairs to the lobby.

Like the rest of the building, it was a mess. The huge windows that ran from the first to the third level of the complex were completely shattered, their blue-gray tempered glass scattered like marbles across the tiled floor. Signs, chairs, and plants were fallen and broken. And the people who had gathered there hadn't fared much better; they were arranged in small groups, some holding split foreheads and broken limbs. Base security had already arrived, helping the wounded and hustling everyone else, including Noel's group, out of the building.

As they stepped outside, an ambulance from the base hospital screeched to a stop. Two medics leapt from the back and immediately spotted Ms. Collins. One of them headed straight over while the other rushed inside.

"Has she been out the whole time?" the medic asked, taking a look under the blood-drenched T-shirt.

"Yeah," nearly all the kids confirmed at once.

"What happened?" Noel asked.

"We don't know yet," the medic said, flashing a light into Ms. Collins's right eye. "There's something—"

He was cut off by a loudspeaker squelch, then a broadcast instructing all personnel to immediately move to the rally points. As the echo from the announcement faded, Ms. Collins let out a soft groan.

"All right," said the medic to the three boys carrying their teacher, "you come with me. The rest of you need to get over to the parking lot right away." He pointed in the general direction.

"I'm not a chaperone or anything," Noel said. "I work here on base."

"Great, then you know where to go," the medic said, dismissing Noel as he helped the boys load Ms. Collins into the ambulance.

Noel waited for the boys to return before moving on. Despite what she had said to the medic, she *was* a chaperone now that Ms. Collins was unconscious. For the moment at least, she was responsible for these teens.

She led them across the cracked and crumbled asphalt to a growing group ahead of them. As they got closer, Noel noticed that everyone was looking in the direction of the base's antenna array—and some of them were covering their mouths as if in horror. She looked over to see what they all saw, but a cluster of trees blocked her line of sight. She hurried the kids forward until she got a clear view.

Not surprisingly, the antennas were heavily damaged and off their angles. Under normal circumstances, that would have been a disaster. But Noel doubted anyone was actually paying the slightest attention to the array, for hanging high above them was something incredible.

It was an object that seemed to be made of light, an ultraviolet aberration that sent a shiver of fear rippling through her despite the midday heat. Noel stared at it until her eyes watered and burned, and then she stared at the afterimage vibrating on the inside of her eyelids. She was afraid to open them again, her brain scrambling to make sense of it, to reconcile the object in the sky with her earlier tables and charts and graphs, until she felt a familiar, moist hand slip into her own.

"What is it?" Aster asked, squeezing Noel's fingers like a stress ball.

"I don't know," Noel said, glancing up at the object again.

"I'm pretty freaked out."

Noel looked into Aster's tear-filled eyes, which darted back and forth between the sky and her.

"Me too," she said, drawing the terrified girl against her side and wrapping an arm around her quivering shoulders, as much for her own benefit as the girl's.

6

Bruce Clarke, the owner of the Crispy Biscuit and its head cook, burst through the double doors from the kitchen and found everyone pressed against the diner's big front window.

"What the hell was that?" he said.

He had just lifted the hinged portion of the counter so he could join everyone at the window, when the doors behind him were blown off their frame, followed by a blast of heat. Flames fed by decades of splattered grease and thick, black smoke belched out of the kitchen, smelling of bacon and propane. Everything taped, tacked, or hung behind the counter was instantly ablaze, including the pictures of the 1996 and 1998 Fightin' Biscuits Little League Team, Bruce's framed first dollar, the Colorado Department of Health's latest grade of 'A', a picture of Franklin High's class of 1986 featuring Rose in her first pair of red pumps, and a photo from Bruce's hunting trip where he bagged his only-ever eleven-pointer. The flames consumed it all as they climbed the walls and reached for the ceiling, igniting the stained and drooping tiles that should have been replaced years ago. The entire diner was going up like an old newspaper, accentuated by the crashes from the kitchen as shelves buckled and cookware, plates, glasses, and mugs hit the floor.

But Bruce observed none of this. The explosion had flung him across the diner and into the wooden corner of one of the booths. Jimmy ran over to him, only to find that the man's shoulder and collar bone had caved in from the impact. When Jimmy reached his hands under Bruce's armpits to drag him away from the fire, Bruce howled and then passed out.

"Gimme a hand!" Jimmy screamed, and one of the municipal workers grabbed Bruce's feet while everyone else stumbled and pushed to get out of the burning building.

Edith McKenzie was on her knees and slipping in a mixture of fruit filling and gushing blood from where the shattered pie case had sliced open her cheek. "I got you, Edie," Rose said, grabbing Edith's elbow and helping her up. But they didn't get far.

"Look out!" Michael yelled, barreling them out of the way of a flaming ceiling tile.

The three of them lay on the warm linoleum looking up through the empty space in the ceiling. The insulation among the rafters was now ablaze, and other tiles would soon shear loose from the ceiling grid. Michael and Rose got Edith to her feet and hustled the hysterical woman out of the diner just before most of the ceiling came down.

Everyone had made it out safely, but nothing about this moment felt safe. They had barely gathered together in the street out front when the church bell rang out a single, truncated note, drawing everyone's attention.

Michael almost let go of poor Edith when he saw the fissure that had split the heavy stone face of St. Anne's. It traveled at a forty-five-degree angle, all the way from the original cornerstone, set down in 1912, to the new steeple dedicated on the church's one hundredth anniversary.

How in the world am I going to afford to fix that? was Michael's initial thought. But only for an instant. As he watched, the fissure grew, and the structure groaned under its own weight. The steeple tore through the roof and crashed into the church, the bell ringing out its last notes in the pews below. Then the circular stained-glass window at the peak exploded, sending a rainbow of glass skittering across Main Street. Finally, the entire structure effectively split in two along the fissure line, and the top half slid off the bottom like a piece of ice cream cake. It started slowly, but picked up speed.

Then young Theresa Donnelly came stumbling through the front doors.

She was covered in dust and dragging her partially zipped backpack behind her, leaving a trail of books and papers in her wake. Her hair was matted in blood, which was the only proof to the patrons of the Crispy Biscuit that she wasn't a ghost fleeing its tomb. Behind her, the church's death throes continued, the cracking and crumbling intensifying.

Michael shot toward her. Debris was raining down, but Theresa was dazed or in shock; she didn't respond, didn't move, just stood in place, teetering. Michael scooped her up in his arms and pulled her away only moments before a sliver of blue-grey roof slate would have impaled her. He stumbled backward, and was relieved when Jimmy appeared at his side. Together the two of them got Theresa back to the others, who had moved down the street a bit, away from the Biscuit's fire and the church's rain of destruction.

Jimmy and one of the municipal workers checked over Theresa, and Michael turned to watch his beloved St. Anne's die. What little was now left of it crumbled and crashed to earth, sending up a massive cloud of dust. Pages from hymnals, Bibles, and church bulletins fluttered like pigeons looking for a safe place to land.

The rumbling slowly died away, and Michael was overcome with sadness over the loss of the church he'd attended his entire life. But that sadness was challenged by another emotion, this one more visceral, as he looked to the heavens and saw the mysterious object now hanging over his town.

And when he whispered, "My God," it was both an exclamation and a question.

7

"CAN'T the system correct for re-entry variability?"

"Yes, but nothing on the scale we're dealing with," Susan said, wriggling her fingers into the glove connected to the end of her sleeve. "We've never been more than one or maybe two points off our orbit. Right now, we're plus nine percent and climbing."

"Yeah, so let's get the fuck out of here," Anatoly said.

He zipped up the front of his flight suit and started to float toward Yanez, who was furiously scribbling with an Expo marker on the glass tabletop where they had shared meals for the last eight months. But Susan stopped him.

"Leave her be," Susan said. "If she doesn't get the sequence right we could land in the middle of the ocean, or worse, we'll skip off the atmosphere entirely."

The cut on Yanez's chin throbbed as she tried to redesign the emergency protocol for the Soyuz. She palmed away a portion of the equation and scribbled a new set of numbers. There were so many variables, and it was hard to see the signal through the mathematical noise. To make matters worse, her beads of perspiration were drifting around her head like fat, lazy flies in summer, and as the International Space Station drifted off into the universe, she had to keep stopping to swat them away.

She closed her eyes and ran through the latest sequence. She did this every time she had to land on the deck of an aircraft carrier—she'd always trusted the arithmetic in her head more than the instruments at her fingers. After taking a few deep breaths to slow herself down, the equation resolved in her mind, the numbers becoming crisp and clear. And that clarity brought calm, because she knew the answer was right.

Unfortunately, the answer wasn't a good one.

She pushed away from the table, floated to the nearest terminal, and started punching away at the keys, entering her equation. The computer confirmed her calculations, and the most important countdown of their lives was initiated. Yanez watched the green numbers spin backward to 16:25, at which point she turned and faced her crew.

"The two of you need to get to Pirs right away," she said. "Get on board the Soyuz and prepare for an emergency ejection. We need to leave in just over sixteen minutes."

"There's no way to go that fast," Anatoly said, looking to Susan for support.

"We have to or we won't get another chance," said Yanez. "This is our only window to get back home." She ushered them toward the door that would take them to the Pirs Module and their lifeboat. "I'll meet you there."

"You're not coming with us?" Susan said, grabbing Yanez's sleeve.

Yanez gently pried the women's fingers off her suit. "I need to get our data from Kibo Module first. It could be the key to figuring out what's happened. Don't worry, I'll make it. But we all have to move, right now."

Anatoly and Susan nodded and left the module. Yanez twisted on her gloves, screwed her helmet into place, and then left the Unity Module heading in the opposite direction of her crew. She propelled herself through the connecting modules, once again kicking off anything she could to gain momentum. As she flew back through Destiny, she glanced over at the Glovebox. Her tomato plant was pressed up against the glass like a puppy in the window, begging to be taken home. She regretted leaving behind the little plant that had become a companion of sorts, but she also couldn't help but smile at the thought of her little tomato plant being the solo living passenger aboard the ISS as it hurtled away from the Earth and maybe even the solar system. A tiny bit of Jersey born to run through the stars.

Kibo was where they controlled much of the heating, cooling, and electrical power for the station. It was also where they housed the interface for video and data exchange with Earth. And because a software update had stalled yesterday's transfer down to Houston, they had forty-plus hours of potentially critical information that scientists on the ground would need.

Yanez went to the control terminal and tried one last time to establish a link with an Earthbound relay, any Earthbound relay, but everything was offline. That left her with no choice but to force-crash the computer and yank out the drive. This process took a few minutes, as she wasn't willing to remove the drive until it was completely offline. But as soon as she was able, she tore open the front casing, pulled the drive free, and propelled herself back out of the node.

According to the countdowns on virtually every screen, she now had less than seven minutes left.

She flew back through Destiny and into Harmony, the node she and Susan had called home. She went to her berth, opened a drawer, and pulled out her Howard University sweatshirt, which she wrapped around the drive for protection. From a different drawer she removed her backpack, complete with lucky blue rabbit's foot hanging from the front zipper. With the bundled drive in the backpack and securely zipped, Yanez gave the rabbit's foot a squeeze and then kicked off toward the hatch.

She had to get to Pirs quickly, but in the docking and cargo port, a large spool of cable had become uncoiled and filled the air, blocking her way. Trying to go straight through it would be like swimming through spaghetti, so instead she had to navigate along the walls, pulling herself hand over hand around the perimeter, using the stowed equipment and anchor points as leverage.

Halfway around, she passed the nadir window, and all thoughts of crew and countdown and answers evaporated at the sight of the object that now hovered over Earth. At first she thought it was some sort of visual anomaly created by the sun, or maybe a rogue comet with its icy tail ripping unannounced through the neighborhood. But its size and positioning over the planet screamed that it was something else entirely. Something more.

She watched it grow in the window as their apogee increased, her confusion turning to shock and then fear. And she might have stayed there and stared at it for the rest of her life had Anatoly not bellowed, snapping her back from the brink.

Yanez averted her gaze and reached for the edge of a nearby rack. She pulled herself the rest of the way around the port to the hatch that would take her to Pirs and the Soyuz. Before she left, though, she glanced back once more toward the window. It was aglow with light streaming in from the outside, its intensity growing by the second. She wanted to turn her face toward that light, to bask in its warmth and give in to its mystery.

"We gotta go!" Anatoly screamed.

Yanez pushed herself through the connecting node to Pirs. Susan and Anatoly were already strapped into their seats and looking up at her from inside the Soyuz, desperation in their wide eyes. Yanez pulled her legs to her chest and rotated her body so she was heading to the Soyuz feet first. When she reached the edge of the capsule's door, Anatoly grabbed her ankle and pulled her inside.

"Did you get it?" he asked.

Yanez settled into her seat, fastening her over-the-shoulder straps, and then nodded toward the backpack. "I got it." She didn't mention what she'd seen. *Not yet*, she thought.

Above them, the Soyuz hatch hissed closed.

"Thank God," Anatoly said, making a sign of the cross, kissing his fingers, and then resuming the emergency sequence. The Soyuz thrummed to life. The countdown ticked past two and a half minutes.

They all double-checked their harnesses and rattled off procedural items, focusing only on the things that were most critical—as in, the procedures that, if not done properly, would lead to their immediate and violent deaths.

Anatoly then held his finger poised above the ignition key.

"Wait until the countdown zeroes out," said Yanez. "Not before."

"Where will we touch down?" Susan asked.

"My best estimate has us somewhere in the southwestern United States."

Susan forced an uneasy smile. "I've always wanted to go to Vegas."

8

"BUT I'M the SATCOM specialist on this shift!" Noel snapped.

The young soldier looked nervous. Splotches of angry pink and red blossomed from his collar and climbed up his barely stubbled cheeks. But he didn't relent.

"I'm sorry, ma'am. All civilian employees have to exit the base at once. Direct orders from General Tate."

"But this is clearly a *special fucking circumstance*," Noel said, her finger aimed at the object in the sky. "I can help figure out what's going on."

"Ma'am, I have my orders."

Noel pushed back again and again, but the young airman held his ground. She eventually gave up and headed for the employee parking lot, where the kids from the field trip were being loaded onto their school bus. Aster stood at the back of the line, and Noel caught up to her.

"Hey, you okay?" Noel asked.

"I think so," Aster said, fighting the urge to look up. "What happens next?"

Noel put her hands on Aster's shoulders and turned her so that the object in the sky was at her back. "What do you know about the scientific method?"

"Uh, in case you didn't notice, I'm a total blerd."

When Noel gave her a puzzled look, Aster elaborated.

"I'm just an Uhura looking for her Spock. Get it?"

Noel smiled and held up a Vulcan salute. "Okay then, what do we know so far?" she asked.

"Nothing," Aster said.

"That's not true. We have information we can use to form the beginnings of a hypothesis."

Aster decided to play along. "Okay, well, it's big. Like really big. And light bounces off of it. So it could be made out of metal or have some kind of mirror-like surface."

"What else is reflective?" Noel asked.

Aster thought for a second. "Water, but it's cold up there in the atmosphere. Could be ice, I guess."

"Good. What else?"

Aster waggled her index finger around as she triangulated their position. "It's in the northeastern part of the sky, like two o'clockish. And it caused an earthquake when it appeared. Though I can't say that for certain because I was in the building with you. But it's probably a safe assumption, right?"

Noel nodded, but wanted more. Aster thought for a few more seconds, then it hit her.

"The satellites," she said, actually palming her forehead like a character in a sitcom. "There's definitely something going on with the communications satellites. Which is why no one can get service on their phones."

"You got it," Noel said with a broad smile. "Seems like a good place to start, right?"

Just then the driver leaned out of the bus doorway and waved Aster aboard.

"I hope you figure it out," Aster said.

"Me too."

Aster boarded the bus, and the doors hissed shut behind her.

As the bus lurched away, the loudspeakers crackled to life and a shrill voice informed all nonmilitary personnel that they had to go immediately, without delay. Soldiers were now ushering people to their vehicles. The powers that be were trying to lock the situation down, and the first step was to get rid of anyone they couldn't order around.

Noel walked to her normal parking spot, in the shade of the big oak. But when she got there, she found her cycle lying on its side. It was her most prized possession. An original 1961 Indian Chief that took her years to find.

"Sonofabitch!"

She knelt next to it like a medic beside a fallen comrade.

A jeep pulled up next to her. "Everything okay, ma'am?"

"Can you help me get this up?" she said.

The soldier hopped out and grabbed the rear of the bike while she took the handlebars. The thing was a beast, but between them they managed to hoist it back onto its wheels.

The bike was dented, a deep scratch carved into its strawberry-red paint. The chrome on the headlight was also dinged, and a rearview was cracked, but the rest seemed okay.

"I'm good here," she said, patting the seat for emphasis. "Thanks for your help."

The soldier took a few steps back toward his jeep, but didn't get in. He just stood there, wiping sweat off his slick forehead and flicking it away.

"Okay, Private Walsh," said Noel, reading the name on the soldier's breast pocket. "I'm good here."

"Sorry, ma'am," Walsh said. "I just need to make sure we get you on your way."

"And then what?"

"Ma'am?" he said. But just then a static-riddled voice burst over his jeep's radio, the person speaking so fast she'd probably have been unintelligible even if the reception were cleaner. Noel waited for it to end, then asked again.

"After you get rid of all of us civilians, what's next?"

"That's way above my pay grade," Walsh said.

"Sure, but what do you think?"

Private Walsh looked up at the object, shielding his eyes against the intensity of the light shining off its surface.

"I think people are surely gonna lose their shit," he said, leveling his gaze at Noel. "So I'd buckle up and get ready for that. 'Cause it's comin'."

9

BRUCE SNAPPED back to consciousness when the roof collapsed. Rose was kneeling next to him, trying to keep him calm, but when he saw the Crispy Biscuit, his life's work, going up in smoke, he shoved her aside and tried to get up. He shifted his weight onto his ruined shoulder—only to let out a howl more raw and powerful than one caused by pain alone.

Michael understood how he felt. He held Rose's apron to the gash on Theresa's head and looked over at the remains of his church. Dust hung in the air around the piles of rubble like fog over a lake. Sunlight streamed through the dirty cloud and dappled the destruction. No matter how long he stared, it still didn't seem real.

Next to him, Jimmy tended to the cut on Edith McKenzie's cheek. Her arm was flung across her eyes, and she shook with deep, quiet sobs.

"Jimmy, come in," said Officer Ken Newsome, a rookie whose voice was barely more than a whisper on the walkie-talkie. Jimmy squeezed Edith's hand, then stood up and keyed his shoulder mic.

"What's happening, Kenny?"

"I'm at the station. We took a hit."

"Same over here at the church."

"No, that's not it, Jim . . . the sheriff's dead."

As Jimmy stood there stunned, Kenny explained what had happened. Sheriff Anderson liked to change the oil on the patrol cars himself. He had been in the middle of swapping out a filter when the shit hit the fan. The car fell off the jacks, and the sheriff was crushed underneath it.

"You're senior now," Ken said. "What do we do?"

Jimmy managed a weak "Stand by" before putting his hands on his knees and taking a few deep breaths, trying to contend with the sheer tonnage of responsibility for this place and its people, everything he'd never wanted, pressing down on him. He felt like bolting, running from all of it.

"Shit, Mike. What am I gonna do?" he said.

"Same as always," Michael said, his voice firm. "You're gonna step up. We both are."

Michael had always been able to convince Jimmy of almost anything. Playing third base in Little League, running for student council, asking Jodie Thompkins to the senior prom, even the police academy when it seemed college wasn't in the cards. None of those things would have happened if it weren't for Michael's unwavering faith in his best friend. And at that moment, despite the chaos swirling around them on the ground and in the sky, Jimmy saw in Michael's eyes the same well of strength and belief in him as always.

He switched his radio to the open channel and keyed the mic. "Listen up, this is Bell," he said. But that didn't feel right. So he started again.

"Guys, it's Jimmy. Sheriff Anderson's dead, St. Anne's and the Biscuit are gone, and who knows what else. There will be time to talk about everything we lost and debate what the hell that thing up there is later on. Right now we need all available officers to do a sweep of the town. Go door to door. Be thorough and be careful. Check in on this channel and with each other regularly. That's it for now."

No one replied at first, but then a series of rogers came over the walkie.

Jimmy called for an ambulance and a fire engine for the Biscuit. Sirens already echoed across the town. And they weren't the only ones coming. The people of Franklin started arriving as well. They came in ones and twos at first, but as word about the church and the diner spread, larger groups descended on Main Street. By the time the ambulance arrived and the pumper truck started pouring water onto the Biscuit, the crowd had grown to nearly seventy-five.

They cried and hugged and consoled each other, comparing notes on what had happened to them and where they were when it happened. They traded theories, tried to keep each other calm, and tended to those who were failing at it. They watched as the paramedics loaded Edith and Theresa into the ambulance. They gasped in unison when Bruce went into convulsions, then screamed and cried when it was clear that he was gone. They watched as the firefighters battled and ultimately put out the blaze. And for a time, they were a unified people, especially about one thing in particular: the object in the sky was to blame.

After a while, Jimmy and several officers tried to get everyone to return to their homes, but it didn't work. People just wanted to stay together, especially when the first fighter jet ripped across the sky, heading toward the base. Others followed in steady succession.

"We need to find out what's going on," Michael said as the rumble of the last jet's engines faded.

"Got any ideas?"

As if on cue, they saw a motorcycle coming down Main Street.

"Is that your sister?" Jimmy asked.

"Looks like it," said Michael. He couldn't see Noel's face underneath the helmet, but her strawberry-red bike was unmistakable.

Noel was making slow progress, thanks to the jagged crevice that cut through the road and the fissures that snaked out and split the curbs on either side, knocking over parking meters, newspaper boxes, and light poles all along the main drag. When it became too difficult to navigate, she pulled her bike in front of the Grand Theater and cut the engine. Michael and Jimmy jogged over to meet her.

The three of them hugged and Noel kissed each one of them on the cheek and then hugged them again. When they finally let go, she gazed at the ruins of her brother's church and the diner.

"Mikey, I'm so sorry."

"Me too," he said, finally letting the tears come.

"Was anyone hurt?"

"Fortunately Mike and I were at the Biscuit when it happened," Jimmy said. He told her about Theresa, and Bruce and Edith and Sheriff Anderson. She hugged them both again, then Michael asked, "How're things at the base?"

"They're locking it down. That's why I'm here. They kicked all the nonmilitary people out."

"Do you know anything?" Jimmy asked.

Noel glanced up at the massive object cutting across the Colorado sky. Sunlight gleamed off its surface, creating the appearance of a white fire, a penetrating luminescence that burned through the eyes and brain and soul of the onlooker. Around it the sky itself seemed to quiver, vibrating and pulsing in a steady rhythm, the surrounding clouds nearly vaporized but never dispersing, caught in an endless erasure.

"There's not much to go on yet," she said, lowering her gaze to the two people she loved most. "But one thing is clear. Whatever it is, it stopped the world."

"What do you mean?" Michael asked.

"I mean the Earth isn't spinning anymore."

PART II

10

Lieutenant General Walter Tate was leader of the 50th Space Wing and fourth-generation military. He had outdone his father, grandfather, and great-grandfather in terms of rank, but his dad had fought in Korea, grandpop in World War II, and great-granddaddy in the OG war of them all, World War I. So you could put as many shiny stars as you'd like on Tate's shoulders, but it didn't amount to all that much in his family.

Now, however, Walter might have the chance to change that, to even the score with the great men who had come before him. And when his number finally came up and he punched his ticket to the big officers' club in the sky, he'd be able to look his forefathers in the eyes and say, *Yeah, but none of you had to deal with the big sonofabitch in space.*

"Who do we got?" he asked O'Neal.

Second Lieutenant Jill O'Neal walked with him toward the briefing room. "Sir, in the room we have Colonels Hart and Dinesh of Space Command, Dr. Eugenia Sang from the physics department at Denver, and a handful of officers from satellite control. We also have the NASA administrator and her deputy on the hard line from Houston."

"Sounds right."

General Tate was about to enter the room when O'Neal broke protocol for the first time in her distinguished career. Just as he was about to open the door, she placed her hand atop his on the handle—which might very well have been the only time they had ever touched in the two years she had served at his side, apart from the occasional handshake.

"Jill? What is it?"

"It's my mother, sir. She's in Seattle," O'Neal said quietly, struggling. "She gets confused a lot, especially since my dad passed."

He turned to face her, the conference room and its inhabitants forgotten. "It's almost a year now, right?"

It was no surprise to her that he remembered she was approaching the one-year anniversary of her father's death. She'd seen it from him time and time again with so many people. That was just what he did.

"Never mind," she said with a quick, tight shake of her head. "I'm sorry to bring it up."

But Tate wasn't having it. "I can take it from here, Lieutenant," he said. "Tell dispatch I want them to use the priority landline and route you through Lewis-McChord. That should get you where you need to go. You're dismissed."

He turned and struck the handle hard to send a signal to those in the room that he was coming in—and as a mercy for the soldier now struggling to hold back her tears in the face of his kindness. Her quiet "thank you" was drowned out by the screech of chairs across the floor as everyone jumped to attention.

One wall of the conference room was lined with video screens. Most showed different angles of the vast object now dominating the sky over the southwestern United States. The rest had shaky video taken from fighter jets flying sorties above Denver and the surrounding area to assess the chaos on the ground.

Next to the video display, Dr. Eugenia Sang stood at a whiteboard covered with numbers and hastily drawn diagrams, a blue streak of dry erase marker on her left cheek. She looked like they had just plucked her out of bed, because they had.

"As you were," Tate said, waving the room back to their seats and taking his. "Dr. Sang, why don't you get me up to speed."

Eugenia looked to the ceiling, the ground, the video screens, the ceiling again, and then the board. She uttered a few "umms" and thrust her fingers through her hair. Finally she began hunting around for an eraser, and not finding one, scrubbed off a portion of the whiteboard with her palm.

The room watched all this in silence, but Mina Blank, the newly appointed NASA administrator, chimed in from the telephone to ask if they were still there. Eugenia barked out a "hold, please" and kept on scrubbing, licking her discolored palm to get at a particularly stuck-on mark. Colonel Dinesh finally got up and offered her his handkerchief. Without a word of thanks, she snatched it and finished wiping the board clean. Then and only then was she was ready to begin.

"The first thing you have to understand is there's no math for what's happened," she said. "We don't know what the object is, where it came from, how it got here, and we haven't had any communications from it. But we do know what it's done. And what it's done is impossible."

Eugenia wrote *1100 MPH* on the board. "It varies slightly, but this is the speed at which the Earth rotates," she said. "Suddenly stopping the rotation of the planet would not stop the atmosphere, which would continue moving at eleven hundred miles per hour. And that means that everything not connected directly to bedrock would be ripped from the surface of the planet. Buildings, topsoil, every tree on every continent. All of it would be ejected into the atmosphere, along with every single human being."

"Don't forget the oceans," Mina chimed in from the phone. "They would also continue moving along Earth's original rotational path, which means tsunamis should be sweeping across land all over the world right now."

"Yes!" Eugenia said. "We should be underwater right now. Entirely swamped by the Pacific Ocean."

"That's preposterous," said Colonel Hart. "We're a thousand miles from the coast and a mile above sea level."

"With that volume of water moving across the continent at the speeds we're talking about," Eugenia said, "debris from Los Angeles would be washing up in the Bronx. And yet that actually *would* be preposterous, because as I said, there should be no debris from Los Angeles. It should all be in space."

The room erupted into shouting. Mina and her deputy at NASA kept trying to break in over the phone, only to be drowned out by Colonels Hart and Dinesh and the crew from satellite operations.

"Enough!" Tate said, his voice booming. Everyone fell immediately silent.

"Not you son," Tate said, pointing to a young man who had fallen to his knees. "You finish up and then take your seat."

The room sat silently through "Holy Mary, Mother of God, pray for us sinners now and at the hour of our death." Tate's amen was in unison with the soldier's.

Tate addressed his NASA administrator. "First things first. Mina, can you confirm that the planet has stopped spinning?"

"Yes, General," she said. "We've lost contact with every satellite in orbit, private and military. But solar positioning—"

She was suddenly cut off.

"Mina?" said Tate. "Did we lose you?"

"Hold please!" she yelled, her echoey voice indicating that she was on speaker and some distance from the phone. After a moment they heard her running back toward them.

"I'm sorry, General, that was ECSAT. We've been trying to reach them via the old transatlantic cable system. The whole thing went fubar when . . . it doesn't matter. ECSAT has also confirmed that the planet's rotation has ceased. As it's currently night in Europe, they can see the stars, which gives another method of measuring planetary movement. And there isn't any. We've stopped."

Tate walked over to Eugenia and her whiteboard. He stood before it. She was scribbling furiously, practically vibrating in her intensity, but he couldn't make sense of a thing she'd written.

"It's thermal dynamics," she said when he asked her to explain. "But it's based on normal atmospheric conditions, and I have no idea if that's even a viable approach."

"What exactly are you trying to figure out?" he asked.

"How hot it's going to get," she said. "There's so many things to figure out, I don't even know where to begin, but when Mina mentioned night in Europe, I was wondering if it will now *always* be night in Europe, which means it's always daytime here, and so I started to wonder about the heat build-up resulting from persistent sunlight."

Tate left her to it, and turned to the group, who were desperately looking to him for orders. He started with NASA.

"Mina, I need you and a small team here in Colorado. Whoever you think you'll need to figure out whatever the hell happened and might yet happen."

"Understood, General. How long do I have?"

"As soon as humanly possible. I'm ordering all operations moved into the Mountain."

11

FRANKLIN WAS AN OLD COLORADO TOWN. And like many old towns in the state, mining was central to its history. For nearly one hundred years, coal had sustained the community. When one coal mine ran dry, another would spring up like clockwork. Four generations of Franklinites prospered from the rich bounty in the surrounding hills and mountains. Life was steady and predictable. But then one afternoon a crew expanding an old shaft stumbled onto a vein of coffinite, and everything changed.

Back then, you'd rather unearth a vein of coffinite than gold. The uranium-containing mineral was in high demand, as the United States was arming itself against the red menace. But it was more difficult to mine than coal; it required a different process and specialized equipment. So it was no surprise when, seemingly overnight, all the mom-and-pop mining outfits that had employed Franklin's workforce were acquired by one of the large national companies. Coal was officially out, and coffinite was in.

After that, people came from all over the Southwest to work Franklin's coffinite mine, and the once humble town grew into a bustling city. Houses went up all over, and for the first time in the town's history, it was hard to know all your neighbors. But if you asked most of the original townies, the truest sign of Franklin's transformation was when Whitey's got competition.

Whitey's Market had served as Franklin's sole grocer and general store since the early 1900s. It had been there through prohibition, the brutal depression years, and the dark days of two world wars. But along with the caravans of new miners and their families, there came a Stuckey's—one of those upstart national convenience stores that were becoming all the rage in 1950s America. The stage was set for an all-out turf war. Yet for a long while, the two stores managed to coexist. The "west-enders" stayed loyal to Whitey's, while the newbie "east-enders" opted for Stuckey's. Both stores were thriving well enough that they didn't need traffic from the cross side of town. And then the supermarket rolled in. It signaled the end for Whitey's and Stuckey's, but it was also an undeniable sign that Franklin had arrived.

As the 1950s turned over into the 1960s, and the drive-in theaters, bowling alleys, and big liquor stores opened their doors, the Franklin renaissance hit its peak. But just as quickly and unexpectedly as the town's fortunes had risen, they fell again when the coffinite vein dried up.

Operations were scaled back. Many of the mining families picked up and moved to other parts of the state; miners with uranium experience were still in high demand during what was then the height of the Cold War. Streets became lined with "For Sale" signs, and of course, no one was buying. The town wasn't only shrinking, it was dying. Even some of the founding families left. Franklin was on the cusp of disappearing altogether.

The Mountain saved it.

Construction of the hardened bunker inside Cheyenne Mountain, just to the northwest of Franklin, began in 1961. It would be the new home for NORAD—the North American Air Defense Command. The miners who hadn't left town soon found themselves working for the Utah Mining Company, which had the government contract to excavate Cheyenne Mountain under the direction of the Army Corp of Engineers.

That turning point marked Franklin's transition into a military town. Heavy equipment trundled down Main Street. Army officers and engineers moved into the vacant homes. Whitey's reopened and started stocking military surplus. Dynamite blasts became the soundtrack to baseball games and harvest festivals. And when the facility opened six years later with no end in sight to the iciness between the United States and the Soviet Union, people felt like the town was there to stay. Sure, the idea of living near one of the prime targets for a nuclear strike scared off some. But life in Franklin was vibrant again, thanks to the Mountain.

Corporal Jed Williams arrived in Franklin in the fall of 1962, shortly after President Kennedy's misadventure in Cuba. Jed was part of the team tasked with establishing the Mountain's communications infrastructure. He was a solid engineer with a high aptitude for long-range radio transmission and the budding field of satellite communications, which earned him several promotions during the five years that he and his team snaked hundreds of miles of cable through the Mountain's primary and secondary shafts.

Once the Mountain opened, Jed was permanently assigned to air defense command as an aerospace surveillance analyst. Now a sergeant first class, he was also permitted to live off base. He chose Franklin, where after a few years of playing the field he met and fell hard for Claire Driscoll, a fourth-grade teacher at Cheyenne Elementary.

Their love affair burned hot, much to the chagrin of her father, Franklin's sheriff, whose job had gotten tougher after the military moved in; men who spent their days looking for intercontinental ballistic missiles tended to want to blow off a little steam at night. Even Jed had spent a few nights in Sheriff Driscoll's jail cell. But eventually Jed convinced the sheriff he'd left behind youthful transgressions and had only the best of intentions for his daughter. The couple was married in the spring of 1973.

Claire and Jed had two children: Michael and Noel. And as is often the case, each child gravitated toward a different parent. Michael was always Claire's, inheriting her charitable and giving nature. In Cub Scouts, he volunteered at the Franklin old folks' home. In high school, he tutored after school, which was where he met his best friend, Jimmy Bell. He worked at the town library, shelving books and keeping the card catalog in order. On Saturdays he read to the kids during story time; on Sundays he was a youth leader at the church. And when he decided to forgo his scholarship to the University of Denver and instead opted to study divinity at Colorado Theological Seminary, Claire's joy knew no bounds.

By contrast, Noel belonged to Jed. Her favorite childhood toy was her Radio Shack catalog. Instead of drinking wine coolers and listening to hair metal with her high school friends, she would spend her weekends with her dad on Blue's Bluff, refurbishing the old radio tower he'd purchased when the station went bankrupt. They'd flip out circuit boards, consult Jed's collection of hobbyist magazines, and make trips to Colorado Springs for parts. Jed beamed with pride when she enrolled in Colorado Technical University and cheered from the front row at her graduation. And when she was accepted into the graduate engineering program at MIT, he took her acceptance letter to the Mountain and showed everyone, including all the brass. And if Claire hadn't been diagnosed with an aggressive form of glioblastoma and died six months later, everyone was sure that Jed would have been front and center when Noel earned her master's degree. But that never happened.

By then, Michael had been assigned to a small parish in Nevada, and Noel couldn't stand the thought of her dad living in that big house all alone. So she stayed with him. Jed made a show of protesting her not going to Boston. After all, that's what fathers are supposed to do, no matter how badly they want the opposite. But when she insisted, he helped her land a job as a civilian communications technician at the Mountain. They commuted to work together and spent nights and weekends on the radio tower, just like old times. Michael would come home every chance he got, and for a time, things were good.

But then the US Space Command was reorganized, and as a result, Jed was relieved from duty. Without either Claire or the Mountain, the two poles of his life for almost three decades, he was lost. And now the fact that Noel still had her job at the Mountain—the job he'd helped her get—caused feelings of jealousy and drove a wedge between them. When NORAD operations were moved to Peterson Air Force Base and Noel was offered a role in satellite operations, their relationship grew cold. Jed grew more obstinate and insular, spending all of his time at the radio tower, talking on the ham setup with anyone who'd listen.

That was when Michael decided it was time to come home.

He petitioned the Diocese of Colorado Springs, and with Father Morgan's help was able to land the post at St. Anne's. Together, he and Noel tried to break through to their dad. But there simply wasn't enough time. They'd lost a good bit of him when their mother died and a giant chunk when he lost his Mountain. Ultimately they lost the rest right before Christmas 2009 when Noel found him at his workbench in the station, dead from a stroke, his soldering iron burning a hole in his cheek. Noel gave the eulogy, Michael led the service, and they buried him alongside their mother.

That was twelve years ago.

A smear of engine oil and blood had left a jagged trail across the concrete from the police cruiser that had crushed Sheriff Anderson to where his body now lay, covered with a Denver Broncos blanket from the station house. Kneeling at the sheriff's side, Michael made the sign of the cross and asked God to take into his bosom his noble servant and dedicated protector of the people of Franklin. He rested his hand on the blanket and concluded his benediction, which was followed by a chorus of choked and broken amens from Jimmy and the other officers who stood nearby, hats in hands and heads bowed.

Michael's knee buckled a little as he stood up.

"You okay?" Jimmy asked, grabbing his arm to steady him.

"Yeah. Just been a long day."

Michael held Jimmy's shoulder as he tried to force some blood back into his right leg. He'd been kneeling over dead bodies for most of the last four hours. He and Jimmy had crisscrossed the town as the calls came in.

"Let's head out," Jimmy said.

"Sure you're not needed here?" Michael asked.

"The mayor and some others are gathered at Whitey's. We should get over there."

"He was a good man, Jim," Michael said. "You're gonna do him proud."

"I hope so."

Whitey's was just across the street. They found Mayor Alice Antonelli, a bandage on her forehead, already holding court before most of the Franklin town council. Noel sat nearby, fiddling with Whitey's ham radio.

"I don't think that's a good idea," Mayor Antonelli said. "We should stay here and wait for instructions."

"From who?" asked Tom Kaplan, head of the town council. "It's been hours."

"I know, but—"

"No one can get a signal. TV is dead. Internet is dead. And we have a bunch of *people* dead. We need to do something."

"We are, Tom," Jimmy said as he and Michael approached the group. "Our first priority is securing the town and making sure people are safe."

Tom looked like he was about to launch into a rebuttal, but hesitated at the sight of the bloodstains on Michael's and Jimmy's clothes.

"How is it out there?" Alice asked.

"Thirty-four dead," Jimmy said. "We've converted the

community center into a morgue. Power is spotty, but the hospital generators are up and running."

"Thank God for that," said Zadie Bennett, one of the newest council members. She looked disappointed when Michael didn't echo her sentiment. He wasn't in the mood to be thankful for the little things from above today.

"Look, right now everyone is still in shock," said Tom. "But that's going to wear off soon, and then the fear will set in. I agree with you, Jim—safety has to come first. But how are you going to keep everyone safe when people think it's the Rapture?"

"That's nonsense," Noel said without looking up, continuing to fiddle with the dials on Whitey's old set. "We don't know anything yet. I'm gonna need a lot more evidence before I'm ready to concede that we're dealing with some sort of wrath of God or Rapture or whatever."

"I'm with you on that, but you know as well as I do that not everyone is going to be so careful about jumping to conclusions. Things are going to get crazy out there, and before that happens, we need to *do* something."

"Like what?" Michael asked, failing to disguise the exhaustion in his voice. "What do you think we should do?"

"Let's go to the base," Tom said. "We'll get some people together and drive over."

"I told you already, they locked it down," said Noel.

"Yeah, and what are they going to do? Shoot us?"

"No, they'll just ignore you. It's a waste of time."

Noel returned her focus to the radio, but Tom was spoiling for a fight. He took a step toward Noel, and Jimmy stepped in to block his way.

Apparently that was the signal for the entire room to explode into arguing. In mere moments Tom and Jimmy looked like they were ready to come to blows, and tensions between everyone else ran only slightly less hot. But just as the arguing hit its peak, Noel's piercing whistle cut through the din.

"Shut the fuck up!" she said. "They're broadcasting."

She turned up the volume, and everyone fell silent and listened.

"This is the emergency broadcast system. A national emergency has been issued for all fifty states. Citizens are advised to remain in their homes or in designated shelters until the nature of this event can be ascertained. All air and rail travel has been suspended. All interstates are hereby designated for use by emergency vehicles only. Local travel on county and state roads is permitted only if necessary. All national television, cellular, and internet services are currently disrupted. Information pertaining to the event will be transmitted via radio communications only. Remain on this channel or any other major frequency for future updates. This message will repeat. This is the emergency broadcast system. A national . . ."

They listened to the message twice more before Noel shut it off. The gravity of the situation was settling on them fast and heavy, like food poisoning.

"Okay, there it is," Alice said.

"I'll have people go door to door and tell everyone to stay put," said Jimmy. "We'll also get a generator going and fire up the old PA system at the station. That way we can at least communicate to the families within earshot." He looked to Tom, whose anger had dissipated, the red in his cheeks slowly fading. "Tom, how about you give me hand?"

Tom nodded his agreement, the fight of a moment before forgotten.

A rumble began to build outside, growing louder by the second. The room started to shake.

"Oh my God, it's happening again!" Zadie said.

Noel jumped out of her chair and ran for the door. She threw it open and looked up. "Jets!" she yelled above the sound of the sky being shredded. "They're haulin' ass."

Everyone filed out of Whitey's to look. Above them streaked the 5th Air Wing, heading east beneath the ominous object. When the sound finally receded, Noel pulled Jimmy and Michael aside.

"Tom's a jackass," she said. "But he's right that the calm will only hold for so long. We need to know what's happening out there."

"What are you thinking?" Jimmy asked.

Noel reached into her pocket and pulled out her keys. She grabbed the one attached to a red rabbit's foot and held it up for them to see.

"Dad's radio tower," Michael said. "Does it still work?"

"Don't know. But I'm going to find out."

12

THE FORMATION RIPPED across the sky. Tate shielded his eyes, squinting against the piercing sunlight reflecting off the object and searching through the forward guard's vapor trail for Air Force One.

". . . confirmed it's maintained its relative position."

Tate turned toward the NASA administrator, who had arrived from Houston about an hour earlier. "Sorry, I didn't catch that," he shouted as the noise from the jets echoed off the surrounding mountains. "What has?"

"The moon, General," Mina said. "Three observatories on what is now the dark side of the planet have confirmed that the moon hasn't moved."

"What does that mean?"

"That this isn't just an Earth-based phenomenon," she said. "The object has somehow halted the moon's orbit as well."

The ground crew scrambled. Dollies, belt loaders, and a stair car zipped into position alongside Humvees and gun trucks.

"Are you ready?" Tate asked as he led the way onto the tarmac.

"I think so," she said. "But I'll warn you, we still don't know much."

"Listen, when we get in the room with the others, don't hold back on the math."

"I'm sorry?"

"The woman has a Nobel in economics. I've been in meetings with her about troop readiness and force depletion estimates. I'm just telling you, she's gonna want to go deep on the numbers."

Air Force One touched down.

"Who's she got with her?" Mina asked.

"Most of the cabinet," he said. "Secretaries of defense and homeland security are holed up in Washington so they can stay close to the rest of the apparatus. The secretary of state is in Italy. But the comms team at the Mountain is trying to track her down as we speak."

"Sounds like a party."

A black Suburban crossed the runway and pulled up to Tate and Mina. Jill O'Neal got out of the passenger-side door and walked to Tate with a tablet in hand.

"Everything's ready, sir. Just need your authorization."

He took the tablet from her without breaking eye contact with Air Force One. Once it stopped and the door swung open, he turned to his aide. "Did you get through?"

"Sir?" Jill said, distracted by the appearance of the president walking down the stairs to the tarmac.

"Did you reach your mom?" he asked again, pressing his thumb to the face of the tablet, eliciting a small beep.

"Yes, sir," Jill said. "Thank you again. My brother's there, thank God."

"That's good. I'm glad he's with her." He handed the tablet back to her but kept hold of it for a brief second to draw her attention. "Because we don't know how this thing's gonna go. And I need my best people here with me."

Jill met her boss's gaze. "Of course, sir."

They both turned their attention to their commander in chief.

"It's good to see you again, Madam President," Tate called out before President Bonita Reyes was halfway to him. "What's new in Washington?"

"Very funny, Walter," Reyes said, extending a hand to him and grasping his forearm. "You still doing the eleven thirty slot at Chuckles?"

Tate directed her attention to Jill. "You remember my aide, Lieutenant O'Neal?"

Reyes nodded to Jill, who was standing at attention. "Good to see you again, Lieutenant."

Jill nodded sharply in reply. "Madam President."

Mina then spoke up. "Madam President, we've prepared a full briefing for you and can begin at your earliest convenience."

"Certainly none of this is convenient, Dr. Blank. And I want to start right now," Reyes said, beelining for the Suburban.

"Yes, ma'am," Mina said, quickening her step to keep up. They climbed into the SUV, Jill up front with the driver and the other three in the back. The president launched into it before the back doors had even closed.

"What do you think has happened?" she asked as she opened the cold bottle of water waiting for her.

"Well, ma'am, despite the scientific improbability—"

"Impossibility, you mean."

"Right, ma'am," Mina said. "All empirical evidence suggests a complete cessation of the Earth's rotation."

"Yes, but that's not what I asked, Dr. Blank." The president took another swig of water, screwed on the cap, set the bottle aside, and then settled back in her seat. All the while, Mina squirmed in hers.

She tried again. "None of this . . ." she started, then shifted tack. "You have to understand, ma'am, that all of this is purely theoretical. Every mathematical model shows—"

"The atmosphere isn't moving, which it should be," Reyes said. "There are no tsunamis sweeping across the United States, not a single supervolcano has emerged, and none of the people in this car are drifting dead and frozen through the universe."

Reyes hit the button to lower the darkened window. As sunlight streamed in through the opening, she stared straight up at the object.

"I have scientific advisors in Washington, Mina," she said, squinting but not breaking eye contact with the ultraviolet surface of the thing violating the Colorado sky. "I heard all about what *should* have happened when this thing arrived. And I'm certain we'll be spending a good bit of time on it again when we get to the Mountain. Until then, I want to know what *you* think happened."

Mina looked at Tate for support, but he offered only a slight shrug. Then she looked to President Reyes, her gaze still on the object, her fingers impatiently drumming on her thigh. Mina took a deep breath, then answered her president's question.

"I think we got fucked," she said.

Reyes finally looked over at Mina. She smiled as she hit the button to close the window, the sunlight shrinking in its wake.

"I think so, too," she said. "The question is, by who? Or what?"

13

"Oh, FUCK!" Susan yelled as the hammering started somewhere beneath their seats. The capsule shuddered.

"That's just the explosive charges from the bolts," Anatoly said. "We're starting the final phase."

The last bolt popped and the latch assembly disengaged, allowing the propulsion module to separate from the descent vehicle. As soon as they were free, the shaking stopped, and Susan breathed a sigh of relief.

"Speed?" Yanez asked.

Susan tapped the console in front of her seat. Yanez's calculations required them to override the normal de-orbital burn procedure. Instead of the standard re-entry speed of 120 meters per second, they were traveling at 150 meters per second.

"We're right on target," Susan said.

"Are you sure we'll be able to slow down?" asked Anatoly.

Susan shrugged. "We're within the margin of error."

"What about the pilot chutes?"

"The tolerances are close, but I think they'll hold."

The sudden pull of Earth's gravity sucked them back into their seats. Yanez strained to reach the hand controller on the central console.

"Be sure to adjust your shoulder straps," she said, detaching the controller from the console and quickly settling back into her seat. "We'll be pulling a lot of g's. It's okay if you go out for a bit. Once I initiate the final sequence, we'll be in gravity's hands."

"Why'd you go with a ballistic re-entry?" Susan asked.

"With no support crew to meet us, it gives us our best shot at a safe landing zone that isn't in the middle of nowhere."

"It's too bad we're not landing in Kazakhstan. I was really looking forward to the beshbarmak," Anatoly said. "My wife makes a nice one, but you can't beat getting it right from the source."

Before Yanez could ask what beshbarmak was, Susan cut in. "Wow, look at that."

She was pointing at the small window next to her. Red, orange, and pink streams of plasma crawled across the glass as they streaked through Earth's atmosphere.

Together they settled in for the ride. Susan continued to watch the color show, but Anatoly made the sign of the cross and closed his eyes. Soon, fire from the heat shield wrapped up the sides of the descent vehicle.

"Here we go," Yanez said.

They tumbled and tore through the atmosphere. Yanez held the controller close to her chest as she adjusted thrust vectors. The gravitational forces were extreme, pushing her body to its limits, narrowing her vision. Finally she simply closed her eyes. *Trust the numbers*, she thought, pushing the buttons on the controller in the sequence determined by the equation in her head.

She made the final adjustment just before the blackness came.

———

Her mother's words were muffled, but Yanez could still hear the urgency in her voice.

Her mom had told her to stay away from the deep end, but Yanez didn't listen. She hopped into the pool a foot past the rope with the red buoys, touched her toes to the bottom, and pushed herself under the rope back to the shallow end. Then she climbed out and did it again, this time another foot farther, the sloping bottom of the pool a little bit deeper. But the third time, her toes didn't touch. The slope of the pool's bottom was too steep, and she'd gone too far, always pushing herself, always trying to go a little bit farther.

She searched out the bottom with her toes, but felt nothing. She tried again, and this time they caught but slipped as she kicked against it, and she was disoriented, not knowing which way was up, the blackness all around her, seeping in with the cold, closing in, her lungs screaming for air that wasn't there, her mind panicking.

And then came the splash as her mother hit the water. She felt her mom's grip on her forearm, felt herself pulled back toward the sun.

Yanez's teeth rattled in her head as the pilot chutes deployed, chopping the capsule's velocity off at the knees. The air smelled like the underside of a Jiffy Pop before the kernels started to sizzle. Her harness dug deep into her shoulders, and when she opened her eyes the capsule swirled around her, making her gorge rise in her throat. She picked a point on the console and tried to focus, taking deep breaths to make her vision settle. The red glow clarified into numbers and she saw that they were at twelve thousand feet and descending.

"Are you okay?" Yanez asked her crew.

"What did we pull?" Susan said groggily.

Anatoly punched keys on the console. "Almost nine g's," he said with a chuckle. "Nicely done, Commander."

"Any idea where we are?" Susan asked, straining against her shoulder straps to peer out the Soyuz's window, the colorful light show now replaced by gray and black streaks of soot.

"We'll find out in about ten minutes," Anatoly said.

Yanez was less concerned about where they were than she was about what they'd be facing once they landed. She couldn't rationalize what she had seen hanging over the planet any more than a caveman might make sense of an iPhone. For the first time in her life, she didn't trust her own eyes. She needed more information. She wondered if anyone had any.

The main chute deployed, rocking the capsule backward at a steep angle to allow the heat to dissipate before landing. The crew sat silently, the anticipation mounting. Minutes later, the heat shield was jettisoned and excess fuel began to stream from the vehicle to prevent an explosion when they hit the ground.

"What are you going to miss most?" Anatoly asked once the deafening hiss had stopped.

"Living in zero-g," Susan said. "I liked having perky tits again."

"That's a plus, for sure," Yanez said. "But for me, it's gonna be the brightness of the stars. God, how many times did you guys find me asleep in the cupola?"

"I'm gonna miss it all, I think," Anatoly said.

"Even the tiny bathrooms and having to sleep upright?" Susan asked.

"Sounds crazy, but yes, even that. And the two of you. But only until you come to Moscow to visit."

"I wish . . ." Yanez began, then lost her words. "As difficult as it was at times up there, it was still the best thing I've ever done. And I'm glad it was with you both."

Yanez, Anatoly, and Susan held hands until Anatoly called out, "Ten seconds." Then they crossed their arms over their chests, trying to get as small as possible in their seats in preparation for the retro rockets, which would fire just before they touched down to soften the landing.

But the rockets didn't fire.

14

THE RADIO TOWER atop Blue's Bluff was one of the first things built during the construction at Cheyenne Mountain—and it was, for a time, critical to the Mountain's operations. But satellites ultimately made it obsolete, and the military sold the tower to a local radio station, giving it a second chance at life. KZZA operated the tower for another decade, sharing "the sounds of our lives" with Franklin and the surrounding area. On a clear summer day, you could pick up Dean Martin and Frank Sinatra all the way over in Beaver Creek. But the station fell on hard times in the 1980s, when all of the advertising dollars started to flow into Denver's pop and glam rock stations. The local station did its last broadcast on Christmas Day 1984, and then put the station and its tower on the block once again. But this time there were no buyers. No one wanted such outdated tech. No one but Jed Williams, who eventually bought the whole thing for pennies on the dollar.

Noel hadn't been to the station since her father died. She had no idea what state the equipment was in. But she thought she could resuscitate the main board and receiver without too much effort, so long as the utilities guys were right about the power being online in this part of the grid.

She used to know every dip and turn in the dirt road to the

bluff by heart. Now she had to weave her motorcycle through the rocks and weeds with caution. The service road on the opposite side of the bluff might have been clearer, but even so it would have taken longer than navigating the overgrown path, and she needed to get things up and running as quickly as possible. The tower was their best chance at getting any real information about what was going on.

She crested the top of the bluff between Scylla and Charybdis —two massive boulders she'd named during her senior year in high school after she was forced to read Homer. Her cycle leveled out, and she skidded to a halt and cut the engine.

She tried to look up at the tower, but was practically blinded by the enormous, mysterious object hanging in the sky behind it. The sunlight bending off its surface made it look like it was on fire. Noel held her palm up and peeked at the scene through her fingers. It was like watching a two-second GIF on auto-repeat. The clouds would try to escape the intruder, only to get pulled back again and again, never getting away but determined to keep trying.

As Noel set her kickstand and got off the bike, she heard a clang from inside the station. *What the fuck?* There shouldn't be anyone in there. She and Michael had boarded this place up long ago.

She opened her leather tool roll, grabbed a wrench, and then strode toward the station. There were no vehicles parked in the small weed-strewn lot in front of the building, its surface cracked from decades of baking in the Colorado sun, and when she got to the main door, she saw that the heavy iron bar was still bolted across the entrance and the padlock was closed. The window next to the door also remained covered in thick plywood.

For a moment she thought she must have been mistaken. There was no one inside; of course there wasn't. But when she put her ear to the window, she heard a faint noise. It sounded like something was sliding across the floor inside.

She headed around to the back. The door there was also locked tight. But there was one other way into the station, and it took only a glance to see that it had been used. On the south-facing side, a steel ladder led up to the roof. A metal box was built around the bottom of the ladder, preventing anyone access to the lower rungs, but someone had leaned a six-foot ladder against the box to get to the steel rungs above it. Not only that, an old purple-and-orange Huffy was lying nearby.

Fucker, Noel thought.

She climbed the wooden ladder and then the steel one to the top of the station. The service door leading inside had been propped open with a rock, its padlock discarded on the ground, cut open. Noel gripped the wrench tightly as she opened the door and shouted down into the station.

"I don't know who the fuck is in there, but I'll give you until the count of five before I lock this door and leave you in there to rot."

Something scraped against the floor down below. It sounded like someone was scrambling.

"I'm not fucking around!" Noel yelled.

"Okay," a voice finally said. "I'll come out."

Noel stood back from the service door, holding the wrench out in front of her. Sunlight gleamed on its surface, making her feel like she was wielding a flaming sword. And part of her really wanted to use it too.

Until Aster poked her head out of the opening.

"Aster?" Noel said. "What—what are you doing here?"

"I'm sorry," Aster said, half in and half out of the opening. "I'm not doing anything bad, I promise."

Noel lowered the wrench and stepped toward her. "Why should I believe you?" she asked, taking the teen's hand to help her step onto the roof. "After all, I haven't forgotten what you did to my satellites."

Aster gave Noel a sheepish grin. "That was an accident."

"You *would* say that," said Noel, keeping up the gag. "But seriously, what are you doing here?"

"I come here to use my telescope. I got tired of lugging it on my bike. And no one is ever up here. I mean like, ever. So I just decided to keep it inside the building."

"You live nearby?"

"My Grandmom and I live in the trailer park outside town," Aster said, embarrassment flushing her cheeks.

Noel knew the place. "Park" was a generous term for the haphazard collection of campers, RVs, and actual trailers that made up the poorest section of the county. And this nugget of information completed the puzzle Noel had been piecing together. She'd seen Aster's status among her classmates, but had chalked it up to the pretty-and-popular versus average-and-unpopular dynamic she saw all the time among high school girls. Now she knew there was more to it.

"Why are *you* here?" Aster asked. "I mean—I've never seen you here before. I've never seen anyone here before."

"Believe it or not, I own this tower," Noel said. "My dad bought it when I was about your age. But I haven't been up here in a long time. Come on, let's take a look." She headed for the ladder leading into the station. "Show me what you've done with the place."

The main console was draped in old bedsheets—Noel's stars-and-planets sheets and Michael's Spider-Man ones, back from when they were kids. Noel had forgotten they'd use those old sheets for this, and couldn't help but smile. Adjacent to the console was her father's workbench, just as he'd left it. His tools were still lying out, along with spools of wire, circuit boards, and his soldering iron. The only difference was now all of it was covered in a thick layer of dust.

The other side of the room was obviously Aster's space, and as such was much cleaner. The same old couch was still there, the one Noel had crashed on back in the day, but the floor lamp next to it was new, as was the stack of books and magazines on the floor. And of course the telescope that sat atop its tripod in the corner.

"Couch still super lumpy?" Noel asked.

"I haven't—" Aster began, then stopped herself. "Okay, I have slept here a couple of times. Sometimes I get caught up until it's too late to go home."

"Doesn't your Grandmother worry?"

"Nah, she gets caught up too."

Noel walked over and took a look at Aster's telescope. "Not bad," she said. She felt like this girl was a kindred spirit from days gone by.

"I know it's not a great scope, but it does the trick. At least it does up here, where there's not a lot of light pollution."

Noel plopped onto the couch, bouncing up and down a bit to test the springs. Aster sat next to her.

"So . . . did you figure anything out yet?" Aster asked. "About . . . you know."

Noel shook her head. "No. In fact, that's why I came up here. Wanna help me?"

"Really?" Aster said, immediately brightening.

"Yes, really." Noel grinned. "You broke it, didn't you? Only fair that you help me fix it."

15

MICHAEL CLIMBED through the rubble of St. Anne's, marking his progress through the wreckage by the stations of the cross, or at least where they should have been hanging on the collapsed walls. *Veronica wiped Jesus's face over there*, he thought, *right above where Mrs. Mills would sit with her grandkids every Sunday.*

He had given Mrs. Mills her last rites just two hours ago.

The steeple had fallen straight through the roof and landed midway up the center aisle. Jagged wooden beams and slate tiles were mounded up on either side, but the steeple itself was miraculously intact. Unfortunately, that miracle was now blocking his path. He considered circling around the destruction outside the building, hoping to find a hole in one of the side walls or the vestry that would get him to the altar. But then he crouched down and looked through the shadows in the steeple and saw light on the other side. *The only way out is through*, he thought, a common bit of advice he used to give from the pulpit.

He turned his gaze upward, seeking resolve from above as he'd done so many times in this place. But instead of inspiration or fortitude, all he found was uncertainty as he beheld the object stuck in the sky like a splinter. He looked away and waited for the object's afterimage to clear from his eyes, then picked his way forward into the steeple.

The church committee that oversaw the one-hundred-year-anniversary celebration had wanted to replace the old bell with a modern speaker system that could be controlled by the organist. But when they presented the idea to the congregation, it was almost unanimously voted down. St. Anne's had had a real bell for its first century, and the parishioners would make sure that it had a real one for its next. That bell now lay on its side, a puncture wound through its patinaed copper. Michael read what was left of the inscription.

. . . sound forth and summon the Faithful of Franklin.

Michael let the tears fall. He'd held them back while tending to his flock, seeing to the spiritual needs of those both dead and alive. But now they would be denied no more. He sobbed openly, the sounds echoing in the guano-encrusted remains of the steeple. The bell could be mended, its copper made whole again through the skill of a craftsman. But why bother? It had no purpose. Nothing to hang above.

His church was gone.

He collected himself after a few brutal minutes and stepped past the bell. Wooden beams crisscrossed the space leading to the top of the central aisle. Afraid to shift any of them, Michael dropped to his hands and knees and crawled. His palms were bloodied, but he barely felt the cuts and scrapes. The pain he felt was much deeper.

On the other side, he stood once more. And his breath caught at the sight before him.

Somehow, one of the church's beautiful stained-glass windows remained untouched. Only one. The one depicting Jesus's Sermon on the Mount. Though the heavy milled stones of the walls around the window were cracked and crumbled, the window itself was unscathed, and the light that streamed through it formed a rainbow of colors that danced all around.

As Michael gazed up at his Lord spreading the gospel to his

flock, he felt a glimmer of hope well up within him. He looked back into the darkness of the steeple, then once more at the glory still streaming into his ruined church. The building might be lost, but the people remained.

Jesus spread the good word from a rock, he thought. *Why can't I?*

Michael moved a few stray beams and pieces of slate from the steps leading to the altar. He ducked under and through other parts of the ceiling and stepped over the plaster Jesus that had come off his cross. And then he saw what he'd come here searching for: the gold of the tabernacle glittering through the rubble. It was dented, and some of the ornamentation had been sheared from its surface, but it was whole, its door still closed, the consecrated Eucharist from his last service inside.

He knew that going to all this trouble to retrieve it made no sense. He could have simply blessed more wafers. But he believed that *these* holy wafers could somehow buoy the new ones for his next service and the one after that, like a well-nourished starter for a good sourdough. No matter how irrational, it was the only way he could think of to preserve something of what he'd lost when St. Anne's fell.

He fished his keys out of his pocket and tried to open the tabernacle's door, but it wouldn't budge. He strained against the key, using his shirt for leverage, and twisted so hard that he snapped the key off in the lock.

His fragile, newborn hope was snuffed out, replaced by frustration and rage. He screamed and cursed the sky, kicked at the debris around the altar. He dropped to his knees and swam his arms through the wreckage, found a chunk of rock he could wield, and returned to the tabernacle. Raising it above his head with both hands, he brought it down on the lock, dislodging pieces of the intricate golden design. Again and again he struck the tabernacle, sending bits of rock and gold and blood through the air. And he would have continued like that until he dropped from exhaustion had Rose not called to him.

"Father Williams? Is that you?"

He dropped the rock and struggled to catch his breath. "I'm here, Rose!" he said, glaring at the mangled tabernacle, trying to will his anger to subside.

"Do you need help?"

"No, I'm done."

"I need to show you something," she said. "Right away," she added.

He worked his way back to the steeple, pausing only to gaze down at the fallen Jesus that had hung over the altar since the 1950s, and then crawled through. On the other side of the steeple, Rose pulled him to his feet.

"Is everything okay?" he asked, concerned by her urgency.

"I . . . yes, everything's fine. You just need to see it for yourself," she said, pushing him toward the front of the church.

They picked their way back down the aisle through crushed pews, broken kneelers, and giant sections of the roof. And as they crested the top of a pile of wood and stone that had once been the vestibule, he saw a group of people gathered on the sidewalk. He knew some of them from Sundays, but there were also a few he'd never seen before.

They were praying the rosary together.

Michael was dumbstruck. A wave of shame at his earlier outburst hit him. With Rose at his side, he listened to the people pray until they got to the Glory Be. And then he joined in.

Afterward, the assembled crowd grew silent. They looked up the steps to where Michael and Rose stood. He glanced up at the sky once more, but only briefly. His sights were set on something new. He made the sign of the cross, then he took Rose's hand, and the two of them left the wreckage . . . and joined his church, waiting right where it had been all along.

16

The Soyuz glanced off the mountain peak and twirled like a whirligig falling from a maple tree in autumn, the main chute ballooning above the capsule as it helicoptered down. It bounced and skipped across a ridge before finally snagging on an outcropping of rock and scrub at the edge of a cliff. There, the capsule stopped, and for a minute it seemed like the astronauts' journey was complete.

But gravity wasn't done with them yet.

The chute slowly deflated and floated down into the canyon below. It caught the canyon's thermal currents, and as it filled, it pulled on the capsule. The rocks supporting the capsule on the precipice shifted and cracked under the pressure of the chute's pull, and ultimately gave way, taking the teetering capsule with it. The Soyuz bounced end over end down the rock face, its seams bursting, each impact like a gunshot inside the capsule. Pressurized air exploded out of the vehicle, aggravating its tumble.

The main chute now dragged behind, and after hundreds of feet, it caught on a massive boulder. The capsule jerked to a stop.

Yanez's head swam. The hiss from the escaping air was a freight train in her ears. She tried to open her eyes, but had to squeeze them shut against the swirl and rising nausea. She waited, taking deep breaths. Eventually the vertigo and noise diminished and she could focus. She looked across to the window next to Susan and saw branches from a cypress tree crushed against the cracked glass.

"Is everyone okay?"

"What the hell?" Anatoly said.

"Let's get out of here," she said. "Blow the hatch."

Susan didn't respond. Anatoly shook her arm, but got nothing. He popped the latches on his helmet and flung it off. "She's unconscious," he said. "I'll get it."

He loosened his shoulder straps and leaned forward enough to reach the panel in front of Susan. He keyed in the sequence and the motors spun up to a deafening pitch, followed by four loud pops as the hinges holding the hatch in place blew. But only three of the latches actually opened.

"Son of a motherless—" he cursed.

"I'll check the door," Yanez said. "You get Susan. I won't be able to lift her."

After so many months in space, Yanez's arms and legs felt like bags of sand, her hands like water balloons. She couldn't get her helmet off, but she pawed down on her shoulder buckles and stabbed open the harness with her thumb. Then she moved to the partially opened hatch. Daylight snuck in around the seams.

The metal around one of the upper hinges was wrinkled and warped, which had prevented the explosive behind it from entirely ejecting the hinge. Yanez spun around and kicked the door repeatedly with both feet, taking a few seconds to catch her breath between kicks.

"Commander . . ." Anatoly said softly. "Susan's—"

But just then Yanez's next kick freed the door and sent it crashing to the ground below. The capsule rocked, and the main chute, or perhaps the boulder that held it, broke loose.

The capsule was only about ten feet off the ground, but as it fell, the retro rockets finally fired. The capsule jumped into the air at an awkward angle, and Yanez was thrown out the open door.

She crashed to the canyon floor, a jolt of pain shooting up her left arm, and watched the capsule cartwheel above her before landing somewhere nearby.

Her world blinked in and out. She fought to stay conscious. As her vision narrowed, she saw the object burning in the sky above, the sheer rock walls on either side creating a perfect frame.

"My God, it's real," she said.

Then all was black.

17

THE SIGNAL TRAVELED from the main switch in Denver to Albuquerque, then across Amarillo and Arkansas to a relay station in Memphis, then up through Nashville and Knoxville and Asheville, over fields and streams and mountainsides, neighborhoods and tobacco farms and sand dunes, to the very edge of America. It swam past the unknowable Atlantic Ocean floor and the myriad mysteries in the dark and cold, emerging desperate for air and light along the rock-strewn beaches of Saint-Hilaire-de-Riez. From there it zigzagged through the vineyards and fields of Poitiers and Limoges, Clermont-Ferrand, Saint-Etienne, and Valence, and weaved through the trees and grasses of Parc national des Ecrins and its neighbor, du Mercantour, before diving back under the waves of the Tyrrhenian Sea. It eventually emerged weak and suffering in Capoliveri and then again in Fiumicino. But it grew stronger as it bounced across cables and transmitters in Ponte Galeria, Casaletti Mattei, and Municipio XIII, ending its six-thousand-mile transcontinental journey in a World War II radio room in the basement of St. Peter's Basilica. More specifically, its terminus was the headset of an officer of the Gendarmerie Corps of Vatican City State, slick with sweat from the young man's fear of disappointing his boss.

But joy comes in the morning, even for those in a city doused in darkness.

"I have them!" the officer shouted, flicking switches and turning knobs to broadcast the connection throughout the room. "We have the Americans, sir."

"This is Inspector General Luca Gauzzioletti," the man in charge said into the microphone handed to him by his aide. "With whom am I speaking?"

After a piercing squawk on the line, a gruff voice spoke. "Inspector General, this is General Walter Tate of the United States Air Force. I am here with President Reyes."

"*Ciao*, General," Gauzzioletti said. "I am sorry this took so long. Once we got word through France that you were transmitting on the Dunant cable, we needed to figure out how to blockade the signal from civilian traffic."

"Sorry for the curveball," Tate said. "Google is the sole owner of this line, so it was easier to just work with them."

"Of course, of course. My aide will gather Ms. Frederick now." Gauzzioletti waved off the signal officer and settled into the young man's seat at the console. "Have you been able to reach others?"

"We have open channels with England and Ireland," Tate said. "And we think we'll be able to get Japan soon."

Another voice came over the line. "Inspector General, this is President Reyes. Who have you had contact with?"

"Madam President, it is an honor to speak with you. We have spoken with most of the leaders in the region. However, there has been no word yet out of Russia."

"We're also trying to reach them, through Britain," Reyes said.

Gauzzioletti, not a man who was good at small talk, let the line fall silent. Luckily his aide soon returned down the stairs.

"She is here now, ma'am," Gauzzioletti said, standing up from the chair and swiveling it around to the US secretary of state, who accepted it with a nod.

"Your president," he said, pointing to the microphone.

"Please stay," the secretary said to Gauzzioletti, then keyed the handset. "Madam President?"

"How was the keynote, Maddy?" Reyes asked, eliciting a smile from Madelyn Frederick, Reyes's first appointment after being sworn in last February.

"It went great, ma'am. I literally knocked them out of their seats." She wondered if it was too soon to make light of the turmoil in the conference center and the bewilderment on the faces of the six hundred battered, bruised, and bleeding attendees who had assembled to hear her talk about data security and the global threat to democracy.

"And you're okay?" the president asked.

"I'm fine," she said. "Just glad that Billy and Erin stayed behind on this trip. Can you get word to them?"

"Of course. We've got a secure line to Washington and will get someone on it right away."

"How are things at home?" Madelyn asked.

"Some parts were hit harder than others. We're still gathering intel."

"Any information on the object?"

"No, nothing yet."

"Madam Secretary, this is General Tate. What's the situation on the ground there?"

Madelyn looked at the exhaustion on Gauzzioletti's face. It had been thirty-seven hours since the event. He probably hadn't slept a wink during that time.

"Pretty tenuous," she said. "Obviously it's a special situation here."

"Probably the same at all the major religious sites," said Tate. "The Brits told us crowds are gathering at Notre Dame and Fatima. They also heard Istanbul had to close Hagia Sophia."

"What about the Middle East?" Madelyn asked.

"Still dark."

"Well, it's pretty much *all* dark over here, General."

Static burst through the speakers, and Madelyn pushed back

from the console so that Gauzzioletti's aide could get to the controls. He donned the headset, twisted ivory knobs, then checked circuits that were probably older than his grandfather. After a few minutes, he managed to restore the connection.

"Maddy, can you hear me?" the president asked.

"Yes, I'm here," Madelyn answered, still watching the aide, who was examining the inside of the receiver with a worried look on his face. "We might lose you again. Tell me what you need me to do."

"Get to Bude right away. It's near Cornwall. A bunch of transatlantic and other hard lines feed into that location, including the Europe India Gateway and the Pan-European line. We're setting up European command and control there. I need you to be our representative for North America."

Madelyn turned to Gauzzioletti. "Can you help me get there?" she asked, holding out the microphone so that the president could hear their conversation.

"Yes, Madam Secretary," he answered. Then more loudly, "It is too dangerous to fly without GPS, even by helicopter. We've had reports of several collisions. But we can get you to the French border and arrange ground transportation for you from there."

"Did you hear that?" Madelyn asked into the mic.

"Hold on," Reyes said.

Static flared, but the aide quickly restored comms once more. He shook his head and shrugged when Madelyn looked his way.

"We're losing you again, ma'am."

"Okay, go to Saint-Malo," Reyes said. "Get to the port and we'll arrange for the British Navy to take you across the channel to Bude. Did you hear? Go to the port at Saint-Malo."

Madelyn keyed the mic and confirmed, but then static crashed through the speakers and the signal cut out again. The aide tried to restore it for a few minutes before admitting defeat. The signal to America was lost.

Gauzzioletti gestured toward the stairs. "Madam Secretary, we should go. The longer we delay, the harder I think it will be to get you out of this city."

She nodded and stood. "Thank you," she said, also turning to the young aide. "Thank you both."

The spiral stairs led to a small storage room off the Portico. The secret steps leading to the radio room were hidden behind a shelf lined with leather-bound Bibles, some old and mildewed, others fresh out of the box from the publisher. As they left the room, the two Gendarmerie Corps officers who were standing guard snapped tight salutes. Gauzzioletti gave a quick salute in return and headed for the east exit, but then paused when he realized Madelyn wasn't following him.

She had stopped dead in her tracks, apparently captivated by the sound of voices raised in song. Gauzzioletti stopped dead as well, taken by the wonder that filled her eyes. In an instant, this powerful woman had been reduced to an awestruck child. He smiled as he walked back to her.

"Please, come with me, Madam Secretary," he said. But instead of the exit, he steered her in the opposite direction, toward an elevator. "You have important work ahead of you and will need all the information you can get."

The Dome elevator was designed so that a passenger could look down into the Basilica and see its wondrous architecture and sculptures during the ascent. And currently, there was a lot of activity to see—the church was filled with cardinals, priests, and nuns in prayer, and warm candlelight flooded the nave. Madelyn could have spent hours just riding up and down in the elevator, soaking in the beauty.

The elevator clanked to a stop, and Gauzzioletti stepped out and unlocked a heavy copper gate. He led the way up another set of spiral stairs, unlit, his small flashlight their only illumination. The stairs grew progressively narrower and ended with a tight corkscrew to the cupola. There he unlocked another heavy door and stood aside so that Madelyn could exit first. As she opened the door, she was met with a wave of sound.

She walked forward to the screen that surrounded the narrow walkway along the edge of the dome and looked down on the mass of humanity gathered in St. Peter's Square and the surrounding streets and avenues of Vatican City. Tens of thousands of candles illuminated the people and buildings below. She tried hard not to blink, wanting every millisecond of the image burned into her soul. The words *Non avere paura*—Italian for *Be not afraid*—washed over her. After a few verses, she had to close her eyes, the sights and sounds overwhelming her. She opened them again when Gauzzioletti touched her elbow.

"Thank you for this, Luca," she said. She kissed him on the cheek. "This will stay with me forever."

"You are welcome. But now I think it is time for us to go."

She hesitated. "Is he down there?"

"The Holy Father has not left his balcony since the first of them showed up."

Madelyn took in the sight below once more, placing her hand over her heart, then she let her gaze drift upward, not to heaven, as would be appropriate given the experience, but to the thick, dark shadow that now bisected the moon, a saber of blackness cast by the object that none in this part of the world could see but that everyone knew was there.

18

Noel touched the red lead of the multimeter to the end of one of the wires that spaghettied out from the panel at the base of the radio tower.

"Yellow!" she yelled.

Fifty feet away, Aster touched the black lead to the yellow wire snaking up from the main conduit feeding into the station. The reading on the meter jumped to 0.02.

"Good!" she yelled back through the open window.

Fuck, Noel muttered, wiping sweat from her face with a handkerchief that was already too soaked to do much good. She tucked it into her back pocket and used her shirt. Then she picked a new color and tried again.

"Purple!"

"Good!"

Fuck.

"Orange!"

"Good!"

Fuck.

"Candy cane!"

"What?"

"Candy cane! You know, red and white!"

"Oh! Hold on!" Pause. "Good!"

Fuck.

Noel heard a car crunching gravel as it came up the service road. She stood to greet it, happy to take a break from the search for the busted wire. Jimmy's cruiser crested the hill and pulled into the side lot. He gave a quick honk and got out, a small cooler in hand.

"How's it going?" he said, handing her the red-and-white Igloo stocked with a half dozen of her favorite—lemon-lime Gatorades.

"The console's fine," she said. "We had to swap out a sound board to get the speakers working. Something chewed through some of the wiring in the ceiling, so the lights are out. But overall, things are better than expected. Inside, anyway. Out here's a different story. We've got a bad connection somewhere, and are working to find it."

"Need me to get someone up here to help?" Jimmy asked. "Maybe Sam can swing by after his patrol."

"Nah, it isn't about more hands," Noel said after a long pull on her drink. "We just gotta go through the wires one by one until we find the culprit."

They walked over to the station, and Noel handed a Gatorade through the window to Aster.

"Hi, Officer Bell."

"Hey, kid," he said. "Your grandma is over at the rec center, making box lunches for people. She wants to talk to you."

"You're not gonna take me there, are you?" Aster said, a look of worry on her face. "Ms. Williams and I have got a bunch more of these wires to go through."

"No, no. I just meant you could use the radio in the cruiser. I already tuned it to the right channel. Just pick up the—"

But Aster was already gone from the window, busting out the door of the station two seconds later and running to the car.

"Guess she knows what to do?" Jimmy said.

"She's probably seen cop shows," Noel replied. She pulled her damp handkerchief out of her pocket and dunked it into the cooler. "What's going on down there?" she asked, wringing out some of the water.

"Army's shut down the interstate. Same with twenty-four and twenty-five," he said. "Drove out there myself, but they're not talking."

"Yeah, that's what I expected." Noel swabbed her face and neck with the ice-cold handkerchief.

"We got more of the power back up, though, and the grid seems to be holding."

"That's the benefit of being near the base. Grid's solid. We're lucky."

She held out the handkerchief to Jimmy, and he used it to wipe his brow. "It's getting hotter by the hour," he muttered. "No air either."

"Actually, it's moving again," Noel said. "But different. Usually blows west to east, it stopped dead for a while, and now it's coming out of the south. You can feel it up here."

Jimmy shrugged. "That happens sometimes."

"Not this time of year."

Noel cracked open another Gatorade and took a swig. Jimmy licked his finger and held it up, nodding when he felt the breeze blowing north.

"Listen," he said, "why don't you guys come back with me? You've been at it all day. Start fresh tomorrow."

"Tomorrow?" Noel chuckled. "There is no 'tomorrow.' It's just one long fucking day."

"Okay, sure. But what are you gonna do? It's an inferno up here."

"Jimmy, we need to find out what's going on. That isn't gonna happen eating sandwiches in the rec center."

"You think that's what I've been doing?" Jimmy said, his voice raised, then stopped himself, lowered his voice. "You know how many people we lost, Noel."

Noel held up a hand in apology. "I'm sorry. I know what

you've been doing. But I gotta get this thing working. It's our best chance of getting any information." She glanced up at the object. "I refuse to just sit back and hope or pray for the best. I need to *do* something."

Aster suddenly blasted a few notes on the siren, and when they looked over, she gave them a thumbs-up. Noel tapped the invisible watch on her wrist, which Aster acknowledged with a nod.

"All right," Jimmy said, "I'm gonna head back. Whenever you're done, swing by the center in case her grandmother's still there. And if you get it working, radio down to me."

He turned to walk back to the cruiser, but Noel grabbed his wrist.

"Hey," she said, then paused. "Maybe I can come by later on?" she asked at last.

Jimmy studied her a second or two, looking for the punch line. "I thought you said we had to be done with all that for a while."

"I know," she said. "But the world might be ending, right?"

Before Jimmy could answer, Aster jogged past them into the station. "Thanks, Officer Bell," she said.

Noel smiled at Jimmy. "Thanks, Officer Bell," she echoed. "So I'll see you later then."

She turned back to the search for the faulty wiring.

"Black!"

"Good!"

Fuck.

19

MICHAEL SPENT a lot of time in seminary studying the myriad ways people respond to trauma. Some people curl up tight, refusing to let anything in. Some swing the other way and open themselves up, reveling in the emotional tidal wave. Some seek comfort in others; some disappear into solitude. Some turn to God, while others curse Him as the source of their despair, shaking their fists at the sky. But what if trauma persists? What if it actually dwells in the sky as a constant reminder of what happened and what might yet happen?

What then?

Michael was exhausted after a second day of ministering to the confused and frightened people of Franklin. They had so many questions, and he wished he had better answers for them. But at the very least he felt he had a good handle on how Rose was responding to her trauma. He sat on the stage of the high school gymnasium and watched as she directed the room, checked things off her list, scribbled new things down on her clipboard, and gave orders to the crew she'd assembled. She had lost the Biscuit and Bruce in one shot, and had responded by orchestrating and controlling what she could to compensate for the things she couldn't. Everyone was glad for it, especially Michael.

"I think we should use just the one set of bleachers for now," she said, pointing to where a few people waited to unlock and then pull out the retractable bleachers from the wall. "That way we can keep the crowd off the court as much as possible and keep Coach Kelly from yelling at anyone."

Michael nodded in agreement, and Rose gave a thumbs-up to the bleacher crew. "We can put the podium at center court for you," she said to Michael, checking a box on her clipboard.

"That's okay, I don't need a podium. Just a small table where I can prepare Communion."

Her disappointment was palpable. She'd had it all planned out and he was ruining it. She scratched out something on her clipboard.

"Actually, you know, you're right," Michael said quickly, walking it back. "I think a podium would be nice. Thank you."

She immediately brightened. "We'll do a table too, Father." She never used to call him Father, having always known him as Mikey. But that changed yesterday. "Of course you need a table for the Communion. I'll get right on it."

As Rose strode away, Zadie Bennett came running into the gym.

"Where's Father Williams?"

"I'm here," he said, hopping off the stage.

"Oh, thank God. You need to come right now. Please hurry!" She waved him forward like a third base coach waving a runner home.

"What is it?" he asked as he ran toward her.

"It's Theresa Donnelly. She's on the roof of the hospital and threatening to jump."

Michael burst from the gym. The hospital was only a few blocks from the high school, so he swerved around Zadie's idling car and sprinted straight for it. As he got closer, he could see a small crowd gathered out front, pointing up to where Theresa was standing on the edge of the roof in her hospital gown.

Michael ran into the hospital, slowing only enough to allow

the sliding doors to open in front of him. He knew the layout well, having visited many times to give blessings to Franklin's newest residents and send others on their way. He cut left at the information desk, headed straight to the central stairwell, and took the steps two and three at a time, up the seven flights to the roof. When he got there, the door was being held open for him by one of the residents.

"We tried to talk her down," the young doctor said. "But she's really confused."

Michael stepped through the door and into a convection oven. Heat radiated from both above and below as it reflected off the metal ductwork and pebble-covered roof.

Midge, Theresa's mother, grabbed him. "Mike, you have to help her," she pleaded. She dragged him toward her daughter. "Honey, he's here! Okay, baby? He's here!"

"Theresa, it's Father Williams," he said, shielding his eyes so he could get a fix on her. She stood looking down at the ground, her back to him. He heard her say something very quietly but couldn't make it out.

"I'm sorry, I couldn't hear you," he said, afraid to move toward her. "What did you say?"

"God is mad," she said. "And he's going to punish us."

"That isn't true. You know that," he said. "God loves us."

"Not anymore. Just look," she said, poking a finger at the object in the sky.

"We don't know what that is yet. But even if God did put it there, he didn't do it to hurt us."

She whipped around to face him. "You're wrong! You weren't there! You didn't see him!"

"See who?" he asked, taking a small step forward now that they were facing one another.

"God!" she screamed, her heels dangerously close to the edge. "He was there in the church. Right after you left with Officer Bell."

"Of course," he said, trying to calm her, taking a very tentative, very small step forward. "God's always there in the church. It's His house, after all. Right?"

"You're not *listening*!" she screamed. "He was *there*! When the world stopped, He was *there*!"

More people had come onto the roof behind him, and Michael heard a small murmur rise at Theresa's proclamation. Ignoring them, he held an open palm out to the weeping girl, trying to get her to focus on him, to see him, to listen to the sound of his voice.

"Tell me about it," he said. "Tell me what happened in the church."

She didn't say anything for a while. She just stood there twisting the hem of her gown.

"You can tell me. Don't be afraid."

She looked over her shoulder and then back at Michael, as if checking to see if anyone else could hear.

"After you left, I played for a little while longer. I like being in there by myself. Just me and the organ. And God too," she said. Then she paused, as if lost in thought.

"And then what happened?"

"I turned everything off, like I always do, and I was leaving. That's when I got knocked sideways into one of the pews." Tears streamed down her face. "There was so much noise, and dust everywhere. I couldn't see anything."

He continued to move toward her. Slowly. "What happened next?" he asked.

"I heard cracks," she said. "From everywhere. All around. So many cracking sounds. And it made me scared, so I crawled back to the aisle and got up. And I saw Him."

"You saw God?"

Theresa's breath caught in her throat, followed by deep sobbing. She pulled at her gown, the tendons standing out on her arms.

"He was the light. He came in from everywhere. The windows and the walls. From above. He came in from all over and I just stood there," she said, the remembrance overtaking her, calming her. But just as quickly, the calm evaporated and her face twisted. "Then the cross fell," she snarled. "It crashed onto the altar. It crashed right down where you stand every week, and Jesus popped off. He popped off and *jumped* at me. I was too far away for him to get me, so he fell in front of me. And then he broke into pieces. Jesus broke right in front of me, Father. And that's when I knew what was going to happen."

"Knew what, honey?" Michael said, almost within arm's reach of her.

She looked directly at him then, her eyes resolute and calm, her body standing tall against the force of the sunlight and memory weighing down on her.

"We're all going to Hell," she said.

She took two steps back, right to the edge of the roof, and then pushed back, arms spread wide. Michael lunged to grab her, but she was too quick, and his arms grasped only air. Behind him, Midge screamed.

Theresa was gone.

20

TAP, tap, tap.

Yanez winced, her mind rising and then falling back into the deepness.

Tap, tap, tap.

She focused on the noise, willing herself back. Her eyes fluttered open and she saw the beak descend.

Tap, tap, tap.

She swatted at the bird, and it took off in a flurry of feathers. Light pierced her eyes through her clear plastic visor. She shielded her face with her gloved hand, then slightly spread the fat fingers of her glove. Even through the slits, the intensity was too much, and she snapped her fingers together again. But then she remembered the gold-coated visor.

The release was on the right side of the helmet. She switched hands so that her left could block the light while she slid the sun visor into place over top of the regular face shield. Once it was locked in, the brightness mercifully dimmed, she let her hand fall.

She gazed at the object above.

Yanez had been on the track and field team in high school. A science and math nerd at heart, she made throwing her focus, and she excelled at the javelin. She loved the arc of it as it soared through the sky. She used to practice various launch angles and throwing styles, trying to eliminate wobble or increase it, whatever it took to maximize the javelin's flight. Even back then, math helped her land things. And she loved when the javelin hit the ground, sticking into the green field at an angle equal to her launch angle, trembling back and forth as it came to rest and the measurements were taken.

Looking up at the incandescent object stuck in the sky, she couldn't escape the similarity. But at the moment of its impact, instead of a burst of dirt, clouds had been ejected from the piercing end of the object, which seemed born of and ensconced in sunlight, enrobed in shimmering, purpled translucence.

Yanez was both enraptured and terrified by the sight. Her air was gone. Her thoughts were gone. Her reason and intellect and hopes were gone, erased by the enormity of the thing. Its size and scale and what it could represent strained her comprehension of science and God. The impossibility of what it had done to her home, the one she was now reunited with, the canyon floor beneath her after being flung from—

"The Soyuz," she said, turning her head to see where it had landed, but instead seeing only the inside of her helmet.

It all came flooding back. The re-entry, the chutes, the retros firing unexpectedly, being thrown through the door of the capsule. She started ripping at the latches on her helmet, feeling like she was suffocating and desperate to be free of it. When she flung it aside she saw the capsule. It was across a small stream on the opposite side of the canyon.

"Anatoly! Susan!" she yelled. "I'm here!"

Her voice echoed in the canyon, but there was no reply.

She got to her knees, and immediately her world swam. She stripped off her gloves and began to work her way out of her spacesuit, repeatedly calling for Anatoly and Susan. It took nearly ten minutes of struggling just to free herself from the hard upper and lower torso sections of the suit, and when she was done she lay sweating and exhausted in just her cooling garment, which was leaking fluid from holes in the line near her chest and right leg. She let the bluish water wash over her hand as she caught her breath.

After a few more minutes, she rose to her feet. Her legs were spaghetti beneath her, the effects of full gravity taking a heavy toll. Normally a ground crew would carry astronauts from the Soyuz to a vehicle that would transport them directly to a hospital to recover and readjust to normal gravity. But there was no ground crew here. No one even knew they were back.

Needles stabbed from her heels to hips, her knees wobbly and quivering. She shuffled toward the capsule with her arms thrust out from her sides for balance. But when she reached the edge of the stream, she couldn't adjust her weight fast enough to compensate for the soft sand on the bank, and she toppled into the water. The frigid cold was the only thing that kept her from passing out again.

She rested on hands and knees for a moment, watching the water flow beneath her, sunlight glinting off its surface. Then she was up again and moving to the opposite shore.

The water wasn't deep, only reaching to mid-calf at its highest point. The capsule lay just ahead of her. It had come to rest a few feet above the ground, sandwiched between two large boulders with the open door facing downward.

"Anatoly! Susan!" she called, but again got no response.

In order to get into the capsule, she'd have to crawl beneath it. Yanez touched the side of the Soyuz, giving it a light shove, ready to jump backward if needed. But it didn't budge. She tried again, this time leaning into it more, pushing with all her might. Once again it held firm.

She dropped to her stomach and military-crawled her way forward. Dirt collected in the hoses of her cooling garment, turning to mud where the fluid leaked out. Sunlight streamed from the capsule's window and out the open door, creating a square of light ahead of her. She swiped aside various bits of debris—operations manuals, wiring, insulation, Susan's troll doll —and moved forward.

And then she saw the puddle of blood.

"Can anyone hear me?" she asked, frantic. Stars swam in front of her eyes, and she was forced to stop and take deep breaths.

When her vision cleared and her breathing slowed, she wiggled forward again. It was impossible to avoid the blood, so she ended up smearing it down her torso and across her forearms, thighs, and knees. The door was just ahead of her, light bending around the edges. She pushed forward to get herself right underneath it, and looked up.

Anatoly was nowhere to be seen. But Susan was still in her seat, hanging by her shoulder straps. Her head was tilted forward, the helmet filled with so much blood that it obscured her face.

Yanez choked back a sob, pushed up onto her knees, and stood, coming face to face with her former crewmate. She pushed Susan's helmet back enough to expose the latches near her neck, snapped them open, and pulled the helmet off, ignoring the shower of blood that ran down onto her. She dropped the helmet and felt for a pulse, not expecting to find one. With her free hand she felt around Susan's skull, looking for the injury, and when she felt the deep crater in the back of Susan's neck, she knew her friend was gone.

"I'm sorry," she said, easing Susan's head down to rest against her chest. "I tried."

Susan was gone. Anatoly, missing. The Soyuz wrecked.

But there was one more thing for Yanez to do here. One item to retrieve. The drive, stowed in her backpack in the compartment beneath her seat.

Her seat was higher in the capsule, so she had to find a foothold to boost herself up. She could stand on the edge of the console across from the crew seats, but that would put her at an awkward angle and put too much pressure on her shoulders. She might slip and tumble down through the open door. She had to settle for wedging her foot between the wall and Susan's seat and using Susan's body as leverage.

"I'm sorry," she said again.

Grabbing Susan's left shoulder strap, she hoisted herself up. Susan's head lolled against her stomach, bringing forth another wrenching sob. She felt her world spinning again; she desperately needed to get out of the Soyuz. Quickly she popped the compartment open and reached inside, felt the fur of the blue rabbit's foot attached to the front zipper of her backpack, and yanked on it. As soon as the backpack was free of the other gear, she lowered herself to the ground and knelt in the puddle of blood, her eyes closed.

She waited a full sixty-count before opening them.

Her path out from beneath the Soyuz was clear, her own muddy, bloody tracks stretched out before her. But with the light from the Soyuz window now at her back, she could see that the puddle hadn't just come from above. A rivulet of blood snaked from the adjacent rock face to the pool she now knelt in. And that's when she knew where to find Anatoly.

Yanez resumed her military crawl back toward the sunlight, dragging the backpack with her. She needed to pause a few times as stars lit her vision, but she eventually managed to wriggle her way to freedom. She set the backpack in a patch of shade, pushed herself to her knees, then to her feet. The air in the canyon was hot and thick, but not nearly as oppressive as the air inside the capsule.

She went around the boulder next to the Soyuz. It had been shorn in half by the collision, creating an almost flat surface wide enough for her to stand on. If she could get up there, she'd be able to reach the edge of the Soyuz and maybe get on top of it. It took her a few tries to boost herself up, but eventually she threw a leg over the edge and then rolled atop the boulder. The effort was tremendous, and she needed to rest again as her vision started to narrow. Once she felt steady enough, she scooted to the edge of the Soyuz.

Anatoly was there. Wedged between the bottom of the capsule and the base of the canyon wall. His chest, shoulders, and head were above the lip of the heat shield, everything else crushed beneath it. He was certainly gone. She tried to work her way along the edge of the shield to get closer to him, but lost her grip and landed hard on her shoulder. Pain shot across her collarbone and down her spine. Her vision dimmed and her mind swam, but she stayed conscious and rolled onto her back.

Lying there, waiting for the fire in her arm to die, she let her grief pour out, her deep sobs echoing through the canyon. Her calculations had gotten them home, but not alive. She'd failed her crew. Had they stayed on the space station, bounced off the atmosphere on re-entry, or landed in the Atlantic, her crew, her friends, would be no more or less dead than they were now.

She opened her eyes and saw the object hanging in the sky, the villain that had claimed their lives. It glowed, throwing light in all directions, indifferent to Susan's and Anatoly's deaths. Indifferent to her own survival. She hoped and prayed that something on the computer drive from the station would help them understand what it was and why it was here. So that her friends' deaths would mean something. But in order for that to happen, she had to get it out of the canyon and back to the world. Her work wasn't done.

She eased herself down from the rock and retrieved the backpack. It was caked with blood and dirt, just like her. She unzipped the bag and looked inside. The drive was still nestled in her sweatshirt, undamaged. She zipped it back up and slung it over her shoulder. And with a final glance at the vehicle that had brought her home, she began her next mission.

PART III

21

ABSTRACT #235, Presented at the 32nd Annual Congress of the International Exogeology Society, 2009.

Authors: Parnell, G.; Chin, A.; Kapoor, V.; et al. University of Washington, Seattle.

Background: Sea levels have remained largely constant over hundreds of millennia as a result of two primary astrophysical phenomena: 1) gravity and 2) planetary spin, which is responsible for centrifugal force and the Earth's ellipsoid shape. The mass devastation that could potentially result from a loss of gravity has been well documented by researchers from Oxford and the University of Tokyo.[1-16, 19] This study focuses on the role of Earth's spin rate on global sea levels and ongoing mantle rearrangements.

Methods: We conducted a meta-analysis of hundreds of studies on the determinants of global spin rate, including but not limited to: Munk's enigma of sea level rise; clock error analyses compared to Babylonian,

Chinese, Arab, and Greek eclipse observations; 20th century rotational vector variances; satellite geodetic estimates; and mantle frame references, including measures of true polar wander.

Results: Correlation between sea level rise and decrease in planetary spin rate is abundant. Data across numerous studies are complementary and reproducible. Therefore, it is possible to predict planetary spin rate's impact on global oceanic migratory patterns and mantle rearrangements with a high degree of accuracy, including in the improbable event of the total loss of the planet's rotation.

Conclusion: Total cessation of planetary spin could result in sea water migration to the polar regions of the planet where gravity is strongest and significant mantle rearrangements along the equator. The combination of a diminished ellipsoid shape and migration of the planet's oceans to the poles could potentially give rise to an equatorial megacontinent and two large circumpolar oceans.

"But this is just a theory, right?"

"Yes, Madam President," Eugenia Sang said, then added: "Well—not all of it, I guess."

"Which parts are and which parts aren't?"

"I'm not a geologist. But I think an argument could be made that we'd end up with several large equatorial land masses instead of a singular mass that encircles the globe. I mean, there's no way of truly ascertaining how much or how fast the bulge along the equator will diminish. And the core may still be rotating to some degree, so some sort of subcentrifugal force could be at play. There's a lot of math here that would need to be worked out. And like I said, ma'am, I'm not a geologist."

Bonita Reyes, forty-seventh president of the United States,

lived by the credo that if you're the smartest person in the room, you're in the wrong room. Sitting at a table filled with scientists and some of the nation's top military brass, with scientific and policy advisors from all over the country on a jammed landline, huddled inside a bunker inside a mountain designed to withstand a nuclear blast, she felt confident she was in the right room.

"I recognize that you're venturing beyond your area of expertise," she said. "So the part about the land . . . let's say for now that that's debatable. But what about the oceans part?"

"Oh, that's definitely going to happen," Eugenia said, nodding emphatically enough that her glasses went cockeyed. "Definitely."

"Can anyone say when?" General Dinesh asked.

"No," said Mina Blank, the NASA administrator. "I mean— there's no way *to* know." She slid imaginary glasses up her nose, looking directly at Eugenia while she did it, but the signal wasn't picked up by its intended receiver.

"Ballpark, then. Are we talking days or hours?" Dinesh said, his frustration mounting. "And which parts of the world will be affected first?"

"We can make projections based on relative distances above or below sea level," said Mina, "but there's no way of knowing with a high degree of certainty. As Dr. Sang explained, the science here is sound, but it's a complex system, and there are just too many unknowns."

"Then," said Dinesh, "with all due respect to the *non*-geologist and NASA, why the *fuck* are we talking about this?"

They had been at it for a long time, and this was far from the first outburst. But as Mina prepared her retort, reaching for the heavy binder in front of her to either find additional evidence or pummel the arrogant, well-decorated dick who had just snapped at her, General Tate decided that the time for debate was over.

"Because, Sanjay," he said, "we aren't the only ones talking about it."

Dinesh took a deep breath and turned to the two women.

"Forgive me. That was uncalled for." Then to Tate: "Who's talking about this?"

Tate opened a folder and removed the top sheet. "These are radio intercepts from the surrounding area and initial reports coming out of AWACS surveillance up and down the coasts," he said. "The theory Dr. Sang just went through is one of the most popular out there on the airwaves."

"Wait a minute. How the hell does anyone know about this?" the president asked, holding up the printout of the abstract. "Isn't the internet down?"

"It is now," said Tate, "but there were pockets where, at least for a little while, the net held out. Someone must have dug this thing up, and now it's spreading around."

"So what?" Dinesh said. "There's plenty of other things out there—prophecies about the end times and Ragnarök and who knows what else, for God's sake."

"I'm sure you're right, General," said Reyes, leaning back in her chair and pinching the bridge of her nose. She hadn't slept since landing in Colorado yesterday and was beginning to feel the impact. "And that's what scares me the most. People are desperate for answers. And if we don't have any to give them, they'll start listening to whoever is talking."

A knock sounded on the conference room door, and Jill O'Neal entered. She handed Tate a piece of paper and then took a step back and waited for him to read it. He gave it a quick scan, then summarized for the room.

"Military and state police report a growing caravan of vehicles along the interstate and other roads heading toward us. Some have taken to mountain passes and smaller county roads to try and circumvent our blockades."

He handed the paper back to Jill and turned to the president. "Ma'am, we've completed the transition of personnel and equipment to the Mountain. We've secured dedicated lines of communication to both coasts and the newly designated central command for Europe in Bude, to which the secretary of state is heading as we speak. I think it's time."

"But what kind of signal does that send, Walt?" she asked. "I don't know that I'm quite ready to make that call."

Tate tapped on his copy of the abstract. "Two large circumpolar oceans and an equatorial megacontinent," he said. "If this is even true by half, we're going to be dealing with mass movement of people in and out of the country. Ma'am, we can't plan for that if we're worried about people crashing our gates."

The room fell silent while the president considered the ramifications of locking down the Mountain. And that was when it dawned on her, for the first time since she'd taken the oath of office, that she couldn't live by the rule of the rooms anymore. Because no matter whether she was the smartest or the dumbest, whenever *she* was in the room, there was only one person who had to make all the hard decisions. And that was her.

She pushed back from the table and rose. Immediately everyone jumped to attention.

"I want to see plans to start broadcasting new messages on the EBS starting in the next two hours," she said, rapping her knuckles on the table for emphasis. She turned and headed for the conference room door, but her escape wasn't clean.

"Understood," Tate said. "What about the Mountain, ma'am?"

Reyes paused at the door, released a deep sigh, then made the decision that would define her presidency.

"Button it up."

22

"I THINK you need to get right back on the horse," Noel said to Aster, who was sitting behind the main console and rolling a spool of sixteen-gauge wire back and forth. The smell of solder lingered in the air.

"I don't know," Aster said, staring out the window at the radio tower. "I think you should do it."

"Come on. It can't go any worse than last time, right?" Noel pointed at the switch marked *Show*. "Let's light this candle."

With a sigh, Aster set the spool aside, closed her eyes, crossed her fingers, and then flicked the switch.

Buttons and panels lit up. Needles on the meters jumped back and forth as radio signals streamed into the station from the tower. Fuzz erupted from the speakers, drowning out Noel's and Aster's cries of victory.

They high-fived, then Noel reached over Aster's shoulder to lower the volume. But as soon as she touched the knob, a spark jumped out of the top of the console, followed by a puff of white smoke and the smell of burning hair. And then silence.

"Man, we are not good at this."

"That one's your fault," said Aster.

Noel removed the access panel at the top of the console and

shined a flashlight inside. "I see it," she said, reaching for a screw-driver in her tool belt. "Blew a transformer."

"Can we fix it?" Aster asked.

"If we've got the part," Noel said. She pointed with the screw-driver to shelves along the back wall. "It should be labeled 'power' or something like that."

Aster went over and began searching. In her time using this station as her own personal hideout, she'd left the stuff on the shelves alone. There was just so much of it. Boxes, crates, bags, plastic bins, spools of wire. One cardboard box was just for circuit boards, of every imaginable shape and color. Another bin had just woofers, tweeters, and midrange cones. A crate wrapped in red and yellow tape declared the contents "fragile" and contained stacked egg cartons of vacuum tubes.

"Where did you even get all of this stuff?" she asked Noel, who was still elbow-deep in the console.

"My dad and I used to go around to garage sales on the week-ends. There was also a big electronics show every year in Denver where we could pick up equipment cheap. And once Craigslist and eBay came around, boy, there was no stopping him. Boxes started showing up on the doorstep almost daily. I eventually had to cut him off or he'd have gone broke."

"Is he the one that got you into science?"

"Yep. He was an engineer," Noel said, wincing and then putting her index finger in her mouth. She examined the tip, then shook it off and plunged back into the console. "He even helped me get my job on base."

"He still around?"

"Nah, both my folks are gone," Noel said, pulling out the fried transformer. "How about you?"

"I never knew my dad," Aster said. "He bounced when he found out my mom was pregnant with me."

"And what about your mom?"

"She was in the service, so we moved around a lot. But that was cool. I got to see lots of places growing up before we landed here." Aster pulled down a duct tape-reinforced box, nearly dropping it when its full weight came free of the steel shelf. "But then three years ago she got sent to Afghanistan. I was in school, so I stayed behind with my grandma. About a month before her tour ended, Mom was killed on patrol."

Noel stopped working and looked over at Aster, on her knees and digging through a box that Noel herself had probably dug through at her age. "I'm sorry to hear that. My mom died when I was young too. I know how hard it can be."

Aster nodded silently and kept digging. That seemed to be enough for her right then, so Noel left it there and got back to work.

Aster had taken almost everything out of the big box before she got to a layer of smaller boxes that contained transformers. "Got 'em," she said, pulling one of the smaller boxes out and reading the label. "This one says 'open bracket.'"

"Nah, we need a high-voltage one. It'll say that or 'class A' on the box."

Aster pulled a few more out and then found one that looked different from the rest. "Found a Hammond HV. That work?"

"Yeah, that might do it," Noel said, examining the torched transformer she had just extracted from the console.

Aster came over and traded for the burned-out one. Noel unboxed the Hammond, nodded her confirmation, and set to work putting it into the console. Aster took up her former seat and tossed the ruined transformer up and down.

"How long have you known Officer Bell?" she asked.

"Practically my whole life," said Noel, twisting a screw into place. "He and my brother have been best friends since they were little."

"But now you guys are friendly too," Aster said, smiling. "Right?"

"It's not like that," Noel said as nonchalantly as she could. She didn't think she'd sold it, though, at least not judging by the grin on Aster's face.

A minute later, she twisted home the final screw. "All right, I think we're ready. Third time's the charm, right?"

"Right," said Aster, resuming her position at the switch. "Ready?"

Noel nodded. "Do your worst."

Aster flicked the switch. The console flared to life, static streaming out of the speakers. And this time it held.

Noel pulled a chair up beside Aster's. "Okay," she said, "now let's see who's out there."

The first thing they heard was the emergency message that had been playing for almost two days. Noel tuned in several low-band stations, and all of them were repeating the same message. But then they found regular people—or at least, people who might once have been categorized as regular.

There was a man reading from the book of Genesis and weeping about his third-grade teacher, two women who were clearly drunk and laughing hysterically while watching porn, a young boy and his friend explaining how *The X-Files* was actually the government trying to get people used to the idea of aliens being on Earth, a woman lamenting the wildlife in Antarctica that would drown when the oceans consumed the polar caps, and on and on.

"Let's try some of the official channels," Noel finally said, tuning to the higher bands. After some searching, they stumbled onto a CB conversation on one of the military frequencies.

"*. . . units will stay to reinforce the blockades on the interstate and other highways,*" said a voice.

A second voice replied. "*That's not going to be enough. Those checkpoints are about to be overrun. And it doesn't matter because people are just going around them anyway. It's just too much space to cover.*"

"*POTUS just called it. The palace is closed. Tate ordered twelve MH-139s to assist in turning people back.*"

"*And if that doesn't work?*"

"*Those are the orders, Sergeant. Reports are to be made in thirty-minute intervals. Good luck.*"

"Son of a bitch," said Noel, switching off the console. "That ain't good."

"Why? What's the palace?" Aster asked.

"It's code for Cheyenne Mountain. It means they shifted operations away from Peterson." She rose from her seat. "We gotta go back to town. They need to know about this."

She led Aster out of the station and then locked it behind her. She got on her motorcycle, handed Aster her spare helmet, then kickstarted the bike.

"Who's POTUS?" Aster asked as she adjusted the strap on her helmet.

"The president of the United States," Noel said.

Aster mouthed a silent "Ah," then got on the cycle behind Noel and grabbed her waist.

"I still don't understand. Why is this bad news?" Aster asked.

Noel shook her head. She shouldn't have said anything. She was probably freaking the girl out. "It's probably not. I was just surprised is all. I'm sure it's just procedure. No biggie."

But she heard her own voice, and she didn't sound the slightest bit convincing.

23

MIDGE'S FRIENDS had to pry her off of her daughter's broken body. She twisted away from them, ran a few steps, tearing at her shirt, then fell to the ground, her screams and howls coming from a primal place. She kicked and thrashed and beat the concrete until her fists were torn and bloodied. It was nearly too much to bear for those around her, watching in horror.

It was too much for Midge, too. She didn't stop until she'd exhausted herself so thoroughly that she collapsed, unconscious. Rose, Zadie, and the others screamed, and a few of the hospital staff hoisted her onto a stretcher and rushed her inside. In the aftermath, Michael was momentarily left alone with Theresa.

He knelt next to her and looked down into her green eyes, ignoring the blood that had splattered her face when she struck the ground. He thought of all the Sundays she had played to a nearly empty house at St. Anne's. If he had just done a better job, more people would have gotten a chance to hear her play. If he had been more inspiring, more people would have come and witnessed her amazing gift, heard the beautiful music that poured forth from this small and fragile soul.

"I'm sorry I failed you," he said, closing her eyes.

He made the sign of the cross on her forehead, then stood as two orderlies came to retrieve her body. They placed her on a stretcher and covered her in a white sheet. As they were wheeling her into the hospital, Jimmy's cruiser pulled up.

"I got here as soon as I heard the news," Jimmy said. "You okay?"

Michael nodded and then hugged his friend.

"The whole thing's fucked up, man," Jimmy said. "None of this should be happening." He steered Michael toward his cruiser. "Come on. Let's get gone for a little while."

Michael climbed into the car and wasted no time fishing a pack of Marlboro Reds and a Zippo out of Jimmy's glovebox. He lit one and handed it over to Jimmy, then lit one for himself. For a long time, they just smoked in silence, Jimmy driving away from town, away from the horrors that needed to be left behind, if only for a time.

Michael flicked his butt out the window and broke the silence.

"Did I ever tell you about Ernie Risso?"

"Don't think so," Jimmy replied, getting rid of his own butt.

"I met him during my third year at seminary. Ernie showed up one day with all of his worldly possessions, which amounted to a bunch of clothes in a cardboard box. His wife had just died of colon cancer."

"That blows," Jimmy said, making a smoking motion with an empty index and middle finger.

Michael shook out a fresh cigarette, lit it, and handed it over. "They had been married for twenty-seven years. Ernie decided to devote the rest of his life to Christ—and the vicar assigned me to be his mentor."

"They do that?"

"Not always," Michael said, lighting another cigarette of his own. "But in a situation like Ernie's—tragedy strikes, wife dies, the husband, lost and alone for the first time, decides he wants to become a priest—well, the powers that be make sure someone watches them. Situations like that actually aren't all that uncommon. Usually, once the trauma wears off, so does their newfound devotion."

Jimmy turned onto County Line Road, which wasn't more than a dirt and gravel trail up to Harvey's Butte, where Jimmy and Michael used to drink pony bottles of Heineken they'd boost from Michael's dad.

"And did it?" Jimmy asked. "For Ernie?"

"No. Within six months, he had become one of our most active seminarians. He volunteered at the soup kitchen and thrift store, spent hours at the old folks' home reading to them and visiting. He'd found his calling, and it was great to see. He was happy, man. Just happy."

"Good for him," Jimmy said. They crested the top of the butte, and he put the car into park and cut the engine.

They got out of the car and walked to the rim of the butte. The interstate snaked below them, hosting a line of vehicles as far as they could see.

Michael looked down at the choked highway, then up at the object in the sky. "At Ernie's graduation ceremony, he told me his secret."

Jimmy said nothing. Just waited patiently.

Michael took a long drag on his cigarette. "We were talking about his new life and what was ahead of him. He was being sent to Ukraine to serve as a missionary. While we were talking, I asked him what he thought might have happened if God had answered his prayers and saved his wife. And he told me I had it all wrong. God *did* answer his prayers. He said he'd been asking God to take her from him for years and years. And finally, God got around to it. So he figured he owed Him. *That's* why he joined the faith."

"What the fuck?" Jimmy laughed. "So the guy was nuts?"

"I'm not sure what's sane or insane anymore." Michael waved his cigarette at the lineup of desperate people below. "But I don't think he was crazy. I just think he made a decision, you know? He just decided on a course of action and made it happen. There's something to be said about that."

Jimmy's shoulder mic chirped. "Hey, Jimmy. I mean, Sheriff," the dispatcher said. "You got Father Williams with you?"

"Yeah. What's up, Rob?"

"His sister's here."

"Put her on," Jimmy said, waving Michael closer. They heard Noel take the mic, but she spoke too softly at first.

"Say again, Noel. We can't hear you."

Jimmy and Michael could make out Noel asking the dispatcher for some privacy. A few seconds later, she repeated herself.

"I fixed it," she said.

"You got the tower working?" Michael asked, leaning into Jimmy's mic.

"Yeah, and I've got some news. But I don't want to say on an open channel. I need you both back here. We need the council too. Jimmy, can you have some people round them up and get them over to Whitey's?"

"Is it bad?" Jimmy asked.

"We just gotta get ready," she said.

"Okay, I'm on it. We'll head there now."

Jimmy started walking to the car, but Michael didn't follow. He just kept staring at the line of people down below, going nowhere. After a moment, Jimmy came back to his side.

"You gonna be okay?" Jimmy asked.

Michael answered with a question of his own. "You know what she said to me?"

"Who?"

"Theresa. Right before she jumped."

Jimmy shook his head.

"She told me that God was mad. She said he was mad and that . . . that he was going to punish us."

"She was really messed up, Mike. I'm so sorry."

Down below, a girl vomited on the shoulder of the road, her

mother screaming at her. Not far off, two men were throwing punches next to a box truck that had overheated, white steam pouring from its hood. Behind the disabled truck, dozens of horns blared. One car tried to drive down the embankment to get around the stalled vehicle, but it got stuck on the upslope and then rolled backward into an SUV that had followed it. The driver of the SUV got out, ran to the driver's window of the car ahead of it, and pounded angrily on the glass.

"I've been thinking about what she said this whole time," Michael said. "And you know what?" He took a last drag on his cigarette and flicked the butt toward the chaos below. "I think she was right."

24

"Oh Mister Sun, Sun, Sun, Sun, Sun.
That's a lot of suns up there in the sky.
Mister weird, shiny golden sun.
Hiding behind a bumblebee."

YANEZ HUMMED and tried to keep her mind from slipping away from her as she stumbled along the stream, which wasn't much more than a trickle wending through the gravel and sticky scrub. Huge red rock formations loomed on either side, shadeless skyscrapers, perches for carrion birds that watched her sad parade down a desolate boulevard. The sun and heat took their toll, the tubes of her cooling garment completely dry now, clinging to her and leaving her skin raw. Her body felt thick and alien in Earth's unrelenting gravity, and the backpack containing the drive from the ISS grew heavier with each step.

"These little children are asking you
To please come down here to Earth so we can play with you.

Oh Mister Sun, Sun, you weird fucking sun.
Please stop shining down on me."

Yanez dreamed of floating in the cold and quiet of space, so light and free on the station, her body a feather drifting on the breeze and looking for Tom Hanks and his box of chocolates.

Gravity is as gravity does.

It had been heaven. Just her and her crew. But now she was all alone. Anatoly and Susan were dead. Dead because of her shitty equation that had put them here instead of somewhere safer and softer and cooler. She should have landed them where there were shady trees instead of a sun monster microwaving them in their capsule, melting them like ice cream from Mr. Softee. Their blood was now on her hands, on her knees, on her shoes. Sticking like bubble gum to the bottom of her Bobos that Mom had bought her at K-Mart for a dollar ninety-nine even though she'd wanted the Nikes like her cousin Tessa had because Uncle Brian had lots of money.

Tears streamed down her cheeks as these wild, untamed thoughts butterflied through her brain. Her vision wobbled, the brutal light dimming in her eyes before snapping back. She tripped and stumbled over rocks and gravel, the stream completely gone now, the ground pitted and splintered. *Keep moving,* she told herself, focusing on each step.

She didn't see the narrow fissure that had opened in her path. Didn't see it, but felt the pain from the pop in her knee when she stepped on the edge of the crack.

She went down hard, clutching at her knee. Her world swam and she tasted copper. She swallowed it down only to immediately retch it up, the pain and the flavor mixing in her gut. When she was finished, she lay on her back, the backpack digging into her spine. The world swirled before her, her vision ringed in bright flecks of golden light. She closed her eyes to try and stave off oblivion, taking slow and steady breaths.

She was lying there, thinking about Susan and Anatoly, about how Mom would be mad if she didn't make it home in time for dinner, when she heard the buzzing. She opened her eyes and saw a giant bumblebee floating directly above her, hovering, blotting out the object in the sky.

Hiding behind a bumblebee, she thought, then blacked out.

25

"THE GRID IS GONE," the officer said, unfolding the map and spreading it on the hood of the Range Rover the French border patrol had arranged for her. "Everywhere is out. My cousin who works at one of the nuclear plants up north said the lockdown could last for weeks."

France led the world in nuclear power, Madelyn knew. Close to eighty percent of all of its electricity came from reactors along its northern border and throughout the countryside. But as she looked out beyond the glow of the SUV's headlights, she imagined the only thing France led the world in right at this moment was people scared of the dark.

"Could you please?" he said, handing Madelyn his flashlight so that she could shine it down on the map. The officer uncapped a Sharpie and made a star near the Italian border. "We are here. It is best for you to stay away from the cities. All the roads are clogged with people trying to get in and out. It is a total mess."

He narrated the route as he drew, and she followed it with the light. "I think it is easiest for you to follow the parks. Baronnies provençales, Monts d'Ardèche, Livradois-Forez, Volcans d'Auvergne, all the way west. And then to Millevaches en Limousin and Périgord-Limousin. You see?"

The wondrousness of GPS set in now that it was gone. Madelyn couldn't recall the last time she'd even *seen* a paper map, let alone had to use one.

"From there, you go north to Loire-Anjou-Touraine, and then you just follow the signs." The officer finished with a circle around the coastal town of Saint-Malo.

"How long do you think it will take?" Madelyn asked.

"If you have no trouble?" He shrugged. "Probably fifteen or sixteen hours."

He held out his hand for the flashlight, which she handed over. Then he waved her to the back of the Range Rover, lifting the hatch to reveal six red gas cans.

"Do not stop for anyone. No one. People are very frightened, and you cannot predict what they will do."

"Are you sure I can't convince you to come with me?" she asked.

He pretended to consider her request, but she had a feeling his mind was already made up. "Madam, it would be an honor to escort you on your journey. But I have a daughter," he said. "I need to stay here. Just in case."

She nodded and shook the officer's hand. He gave her a final thumbs-up, got into his own car, and drove away, leaving her completely alone.

She settled in the SUV, started the engine, and just sat there with her eyes closed for a good thirty seconds. She thought about her husband and daughter, thousands of miles away across the ocean, and how much she needed to see them again.

She opened her eyes, folded the map small enough so that she could hold it across the face of the steering wheel, and set off into the darkness.

In the early days of her post, Madelyn and her husband Billy used to fantasize about all the trips they'd take together. They'd talk about tacking on a few days before or after her journeys abroad so that they could show their daughter the world. They vowed to take advantage of the unique privilege that had fallen in their lap when President Reyes asked her to be secretary of state. Billy even quit his job to homeschool Erin so they'd be free to follow her around the globe.

But then the realities of the job set in. Rarely was there a moment not accounted for on one of her itineraries. From the minute she'd touch down in Europe, Asia, South America, or wherever the president needed her to be, to the minute she took off from the tarmac to head back home to Washington, Madelyn's schedule was constant and immutable. The only time she'd ever catch a down day or two on the road was when the trip itself came up so unexpectedly that there was no time for the advance team to plot out her every hour—and at those times, there was also typically no way to mobilize her family fast enough. So for the last eighteen months, Billy and Erin had been left behind. And now here Madelyn was once again—alone. She was driving through one of the most beautiful parts of Europe, but it didn't matter without anyone to share it with.

Not that any of them could have enjoyed it in a world where the sun hadn't risen in three days.

The roads through the parks were narrow and winding, cutting through the hills and forests. The Range Rover's head-lights were the only illumination for miles. Madelyn focused entirely on the twenty feet ahead of her—that plus the occasional road sign, for which she'd inevitably have to slow down so that she could figure out the French, which she spoke only haltingly. Hours passed, the road flowing past in slivers of yellow light. She couldn't remember the last time she'd seen another vehicle, another soul.

She was so focused, or unfocused, that when the fuel indicator dinged, she nearly swerved off the road. She'd have to fuel up from one of the containers in the back. But she was in the middle of a forest, and was too spooked to stop here, so she drove on, watching the fuel gauge carefully. Just when she thought she was going to have to brave it, the trees thinned and ended at a vast meadow.

She pulled onto the shoulder, cut the engine, and rested her head on the steering wheel. She considered grabbing a few hours of sleep in the back seat, but then thought of the boat sailing to get her in Saint-Malo. She couldn't keep it waiting. So she shook off her sleepiness, grabbed the flashlight, and stepped out of the car.

The air was heavy with the scent of rosemary. She breathed deeply, letting the aroma wash through her, calming her rattled nerves. But as she moved around to the back to retrieve one of the gas cans, she realized she wasn't alone. Not entirely anyway. Across the field was a campfire, with a few people gathered around it.

As she peered in their direction, one of them waved to her. She knew she should heed the officer's warning, fill up the SUV, and be on her way, but curiosity got the better of her. Taking a much-needed break from driving also weighed into the decision. So she waved back and set off toward them, her flashlight in hand.

When she was about halfway across the field, she saw they were taking turns looking through a telescope. She waited until she was within earshot, then called out.

"Hello," she said in French. "I was driving by and saw your fire."

"You're only the second car that's come by in the last two days. Or whatever counts as days now," a man said, taking a few steps toward her. He switched to English. "You sound American."

She guessed her French was worse than she thought. "I am," she said, switching to English as well. "I hope I'm not bothering you."

She clicked off her flashlight as she reached the circle of light from their campfire. The man who spoke to her was wearing overalls and had a long gray beard.

"Not at all. The kids like to see it up close," the man said, pointing up at the moon and the dark slash across its belly.

"Do you live out here?" Madelyn asked.

"Right over there," he said, pointing across the field. Madelyn saw only darkness. "When everything happened, my daughter brought her family out of the city to stay with us here where we can be safer."

"I'm Maddy," she said, holding out her hand.

He introduced himself as Francis. His daughter, Judith, joined them at the edge of the firelight. She rattled off the names of her kids, each of them giving her a small wave when their name was mentioned. But she couldn't recall them even five seconds later. The heavy scent of rosemary, her exhaustion, and the cumulative effect of the intense focus required to stay on the twisted road combined to make her head fuzzy.

"Do you know anything?" Judith asked.

"No more than everyone else," Madelyn said, deciding not to divulge too much about herself yet. "I was on vacation when it happened."

Judith nodded, disappointment on her face. "Where are you heading?"

"Saint-Malo. I have a cousin there that I'm going to stay with until this is all over."

"You might be staying there a long time then," Francis said. He nodded toward the telescope. "Do you want to see?"

He led Madelyn over to the telescope. The oldest child, a teen, was peering into it, but stepped aside so she could have a look.

Madelyn put her eye to the viewfinder. A close-up of the moon filled her vision. It was a very good telescope; she could see the moon's topography in great detail, its craters and mountains painted in shades of grays and deep blues. But that pocked and blasted surface was split by a band of darkness, a vast shadow cast by the object that had appeared between the moon and the Earth three days ago.

Madelyn raised her head to look at the moon directly, and then went back to the eyepiece again, as if seeking confirmation that what she saw through the telescope was real and not some sort of illusion created by the device.

"Strange, yes?" Francis said. "We have been watching since the beginning, always from this spot. My grandson marked it with rocks so we are precise," he said, pointing to the circle of stones that surrounded the tripod's feet. "Neither the shadow, nor the moon itself, have moved."

"What do you think it is?" Madelyn asked. She was sincerely curious. Perhaps amateur astronomers would be the ones to figure it out first.

Francis shrugged. "Who knows what it is or why it's done this to us? But we have faith that the sun will rise again. Until then, we will keep—"

The squeal of brakes and grinding of gravel drowned out Francis's words. A truck had rounded the dark corner too fast, had drifted onto the shoulder where Madelyn's SUV was parked. The driver tried to stop, the truck's front end bucking and jumping, but the momentum was too much. The truck smashed into the back of the Range Rover—and the gas canisters stored there.

The fireball lit up the night sky.

26

"I TOLD YOU, I don't have enough people!"

"I'm not talking about your men, Jimmy," Tom said. "We can get volunteers from town to go out there with a few sawhorses and tell folks that there's no room at the inn."

After Jimmy and Michael arrived at Whitey's, Noel had told the town council about the massive influx of people heading toward the Mountain—people likely to end up on Franklin's doorstep once the military turned them away.

"And what happens when someone won't take no for an answer?" Jimmy asked. "I'm not gonna put people in that situation and just hope for the best."

"What's the alternative?" said Tom. "We don't know how long this thing is gonna last, and we need to conserve our resources for our own."

"I don't get it," said Zadie. "Why are all these people going to the Mountain in the first place?"

"Because they know all the smartest people in the world are in there working on the problem," said Noel. "It might not make a lot of sense to you, but some of us want to be part of something that's happening versus just sitting around and wishing for something to happen."

"And how do you think they're going to feel when they get there and find out it's locked down?" Tom asked. "That the president and all those *geniuses* are hiding in there, safe and sound, and keeping all of us out here. Forcing us to roast in this fucking sun underneath that abomination!"

The room erupted into shouting. The problem at hand was quickly getting lost amid finger-pointing and accusations.

Normally Michael would dive in to mediate. But instead he stood by the window, letting their anger simply wash over him, and looked up at the object, searching for an iota of understanding. Three days this thing had now burned in the sky. Was it observing them? Judging them? Was it waiting for them to act? Or was it indifferent to them entirely?

He tuned into the argument behind him. People were talking over one another. Past one another. Their words were falling on deaf ears. No one was listening.

And that was when it hit him.

Clarity and understanding coursed through him like an electric charge. He inhaled so sharply his breath caught in his throat. He coughed it back out with a gasp of relief and joy. And more importantly, resolve.

"No one is listening," he said, shutting his aching eyes. Then louder, "My God, no one is listening!"

Michael's declaration echoed through Whitey's, cutting through the council's squabbling.

"What are you talking about, Mike?" Noel said.

"That thing is trying to *tell* us something," he said. "*God* is trying to tell us something. And no one is listening. No one is paying attention!"

He thrust his finger at the window, smiling widely. No one said a word, until finally Jimmy took a few steps forward.

"Listen, why don't you let me take you home for a while." He put his hands on Michael's shoulders. "You don't need to be here. We got this."

"No. You're wrong," Michael said, turning to face his friend.

"This is exactly where I need to be. I'm sure of it." He gently removed Jimmy's hands from his shoulders and started walking toward the door.

"Mike?" said Noel, stopping him before he could leave. "Are you okay?"

He saw the concern in the lines of her forehead. "Let them come, sis," he said calmly. "I know what I need to do."

"And what's that?"

"I'm going to help us all listen," he said. Then he kissed his sister on the cheek before walking out of the store in silence.

"What the hell was that all about?" Tom grumbled.

"Oh, fuck off, Tom," snapped Noel. "You have no idea what he's been through."

"We've all had it tough! But the rest of us are holding it together."

"That's easy for you to say when you're not the one giving last rites."

Zadie cut in, her voice small. "You should have seen the look on his face when Theresa jumped. He tried so hard to save her."

That quieted everyone.

Noel took the opportunity to pull Jimmy aside. "Listen, I ought to get back up to the radio tower. Can you check on him later? I'm worried about him."

"Yeah, of course. Already planning to." He nodded toward the council. "And what about them?" he asked.

Noel shrugged. "Trying to keep all those people away is going to be like trying to hold back the ocean," she said, loud enough for everyone to hear. "I'd tell everyone in town to get ready."

27

D<small>EL</small> C<small>URLEY'S</small> drone hovered above the injured astronaut, sending
him a crisp 4k image. Her clothes were covered in dirt, grime, and
blood. Sweat streaked her dust-coated face. Something dark was
caked at the corners of her mouth. A moment ago she had been
moving. Now she wasn't. He couldn't even tell if she was still
alive.

He steered the drone down closer to her and then buzzed it
back up, hoping to get some sort of reaction from her. She didn't
so much as flinch. He knew he had better get to her quickly, so he
maneuvered the drone a short distance from her and brought it
down. As soon as the viewfinder filled with the red dust of the
canyon floor, he ran back to his ATV. With the drone controller in
the passenger's seat, he took off down the canyon.

As he swerved through broken boulders and scrub, the growl
of his engine echoed off the high canyon walls. Twice he had to
circle back and choose a different route when the one ahead of
him became too narrow, but eventually he found a clear line of
sight down a dry streambed. He picked up the controller to check
the distance and saw that he was within half a kilometer of the
drone.

He had been atop the ranger outpost adjusting one of the solar panels when he heard the Soyuz's main chute deploy. He stood up and watched it unfurl, terror ripping through him the same way it had three days prior when the object appeared in the sky. But as the distinctive shape of the Soyuz came into view, his fear was replaced by confusion. He knew exactly what he was looking at; he just had no idea what it was doing *here*. As it disappeared into the canyon, he fully expected to hear helicopters and planes, jeeps and tanks racing to retrieve the astronauts inside. But after an hour passed, he realized that no one was coming.

The canyon walls pinched in and the path in front of him splintered and cracked, forcing Del to stop. He cut the engine and got out, shielding his eyes from the blistering sun and the blindingly intense light radiating off the object's surface. He clambered atop a boulder in front of the ATV and looked further down the streambed. The astronaut was just ahead of him, lying on her back, the drone on the ground nearby. He jumped down and ran to her, calling out as he approached.

"Can you hear me?" he asked, kneeling down as soon as he reached her. She didn't respond.

He felt her neck for a pulse and breathed a sigh of relief when he found one. He turned her head from side to side to check for injuries and then checked the rest of her. The front of her outfit was covered in dried blood, but he couldn't see any wounds on her that would produce such a large quantity. He slid his hands under her back, removed her backpack, and gently pulled her into a sitting position. She teetered on the verge of falling forward, then suddenly snapped back up and flailed her arms.

"It's okay," he said, trying to steady her. "You're safe. I'm going to help you."

She pushed away, skittering across the ground like a crab to get some distance from him. He watched as she tried to focus, shaking her head and muttering. He stayed still and held up both hands to let her know that he wasn't threatening, giving her the time she needed to settle down.

"You're okay," he kept repeating. "You're safe."

Finally, she came to her senses. "Where am I," she croaked.

"New Mexico."

"New Mexico," she repeated, picking the crust from the corners of her mouth.

"I'm Del," he said. "Who are you?

"How did you find me?"

"I saw the capsule come down in the canyon."

The mention of the capsule must have triggered something in her mind because she became frantic, searching for something.

"Are you looking for your backpack?" Del said. "It's right here." He picked it up off the ground next to him and held it out.

She snatched it away, unzipped the main compartment, and looked inside. Immediately she settled down.

"I'm sorry," she said, exhaustion thick in her voice as she plopped back down and hugged the backpack to her chest. "I just . . ."

"It's okay. Let's get you out of here."

He leaned down and helped her to her feet, bearing most of her weight. Together they took a few tentative steps, but when it became apparent that she couldn't walk, he scooped her up in his arms and carried her.

"What's your name?" he asked.

"Yanez Prescott. I was in charge of the mission on board the ISS."

"Did anyone come back with you?" he asked. "Are there others?"

"My crew's dead," she said. Then her head fell back and she passed out.

The next time Yanez opened her eyes, she found herself staring at a ceiling with heavy wooden beams and wagon wheel chandeliers. A skylight created a square of sunlight on a stone chimney that stretched from the floor to the roof. An elk's head and antlers hung over the mantel. The room smelled like a campfire and pine needles.

She tried to sit up, but felt a sharp pinch at her right arm, the tubes from an IV dripline pulled taut. She turned to look at it and saw her backpack sitting on a chair next to the IV pole.

"Easy there, Ms. Prescott," a man said, jumping up from a desk. "Go slow."

She settled back down, realized she was lying on a couch. "How long was I out?" she asked.

"About nine hours," the man said, checking her arm to make sure the IV line was intact. "You were really dehydrated."

"Are you a doctor?"

"No, a park ranger. But we get a lot of lost hikers out here, so we keep some basic first aid stuff on hand at all times."

"Where's here?"

"Carson National Park."

Yanez took a good look at the stubbly face and brown eyes of the young man who had saved her. He looked Native American, his long black hair tied back in a ponytail, his wiry arms deeply tanned.

"Thank you for saving me," she said. "I'm sorry, but I don't remember your name."

"Del Curley," he said, holding out his hand.

"I appreciate all that you've done to help me, Del. Please call me Yanez."

She noticed that her cooling garment was gone. She was dressed in a T-shirt and shorts. When she glanced down at the University of New Mexico logo on the front of the shirt, Del was quick to apologize.

"I'm sorry. I had to get you out of that suit you were wearing so that I could get the IV in and wrap your knee. It was swollen up pretty good. And I wasn't sure about the blood all over you either. So I had to, you know, check."

She checked her knee. A bandage was holding a room-temperature ice pack in place. "It's okay."

"So, I guess if that blood wasn't yours, then . . ."

"My crew," she said. "They didn't survive the landing."

"I'm sorry to hear that."

She slowly swung her legs over the side of the couch and sat upright. Her head felt weak and her body empty. She unwrapped the bandage and set it and the warm ice pack on the couch next to her.

"I bet you're hungry," Del said. "Can I make you something?"

Her stomach rumbled at the mere mention of food. It had been days since she'd last eaten. She nodded, and Del put a pot on the stove, then opened the cabinets and fished out a can of soup.

"I hope you like chicken and stars."

She said she thought it sounded heavenly, and they both chuckled. He stirred the soup and then asked the question he'd probably been dying to ask ever since he'd found her.

"What happened up there?"

Yanez told him the story of their escape from the ISS as she ate her soup and an entire sleeve of saltines. She told him everything from the minute it happened to the race to get the drive and get off the station. But everything after landing and finding Susan and Anatoly was a little fuzzy.

"So you think the information on that drive might be able to tell us something about that thing?" he asked.

She was still weak but could feel some strength returning. And along with it, her resolve.

"I won't know for sure until I get it to NASA. But I think so, yes."

Del took her bowl to the sink and returned with a grape Pedialyte. "The IV and soup are a good start, but you've still got a ways to go."

She twisted off the lid and took a long sip. "What about down here?"

He shrugged. "There's not a lot of information to go on. I was at home when it happened, on the other side of the canyon from where I found you. We lost power, then cell and internet. So I came out here. The outpost has a landline and solar. Radio too."

"That's good. I need to get in touch with Canaveral."

"Well, that's going to be problem. We may have a landline, but they're completely jammed." He walked over to the phone attached to the kitchen wall and picked it up. A busy signal rang out. "See what I mean?"

"What about the radio?"

"You can listen, but the handpiece is busted. Damn thing probably hasn't been used in fifteen years, ever since the cell tower went up across the canyon."

"Where is it?" Yanez asked, pushing back from the table and standing up gingerly. Del pointed to his desk and then came to her side to catch her in case she stumbled. But she made it to the chair in one piece.

She flipped on the radio and picked up the emergency broadcast message, which Del told her had been on a loop since the whole thing started. She spun the dial and heard the same thing on many of the other channels. Then she scanned through some of the high- and low-band frequencies, pausing a few times to listen to the insanity being broadcast by a host of random people out there. She was about to push away from the desk, then decided to try the handset. As she pushed the red button on the side, static pulsed through the speakers.

"I thought you said it was broken," she said, holding out the handset toward Del.

"It is. The mic is dead. It won't pick up anything you say. I even took it apart and checked the wiring. I think a capacitor or something is blown."

"But it'll signal," she said, keying the red button on the side and listening to the break in the static each time she pressed it.

"I guess. Why does that matter?"

"I'll show you," she said, and got to work.

28

No one emerged from the truck that rear-ended Madelyn's SUV. They rushed toward the accident, hoping for a miracle, but the heat beat them back, a shock front of gasoline-scented air. There was nothing they could do.

If I had just filled up and been on my way, the person in that truck would be alive and I'd still be on my way to Saint-Malo, Madelyn thought as she watched the black cloud that mushroomed above the burning wreckage.

The woman, Judith, began herding her children across the field. The little ones made a mad dash, and the teen boy walked behind with the telescope. But Madelyn could only stand there, watching the flames in disbelief.

Francis put a hand on her shoulder, gently urging her to follow him. As they crossed the field after the others, she kept glancing over her shoulder at the inferno.

They came over a rise, and Madelyn finally saw Francis's home. It was a small cottage, its porch lit by the warm glow of lanterns, candles already flickering to life in the windows as Judith moved around inside. The hulking shadow of a dark barn rose behind the building. Otherwise, it was all alone out here.

She followed Francis inside, and heard the children upstairs talking about the explosion. They didn't sound upset in the least, more like the whole thing was an amazing adventure. After a lot of giggling, the teenager stomped across the floor and the kids quieted down.

Judith filled a kettle from a barrel of rainwater outside and put it on the stove, lighting the propane burner with a match.

"Are you okay?" Francis asked Madelyn, taking a seat opposite her at the kitchen table.

"I'm fine," she said. "I just feel terrible about what happened. That poor driver never stood a chance."

"That wasn't your fault. It's a bad turn. You'd be surprised how many people come around that turn too fast and run right off the road. If anyone's to blame, it's me for not suggesting you move your car. But like I said, there's been no one through here for days . . ."

They tried to convince each other they weren't at fault. Then they discussed what to do. They couldn't even report the accident —there had been no power, no cellular service, no landline since the event. Francis said that park officials usually patrolled the roads every few days, but Madelyn doubted they would still keep up old habits in this new world.

The kitchen looked like it belonged in a catalog for French fastidiousness. Even in the candlelight, the appliances gleamed and the glass cabinets were unsmudged. Cans, jars, and boxes were lined up neatly on the shelves, which were hand-painted with pastel flowers. Hanging above the sink was a portrait of a much younger Francis beside a laughing woman with a pile of reddish-blond hair. A grade-school-aged Judith flew in front of them, legs flared out in a dancer's leap.

"That's my mother," Judith said when she saw Madelyn looking at the picture. "She died two years ago."

"I'm sorry," Madelyn said to them both, making sure she caught both of their eyes.

"This was her happiest place on Earth," Francis said, circling a finger in the air to encompass the kitchen. "She told me if I messed it up, she'd haunt me. And let me tell you, Maddy. She would."

He smiled and then got up from the table to grab some biscuits from one of the cabinets. They made small talk and drank Judith's tea, and in other circumstances, Madelyn would have found this a welcome, peaceful respite from her busy life. But she had no time for quiet conversation; she needed to get to Saint-Malo. She considered her options and decided these generous, gentle people deserved the truth.

"I lied to you before," she said, setting her cup down. "I wasn't in France on vacation, and I don't have relatives here."

Judith and Francis looked at one another, then Francis said, "I understand. You don't know us. But why are you telling us this now?"

"Because you've been kind and opened your home to me when you had no reason to," Madelyn said. "And because I need your help."

Two of the girls ran into the kitchen, suddenly in desperate need of a snack. Judith handed them the box of biscuits from the table and then pointed back out the door they had dashed through. The girls protested and tried to get Grandpa to let them stay, one even going so far as to climb on his lap and lavish kisses on him. But in the end, Mom won and the girls retreated from the kitchen, casting glances at Madelyn the whole way out.

"Tell us," Judith said, sitting back down next to Francis.

"I'm the American secretary of state," Madelyn said, then paused to let that sink in. "I need to get to Saint-Malo, where a ship is waiting for me. I'm trying to get to the UK, where there's going to be a gathering of European leaders."

"You're the US secretary of state," Francis repeated, as if trying it out. "So you must know something about what happened."

Madelyn shook her head. "No. That part I wasn't lying to you about. All I know, all any of us know, is that the object appeared three days ago and it stopped the rotation of the planet. We don't know what it is, we don't know how it's possible, and we don't know what it will mean for us. That's why I need to get to Saint-Malo. If somebody *does* know something, we need to pool our resources."

Francis's hands were folded in front of him as if he were praying. Judith watched him for a moment, then broke the silence.

"We can give her my car, Papa. The kids and I aren't going anywhere anyway."

Francis paused, then shook his head. He got up from the table and put his hand on his daughter's shoulder. "I have a better idea. Come. Both of you."

Judith and Madelyn followed him out onto the porch. He grabbed a lantern from the post nearest the door and then headed around the house toward the barn.

Judith apparently understood what he had in mind and dashed after him. "Papa, no. You can't. You have no idea what will happen."

He stopped and turned to her. "This is the best way. It's the safest for her. And the quickest." He turned back to Madelyn. "I will take you Saint-Malo."

Madelyn was about to add her own objections—she didn't want to take this man from his family—but Judith was continuing to protest quite adamantly on her own, waving her arms and spitting her disagreement in blistering French. She spoke so quickly that Madelyn couldn't make out a word of it.

Francis, however, had clearly made up his mind. He handed his daughter the lantern, kissed her on the forehead, and then pulled open one of the wide barn doors.

It was too dark to see anything inside. But as he took the lantern back and walked in, his light caught the front of what Madelyn thought was a car. Then she got closer, and she saw why Judith had protested so strongly.

Francis was standing next to a plane.

"It's too dangerous for you to drive all the way to Saint-Malo," he said to her. "I will get you there."

"I was told it's not safe to fly," Madelyn said, glancing at Judith, who was still fuming. "There's no GPS."

"I don't need GPS," he said, waving off the notion. "I flew for the government for thirty years, spraying the meadows in all of the parks from here to the coast."

"What about other aircraft?"

"We won't be very high up, so we don't have to worry."

Madelyn looked to Judith, who threw up her hands and headed back to the house in defeat.

"Francis," Madelyn said, "I think your daughter's right. I would be immensely grateful if I could simply borrow her car. Your family needs you here."

Francis set the lantern down on the ground, walked over to Madelyn, and took her hand. "My family *does* need me. Which is why I insist on going with you. I want those children to have a future. Not endless night and who knows what else. If I can play a part in making that happen, then that's what I'm going to do."

Madelyn touched the man's cheek, marveling at the kindness that could still be found in the world, even when wrapped in darkness.

"I'm ready when you are," she said.

29

Noel had been scanning the bands for hours, listening to a litany of conspiracy theories, including ones about military testing gone awry, China's grand plan to use the sun to burn out the west, alien colonization, and the emergence of a multiverse. There were also many, many people in hysterics about the end times, the anti-Christ, Armageddon, Rapture, Revelations, and death on a pale horse. And of course, there were people in equal numbers who were simply looking for the party to end all parties. Local police and military bands were dominated by reports of people flooding into the area. It was clearly just a matter of time before the masses would flow around the blockades and detours like water around rocks and wash up in Franklin.

After so much insanity, the Morse code people were a welcome distraction, even the sad ones who were just hoping for someone to come play with their dots or self-proclaimed impressively long dashes. Noel jotted down the messages in a spiral-bound notebook before translating them using a laminated card of the Morse alphabet she'd found in a drawer. *Of course you laminated it*, she said, thinking of how many times she'd found her dad sitting behind the main console translating and sending messages.

"There's some people out there setting up telescopes," Aster said as she came into the station. She knelt down and unzipped her bag. "Won't they burn their eyes out?"

"As long as they don't look right at it, they should be okay," Noel said. "That, or use a filter. What'd ya bring me?"

"Rice and beans and some chips," Aster said, taking out a Tupperware container and handing it over. "Anything new?"

"There's a real rager going on out near Colorado Springs," Noel said, popping open the container and taking in the spicy aroma. "Apparently some of the Air Force guys who were on patrol out there gave up trying to control the traffic and are now doing keg stands with the crowd."

Aster brought her lunch over to the console. "What's this?" she asked, pointing with her fork toward the fuzz coming from the speakers.

"It's Morse code. I'm just taking a break from the other channels. I like decoding the messages." Noel turned up the volume. "This one's a little weird. Whoever's doing it is using the static instead of beeps to send the dots and dashes."

"What's it say?"

"Let's find out," Noel said. She had missed the last few lines of the code when Aster came in, but the sender had repeated it a few times already, so she just waited and then jotted down the rest of the message in her notebook. When she recognized it had started over again, she grabbed the alphabet card and demonstrated to Aster how to translate the message.

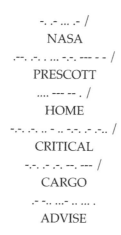

-. .- ... .- /
NASA

.--. .-. . ... -.-. --- - - /
PRESCOTT

.... --- -- . /
HOME

-.-. .-. .. - .. -.-. .- .-.. /
CRITICAL

-.-. .- .-. --. --- /
CARGO

.- -.. ...- .. ... .
ADVISE

"Why would someone be talking about her?" Aster asked, shoveling in a bite of rice and beans.

"Who?"

"Commander Prescott. From the space station."

"You know who's on board the station?"

"Seriously? A black woman in space," Aster said, making the exploding-brain motion with her hands.

"Maybe we're picking up their frequency. It would make sense to use the ham to communicate with the ground since satellites are down."

"Wait—you don't think it could actually be her?" Aster asked, nearly choking on a chip.

Noel set down her lunch, pushed her chair back, and went over to a chart of common frequencies hanging next to the Franklin Savings and Loan calendar from 2006. Astronauts would often communicate with amateur radio enthusiasts and school kids while onboard the International Space Station, mostly to help break up the tedium of a space mission. But according to the chart, they always broadcast at either 144.49 or 145.20 MHz. This signal was coming in at a much higher band.

"Nope, wrong frequency," she said.

"Can we send a message back?" Aster asked.

"We could, but it's probably just someone screwing around."

"Let's find out," Aster said.

"How?"

"Ask her what her pump-up song is."

Noel raised an eyebrow. "Her what?"

"I read an interview with her last year before the launch, and she talked about her favorite song to listen to while training for space. If it's just some asshat pretending to be her, they probably won't know the answer."

Noel threw up her hands in the face of Aster's unassailable teenage logic. She wrote out their question in her notebook, and then together they translated it into the necessary dots and dashes.

When the mystery person's message ended, Noel keyed in their question.

The response was immediate, and Aster translated it letter by letter as it came in.

‾... . .‾.. .. . ...‾ . .‾.

BELIEVER

"Holy shit! It's her!" Aster said. "That's her song!"

"We don't know that for sure," Noel cautioned. "Whoever is posing as her could have also read the same article."

"But why? I mean, what do they have to gain?"

"Who knows? They're saying they have critical cargo. Maybe they're hoping that will get the military's attention or something."

Aster nodded, as if considering the idea. But at the same time, Noel was coming around to Aster's side of things. Pretending to be from the station, one of the few people to have been in space when the object appeared, was a pretty good ploy to get NASA's attention—but it was also a simple bubble to pop. If the guy got far enough to get a response from the bigwigs, all NASA had to do was ask this person a few very specific questions that only the commander of the ISS would know. If the guy couldn't answer, the jig would be up. So why do it?

Noel and Aster debated this for a few minutes, Aster drinking from the half-full part of the theory while Noel sipped from the half-empty portion. Meanwhile the word *confirm* kept being broadcast by the mystery sender. When it was sent for the fifth time, Noel and Aster came to a decision.

They decided to keep talking.

30

FRANKLIN SIMMERED as the sun crushed down on it for the third day. The roads felt soft and sticky under Michael's feet, heat shimmering off every hard surface and wilting every living thing, plant and person alike. Michael walked past the homes of old friends and rivals, former teachers and coaches. Past the laundromat where he got into a fight in eighth grade. Past the ice cream parlor where he'd worked his first job. Past the cracked and weed-choked asphalt of the drive-in theater where he'd had his first real date—and first real kiss—with Gina Wallace. He went to the municipal park and sat on the same swing he'd sat on after graduating high school, head swimming from the beers he and Jimmy had stolen from his dad. So much of his life had been defined by these places. He had always drawn great comfort from that fact. But now it was time to say goodbye.

He finished his trek around Franklin at the same spot where everything had changed. He looked up at the object in the sky, its message now so loud and clear. Then he looked down at the indentation Theresa's body had made in the packed earth beside the hospital.

"You were the real harbinger, my dear," he said.

Staring down at the bloodstained blades of grass, Michael let go of the past and accepted a new reality where the present was all there was and all there could be. Judgment was here, and there was no more time to waste on what had come before. Nothing mattered but right now.

He was ready for it. And he was going to make sure others were too.

He bent down and touched the grass, then strode across the street to the high school. Someone had propped open the double doors to the gymnasium to let in some air, and he could hear Rose and Jimmy arguing inside as he approached.

He entered the gym, walked straight over to them, and embraced them both. "I'm so glad to see you here. We have so much to do."

Rose and Jimmy looked him up and down, no doubt taking in his dripping and crumpled clothes after hours in the heat, whitish salt stains now decorating his black shirt.

"Where have you been?" Jimmy asked after keying his shoulder mic and telling the dispatcher that they could stand down from their search for Michael.

"I'm sorry to have worried you," he said. "I didn't realize you'd be searching. I just needed to spend some time alone, saying goodbye to things."

"Why? Are you going somewhere?"

"We all are," Michael said, chuckling. "The only question is where. Man, and that is a *big* question, for sure."

Rose and Jimmy looked at each other, totally confused. Rose apparently thought it best to change the subject.

"The gym's all set, Father Williams," she said. "Just like we talked about."

Michael looked around. The bleachers had been pulled away from the walls, and his podium and side table were set up at center court. Rose had even put a small arrangement of flowers on the table.

"Some of us have been talking about a memorial service for the people who didn't make it," she said with a catch in her voice. "We were hoping we could do it . . . well, I was going to say tomorrow morning, but those words no longer have meaning anymore."

Jimmy looked his friend over again, then turned to Rose. "How about we postpone until tomorrow night. Give Mike a chance to rest."

"No, no, morning is good. We can't delay these things," said Michael. "Nine o'clock. But it can't be here."

"But we're all set," Rose said, looking around to see if there was something she'd missed. "Did I do something wrong?"

"No, you've done a wonderful job. It's my mistake," Michael said. "We have a church, and I see now that we absolutely need to use it for tomorrow's service—and all of our services."

"Are you sure?" Rose said.

"Completely," he said, and without any explanation as to how they'd manage to hold service in the ruins of St. Anne's, he turned and started walking back toward the gymnasium doors.

Jimmy ran up behind him and grabbed his arm. "Damn it, dude. You need to stop!"

Michael turned back around to face him and Rose. "We aren't going to be like those cowards in their Mountain," he said. "We aren't going to hide in the dark and pretend that it's not up there." His voice grew. "We are going to stand in its light—and *listen* to what it's telling us."

But then he saw their confusion and fear and caught himself. *This isn't the way*, he thought. *Not yet.*

"I'm sorry," he said, smoothing his hair and wiping his face on his sleeve. "I haven't done a good job of preparing any of you for the path forward. But that's all going to change, I promise. And we'll start in the morning. Or whatever we call it—right, Rose?"

He smiled at them, trying to look convincing. Calm, confident —not crazy.

"Mike, come on," Jimmy said. "Let's talk about this."

Michael held up his hands to end the discussion. "We're holding the service at St. Anne's," he said as he walked back out toward the light and heat. "Tell everyone."

31

THEY WENT BACK and forth for nearly an hour before Yanez finally convinced Noel she wasn't an impostor. Only once had someone tried to break into their conversation, and by then they'd already arranged to switch to a different frequency if that happened. It probably helped that they were communicating with Morse code, and that Yanez's radio could only send bursts of static, which certainly didn't make for riveting repartee.

Yanez translated Noel's latest message, then poked Del in the arm. He had dozed off in the seat next to her.

"Hey, got a map of Colorado?" she asked.

Del hopped up and pretended not to have been asleep, sucking back a huge yawn as he walked across the room to the welcome area. He opened a tall cabinet and started rooting through a disorganized stack of local and state maps.

"So what made you want to be a ranger?" Yanez asked.

"My people are from around here," he said, tossing the wrong maps into a pile. "I just fell in love with the land and decided it was what I was meant to do."

"Who are your people?"

"We're Apaches," he said, exhausting his first stack and grabbing another. "I grew up on the Jicarilla Reservation not that far from here."

Yanez keyed *stand by* into the mic. "You go back often?"

"All the time," he said. "My grandparents and my sister's family are still there. I drove out right after this went down."

"Why didn't you stay with them?" she asked, but then checked herself. "I'm sorry. I shouldn't be prying."

Del waved her off. "Nah, no biggie. The family house is just too tight, especially with all this heat. I tried to get them to come and stay with me here, but there was no chance of getting the old heads off their land." He chuckled. "I think they still believe if they leave it, someone will swoop in and take it."

He gave up on the cabinet and moved to a storage closet, which was crammed with hiking gear. "How about you?" he said as he shifted a stack of rain slickers out of his way. "Where's your family?"

"I'm from Vermont, originally. I still got some family up near Killington."

"You a skier?"

"Not for a while. We don't get a lot of snow down near Canaveral."

"Guess not," Del said. He pulled a plastic roll-away set of drawers from the closet. "You married?"

"For a little while," she said. "Turns out I'm not very good at it."

With a triumphant *aha*, Del pulled out a shrink-wrapped stack of maps. He brought them back over to Yanez, tearing the plastic film off the bundle. She took one and unfolded it on the desk.

"Okay," she said, tracing her finger across the folds. "Noel wants us to go to a town called Franklin, which is . . . right here." She pointed to the dot on the map.

"Why there?" he asked, looking over her shoulder.

"Apparently the president and a bunch of others are holed up inside Cheyenne Mountain, which is right here," she said, putting a different finger on the spot so they could eyeball the distance between the two places.

"You mean the one from that movie?" he said. "With the big steel door?"

"That's the place."

"Did they shut it?"

"That one and all the other doors too," she said. "Roads heading anywhere near the Mountain are closed, but Noel thinks she might be able to help us get a message inside. She works at the airbase nearby."

"Can't she just reach out to NASA for you?"

"She says she'd never get through, and even if she did, no one would believe her. We agreed our best shot is to get word about me and the computer drive to the people inside the Mountain."

"We should get a move on then," Del said, nodding at the map. "It'll probably take the better part of a day to get there, especially if we have to stay off the main highways."

He started to get up, but Yanez stopped him.

"Hey, you know you don't have to do this," she said.

He shook his head, surprised. "There's no chance I'm letting you go by yourself. Plus, if you do happen to have information that saves the world, I wanna be on the float in the ticker-tape parade."

Yanez gave him a quick hug then picked up the handset and keyed to Noel that they'd be coming. As she waited for Noel to confirm receipt of the message, she squeezed the rabbit's foot on the zipper of her backpack like she used to do before exams in college. Hope in the midst of chaos was the hardest thing to hold on to. But as she watched Del buzz around the room gathering supplies, this young Apache forest ranger who had saved her from a slow and lonely death in an ancient canyon so she could deliver a computer drive from outer space with information that could save them all, hope somehow felt real and tangible.

Otherworldly, even, she thought. *How appropriate.*

PART IV

32

MADELYN FLEW west across the French countryside. Bonfires and lantern light marked neighborhoods and towns, points of light in the darkness now in its fourth day. They followed one of Francis's old spraying routes from his years tending to the parks, and he'd point out various fields as they passed above them—wild anemones, gourdons, irises, rosemary, betony. He must have been going by memory, because Madelyn couldn't see a thing.

Midway through their journey, they crested a rocky hillside and approached an open field surrounded by a dark forest. Francis, determined that Madelyn experience something of the land before continuing on her mission, angled the plane low enough so that the hypnotic fragrance of lavender filled the cockpit. Madelyn shut her eyes and breathed in deeply, imagining a sea of purple undulating in the spring breeze. She let herself relax for the first time since Rome, the hum of the engine and the dream of flowers a soothing balm for her weary soul. Even as they rose once more, she kept her eyes closed and enjoyed the fading scent.

"You go ahead and rest, Maddy," Francis said. "We will be there soon."

She allowed herself to drift in and out of a fitful sleep, but was awoken when the radio chirped to life. She opened her eyes and found herself looking straight at the moon and the dark, alien band across its middle. Spastic French crackled over the plane's single speaker.

Francis unhooked his handset and responded calmly in French. Whatever he said, it did nothing to soften the tone of the person on the speaker.

"They've seen us now," Francis explained to Madelyn. "They are not happy."

"Who?" Madelyn asked, looking out the window at the town below.

"Saint-Malo police. They're demanding we change course away from the city."

"Let me talk to them," she said.

She took the mic from Francis. "This is Secretary of State Madelyn Frederick. Can I speak with whoever is in charge?"

"I don't care who you are. You must stop flying over the city at once," said a furious French officer in halting English.

"Sir, I am here on behalf of the United States and the European Union. You must let me speak with your superior immediately."

After a slight pause, the officer told Francis to maintain his altitude and stand by for further instructions.

As they waited, Francis told Madelyn about the city's history and the role it played in World War II. It served as a German garrison until the Americans and British nearly bombed it back to the Stone Age.

"So it's ironic, really," Francis concluded.

"What is?"

"That an American is here once again, without invitation, to rendezvous with the British. It's like the 1940s all over again, eh?"

They laughed as Francis banked right and swung over the northern edge of Saint-Malo. Once the plane straightened out, Madelyn saw that one section of the city glowed brighter than the others.

"What's that?" she asked, pointing to fires burning around the edges of a large gathering.

"Saint-Malo Cathedral, most likely," he said. "It is very famous. Do you want to go see?"

Madelyn thought back to the scene in Rome, the mass of people there seeking answers. As much as she wanted to witness that again, to look down on people united in faith and feel their hope, she didn't want to cause any anxiety by flying near them.

"No. Let's go back out over the water and leave them to their prayers."

The plane banked over the Channel, and a new voice came over the radio.

"This is Captain Maurice Dupont. Please tell me your business in Saint-Malo."

"Captain, this is Madelyn Frederick from the United States government. I am here to meet a British vessel in your port."

"Not an American one?"

"If you'd allow us to land, I can explain further."

"Things on the ground are not good. Landing will be very difficult. I recommend you continue across the Channel."

Madelyn looked to Francis, who shook his head.

"Sir, we cannot," she said. "Please, confirm what I'm saying with the British if you need to. But we must land here."

The captain told them to hold while he conferred with the harbor. A short while later, the first officer they'd spoken to came back on. He sounded much more contrite as he instructed them to land in the parking lot at the ferry terminal. He said that a British Navy cutter would pick Madelyn up at the pier.

Francis swung the plane toward their landing zone at the south end of the city.

"I think they're startled by such an important person appearing out of thin air," Francis said. "I know how they feel."

Madelyn grabbed his hand. "You saved me. Thank you."

"Now you need to go save the rest of us," he said.

The police had set a series of flares on the ground, guiding them safely into the lot. They touched down and glided toward several police cars that were waiting for them. Francis was about to cut the engine when several of the officers started windmilling their flashlights around and running toward them. He opened his door just as the captain reached the plane.

"Madam Secretary, you must hurry!" he shouted past Francis to Madelyn. "There is no time to waste!"

"What's happening?" she said.

"This plane has to take off from here immediately! The parking lot will be underwater very soon!"

She got out of the plane and jogged around to where the captain and the other officers were standing near Francis's open door. Francis had also gotten out of the plane to participate in the discussion.

"The water is rising, Madam. Very rapidly."

"In the Channel?" Francis asked.

"Yes, and everywhere else. It has already come over the storm wall and keeps building. The docks will be gone soon."

"Has this ever happened before?"

"Never," he said. "The British are waiting, but the pier is already partly covered. We need to get you to them right away or they will have to cast off."

Madelyn turned to Francis. "Thank you for everything. Now get home to your family. Keep them safe."

"Good luck, Maddy," he said. "To us all."

She kissed his cheek and then watched as he got back into the plane and started to pull away. The officers gestured for her to follow them, but Madelyn waited until Francis's plane climbed safely into the air before she jogged with the officers to the pier— and even then she kept looking back, watching Francis's taillights blink away into the sky.

Her feet splashed through shallow water as they ran. By the time they got to the entrance to the long pier, the water was at her ankles. Now they walked, striding quickly but deliberately, the captain using his flashlight to keep them on the path toward the ship. She could see its lights at the tip of the pier and heard several of the seamen shouting for them to hurry. As she and the officers approached, two British naval officers leapt onto the pier to help her aboard. The police captain wished Madelyn a safe journey and then turned to go.

"Captain Dupont!" she called to him. He spun around. "What will you do?"

"Pray, Madam. What else can we do?" And he trotted back through the water toward Saint-Malo.

33

THE CROWD around the radio tower had been growing for hours. At first, it had been just a few people trickling in from town with telescopes hoping for an unobstructed view of the object. But once word spread to the travelers flooding the area that the tower was up and running, people started arriving on Blue's Bluff in steady succession. The promise of long-range communications was a powerful intoxicant to the ham radio set, CB personalities, amateur astronomers, and science-minded folks alike. People had even set up tents near Scylla and Charybdis. It was like an end-times festival for geeks, complete with certain aromatics spicing the air and mingled with the scent of hotdogs and hamburgers.

For a while, Aster was annoyed that people were imposing on the space she and Noel had carved out for themselves. But when her rock star status became clear, her objections quickly vanished. A murmur would go through the crowd each time she emerged from the station. Sometimes she would come out just to create a stir, enjoying the attention and playing into the growing air of mystery about the special teenager who had access to the radio tower. But this time, she actually needed to find Noel.

She made her way through the crowd, asked people if they'd seen Noel, and followed their pointing fingers to the edge of the lot. This was the line that divided the newly established "research section" of the bluff—where the telescopes were set up—and the common area. With help from a few of the newcomers, Noel was installing external speakers on one of the light poles so that they'd be able to broadcast directly from the station.

Aster pulled Noel aside so that the others wouldn't overhear them.

"Officer Bell's on the radio. Says it's important. Something about your brother."

They walked back to the station together, fending off a few questions along the way, and went inside. Noel sat down at the console and keyed the mic.

"Jimmy, what's going on?"

"I need you to come down here," he said. "Mikey's in bad shape. I've never seen him like this. It's like something went out inside of him. Or came on, I don't know. He doesn't even sound like himself. The way he's talking is way off. Rose and I have tried to get him to ease up, but he's not listening to anyone."

"What makes you think he'll listen to me?"

"How about because you're his sister?"

"I don't know, Jimmy. There's a lot happening right now. You should see how many people are here."

"Can't be as bad as town. This place is packed. Please, Noel? We can talk to him together."

Noel looked to Aster, who nodded as if to say, *Go on. I got this.*

"Okay," said Noel, "I'm on my way. Where is he?"

"At the church."

"What do you mean? The actual church?" she asked. Her worry rose from a steady yellow to a solid orange.

"Yes. The actual church."

"I'll meet you there in twenty minutes."

Noel grabbed her helmet and leather jacket from the couch, gave Aster a few instructions on which channels to monitor while she was gone, then strode out of the station and got on her motorcycle. She kickstarted the old Chief to life and slowly wended her way through the crowd. She wanted to take the dirt road back to Franklin, but when she looked over at the people gathered around Scylla and Charybdis and thought about swerving through all the others coming up the switchbacks to the top, she decided the service road was a better choice.

Still, even that route was horribly congested, lined with cars and trucks. People were everywhere, the density only increasing as she moved into the heart of Franklin. Every available parking spot was taken along the main roads, and many people had parked on grass lots, sidewalks, and playgrounds. The town had swelled to the verge of bursting like a tick on an elephant. Whitey's was jammed with people buying supplies. A few of the restaurants were open, with huge lines of customers milling about and waiting.

If Noel were driving a car, she'd never have made it through the chaos. Her Chief allowed her to get as far as the community center, still a half mile from the church, before she decided it would be best from here to proceed on foot. She parked next to the front doors and stowed her helmet and jacket in the bushes.

Although she'd lived in Franklin her whole life, and knew almost everyone in town, she didn't see a single face she recognized as she walked to the church. That was, until she got to the burned-out remains of the Crispy Biscuit where she saw a few guys from the fire department trying to keep people away from the charred timbers and warped metal. She pushed her way across the street to the church, and found Jimmy out front. Rose was with him, fussing over a PA system they'd apparently brought out for the occasion.

"Holy shit, man," she said when she reached him, yelling near his ear so that he'd be able to hear her over the din.

"Yeah, that about sums it up." He took Noel around the side of one of the collapsed walls, and there was Michael, sitting in a cracked and broken pew, thumbing through a hymnal. When Michael saw her, he jumped up.

"I'm so glad you came," he said.

His clothes were filthy, smudged with soot and ash and spots of blood. As he gave her a hug, she noticed he needed a shower, too. Though lots of people were running ripe these days.

"Quite a crowd out there," she said.

Michael laughed. "If I'd have known all it took was knocking down the church to get people here, I'd have had my jackhammer out years ago!"

"Are you doing a service here, Mike? I thought you were going to use the gym. People are going to boil out here. The sun's an absolute killer."

But he just smiled. "That's like Butch and Sundance peering over the edge of that huge cliff down to the boulder-filled rapids and being afraid to jump because they might drown. You're worried about the heat? Because the fall's what's gonna kill us."

An awkward silence hung in the space between them, only the noise of the restless crowd giving them permission to not say anything to one another. Then Noel tried a different tack.

"Listen, both of you," she said to Michael and Jimmy. "This is gonna sound crazy, but I made contact with one of the astronauts from the space station."

"Up there?" Jimmy asked.

"No, she's back on Earth. Her name is Yanez Prescott. She was the mission commander. She says she has data from the space station and needs to get it to the right people. So she's coming here and I'm gonna help her get word inside the Mountain."

She paused for their reactions. Jimmy looked at her with wide eyes, but Michael was mostly blank, as if processing the information.

"Mike, did you hear me?" Noel said. "I mean, think of it. If she actually has data captured from the ISS, we might be able to determine if we're dealing with some sort of lunar fragmentation or a solar ejection, or a comet or rogue planet that's pulling with equal force in the opposite direction of the Earth . . . There's a million possibilities."

He smiled at her then, the type of smile you'd give a child who made a good try at something but fell a wee bit short.

"Well, you're looking in the right direction at least," he said, index finger toward the sky. "But there's only one possibility, dear sister."

Just then Rose appeared, picking her way through the rubble. "Father Williams, I don't mean to disturb you, but I was wondering when you would be ready to start?" she asked in a warbly voice. "People are getting restless out there. I'm worried about what might happen if they stand there too long in this heat."

"I'm coming right now, Rose," Michael said, snapping his hymnal shut. "Let's get this show on the road!"

Michael stood atop the steps that had once led to the church, now just a pile of wood, slate, and stone behind him. Below was a sea of sweaty, desperate faces. Some he knew, but many he didn't. He smiled at the sight, remembering how not so long ago he'd look out from his pulpit at the meager gatherings in St. Anne's, never robust, never so hungry for the Word of God as the hundreds before him now.

He picked up the microphone that Rose had left for him atop the amplifier, creating a squeal that made everyone cringe. He held it away from his face and looked up into the sky, letting the light emanating from the object beat down on him. Tears ran down his face as he gave silent thanks to God and the object in equal measure.

And then he began to sing.

"While he, the king all strong to save,
rends the dark doors away,
and through the breaches of the grave,
strides forth into the day."

As the last syllable rang out across the silent crowd, Michael looked down at Midge, who was right up front, being held together by friends and neighbors, her anguish as palpable as the heat that came off the crowded bodies. He waved for her supporters to bring her forward to stand with him at the top of the steps, and as they did so, her sobs could be heard all the way in the back.

Michael embraced her and then set her at his right hand.

"We are here to mourn the loss of Midge's daughter, Theresa, an innocent and faithful servant of the Lord for all of her short years on this Earth."

Then he waved for Rose and Jimmy to join him. Rose grabbed Jimmy's hand before he could object and pulled him toward Michael, leaving Noel alone to watch from the side.

"And to mourn the loss of our friend, Bruce Clarke, who for decades served us meals made from the heart. And Sheriff Dave Anderson, who protected all the citizens of Franklin with honor and dignity. And many other treasured friends and loved ones in recent days.

"But we will mourn with a glad heart. For their passing holds a purpose. Their deaths tell us something, so long as we are brave enough to listen and accept what we hear. So long as we accept the message that is coming to us like a clarion call, an ultraviolet beacon breaking through the darkness. Coming from up there in the heavens, clear and crisp and true!" he cried, thrusting his open palm toward the object. "My friends, can you hear it?"

Sobs and sniffles came from all quarters, but no one answered Michael's question. So he asked it again. On his third try, he screamed it at the top of his lungs, overloading the amplifier and creating a squawk that made the crowd shrink back.

The refugees from the road didn't know what to expect from this priest, so they looked to one another in confusion. But the people of Franklin, those who knew Michael, were stunned to silence by this new manifestation of one of their own.

Noel looked at her brother and saw only a stranger.

"It's okay," he said in a softer, gentler voice, and everyone let out the breaths they'd been holding in. "Don't worry, it's not your fault. I didn't hear it for a while either. But now I do. And I'm here to share the news with you all."

He reached for Midge, pulling her tight against his side. Her sobs were amplified by the microphone.

"Do you know what that thing is telling us?" he asked her into the mic, draping his arm over her shoulders. "Theresa knew. She told me before she died."

Midge merely continued to sob, racked with grief that knew no bounds. So Michael took it upon himself to share the answer, with her and everyone else.

"It's telling us," he said, "that we're all surely going to burn."

34

It DIDN'T TAKE Yanez and Del long to come upon a highway casualty, a minivan that had fallen victim to the slow-moving traffic and incessant sun. Gray smoke spewed from the hood as a woman stared into the boiling engine. Her three kids milled around on the shoulder and chucked rocks at nothing. With Yanez's silent agreement, Del pulled onto the shoulder behind them, and a small cheer went up from the kids as Del and Yanez got out to help. The mom threw her head back and thanked God, and Del blushed from his cheeks all the way down his neck when she hugged him.

The problem turned out to be a leaking coolant line, which Del was able to repair with some crafty duct taping. While he wrapped the line and refilled the coolant reservoir, Yanez made small talk with the mom—mostly about where they had each been when "it" happened—Yanez made up a story about a business trip—and what they'd heard from others who knew a person who knew a person, all the while trying to stand in the shade of the van and make sure the kids didn't drift too far away. When Del announced he was done and the mom was able to start the engine again, no steam or smoke in sight, they shook and hugged and said their goodbyes.

"Man, Noel wasn't kidding about the logjam out here," Yanez said as she waved to the kids in the back window. Del stowed his gear behind the driver's seat and then stood by her on the shoulder, watching the minivan crawl away.

"I have an idea," he said once the family was out of sight. He went to the bed of his truck, opened the metal toolbox behind the rear window, and pulled out a folded and oil-stained map. He spread it on the hood of the truck. "This shows all of the service roads in Carson National. It's updated every year based on where conservation efforts are focused throughout the forest. That way the rangers are able to direct crews away from the tourist areas, and vice versa." He traced a squiggled, red line north with his finger. "See, the service roads all connect, because the National Forests in this area connect. We can follow the service roads up through Rio Grande National, across Gunnison, and through Pike and San Isabel."

Yanez saw the route he was proposing. "That'll get us pretty close," she said, pointing to the spot on the map where Franklin was marked with a small dot.

"It's pretty remote right around there. So my guess is the roads between San Isabel and the town shouldn't be too bad." He tried to fold up the map but quickly gave up and handed it to Yanez. "Hopefully once we're out of the last park we can weave our way around those little mountain valleys and get over to the town without too many problems."

"That's some good thinking there, Mr. Curley," she said, folding up the map with ease and giving him a whack with it as they got into the truck. "Gotta say, too, it feels good to just be the copilot for once and let someone else fly the ship."

To even get to the nearest service road they still had to crawl along with traffic for a while in the relentless sunlight and heat. They needed to conserve fuel, so they ran the air conditioning very sparingly, mostly driving with the windows down until one of them couldn't take it anymore. Neither of them wanted to end up like the family in the minivan, so they checked the engine temperature frequently. Del also kept a close eye on Yanez, not wanting her to experience a setback in the sweltering temperature.

"How are you doing on your water?" he asked.

Yanez drained off the rest of her bottle and proudly showed Del the empty before crushing it and tossing it into the back. He gave her a thumbs-up, then reached down and opened the drawer underneath his seat, fishing out a fresh one. He cracked it open before handing it to her.

"Thanks, Mom," she said, taking the bottle.

"We should be able to pick up the 577 ahead. That'll get us back into the forest and some shade."

"After spending most of the year in space, I never thought I'd be longing for the dark."

"What's it like?" Del asked. "Space, I mean."

It was the question Yanez had gotten most often since joining NASA, and each time the person asking it would smile in the same way Del was smiling now. For whatever reason, the question always traveled with a touch of childlike giddiness, like when you get a present and ask the person giving it to you what they got you before you rip off the wrapping.

"It's unbelievably beautiful," Yanez said. "When I wasn't working I'd go to this one place on the station called the cupola, which is really just a bunch of windows, and stare out at the stars. You can google images of the universe and see some pretty amazing shit. But being there, in the middle of it . . . it's really hard to describe the feeling."

At the mention of windows, Del raised his and turned on the AC to beat back the heat in the cab. "That must be awesome."

"It is, but it can also be pretty unsettling," Yanez said, raising her window too. "You just can't wrap your head around the size of it. It's pretty easy to feel small and insignificant up there, especially when you and your coworkers are crammed into what feels like a high-tech shoebox."

She got quiet at the thought of Anatoly and Susan, lying dead in the New Mexico canyon where they'd crash-landed. She would insist on the retrieval and proper burial of their bodies when she got to the Mountain and could talk to NASA or the military.

"I'm really sorry about your crew," Del said.

She smiled at him and then took a swig of her water, swallowing loudly to lighten the mood. She reached for the radio and searched out something they could listen to on the AM bands, settling on a lone-gunman-type operator out of Amarillo and his theory about NASA's complicity in the ongoing alien invasion. As they drove to the forest, they learned about how the government was in contact with the aliens and that the object was going to open any day now, spewing forth the invaders.

"So this is *your* fault," Del said, giving Yanez a suspicious side-eye.

"For sure," she said, reaching down and touching the top of her backpack, which was resting at her feet. "This baby is just the final set of instructions for the aliens."

Del took the opening as if he'd been waiting for it. "All right, I'm gonna say it. *This* dude is obviously nuts. But . . ."

"But could it be aliens or some shit?" Yanez finished.

"Yeah."

"Sure."

"Seriously?" he said.

"Del, that thing up there stopped the Earth. Whether it's aliens or God, busted physics, or an enormous pushpin on somebody's corkboard, it is definitely 'some shit' we're dealing with."

Del turned off the main road and into the forest. The shady trees offered instant relief. He flipped off the AC and rolled down their windows, letting fresh air into the cab.

"Well in that case, Commander Prescott, I hope you'll put in a good word for me with our new alien overlords."

They reached the gated entrance to the nearest service road after a few miles. Del's key card wouldn't work—the power was down, and the battery backups were only meant to last a few days—but he got out and used the hand crank to manually swing the gates open wide enough for them to get through. They continued in that fashion, every now and then stopping to crank open a gate along the way, as they crossed into Colorado and Rio Grande National Forest. The heart of the forest was a few hours north, so they were able to make good time in the largely wide-open southern portion.

Shortly after they stopped to eat and refuel at one of the ranger outposts, they saw a truck pulled over. It was towing a small Airstream, the kind designed for a couple of people to sleep in and store a few things, but not much else. A man standing near the open hood looked up when he heard Del's truck approaching and waved them down. They pulled in behind the trailer, and Del leaned out his window.

"Engine trouble?" he yelled.

As the man wiped his hands on his jeans and walked toward their truck, a woman appeared out of nowhere at the open passenger-side window and pointed a shotgun at Yanez's head.

"Get out! Now!" she shouted, her voice cracking as she screamed. "We need your truck."

35

THE BRITISH NAVY vessel pushed its engines to the limit as it crossed the English Channel. The seas were running high and the chief engineer urged the captain to ease up. They'd been docked near Bournemouth for repairs when the orders came down from command and now a misaligned turbine was creating a troubling shimmy in the engine block that could cause permanent damage. But the fleet commander's orders were exquisitely clear. They were to retrieve the American from Saint-Malo and deliver her to Bude as fast as possible. And given how much vomiting she'd been doing in the last eight hours it was probably best to get her back to land quickly to avoid permanent damage to *her*.

Madelyn wiped her mouth and sat back on her berth. She'd tried to sleep, but the lurching of the ship had made that a pipe dream. So in between sessions with the bucket, she'd been composing a letter to her daughter, trying to apologize for all the time she'd spent away and all the things she'd missed. Fear of drowning and puking out major organs, it seemed, made one especially contrite.

A knock sounded on the cabin door. A threatening belch rose up, but Madelyn swallowed it down and weakly called out for the person to come in.

"Ma'am, the captain has requested your presence on the bridge," the petty officer said. He tried not to glance down at the bucket, but Madelyn saw his eyes stray there for a beat. "At your earliest convenience," he added. She thanked him, waited for him to leave, and then very carefully got up.

She walked the narrow corridor with a hand on either wall to steady herself. After two pauses to close her eyes and count to ten, she made it to the bridge. The captain took one look at her and then helped her to a chair.

"Ma'am, I apologize for the ride," he said. "The waters have been remarkably high in the Channel. Hopefully things should smooth out as we make our way north."

She smiled and gave a brief and unconvincing thumbs-up. "Any word?"

"That's why I summoned you," he said. "We've rounded the southern tip near Penzance. It and nearby St. Ives have been evacuated. Flooding."

"How bad?" she asked.

"Biblical."

Just then the radio officer flipped a switch and spun around to face the captain. "Sir, I have Bude."

"This is Captain Davies. What is the situation?"

The harbormaster's frantic voice crackled through the bridge speakers. "Captain, the docks are gone and the harbor is littered with rogue vessels that broke their moorings. Do not approach."

"What about the town?"

"The evacuation is underway. The water has been rising almost a meter per hour."

"I need to speak to the delegation," Captain Davies said.

"They've moved to a new site. We're rerouting communications, so we can't get them right now. You must swing west away from the harbor and head north to Vinegar Cove. Drop anchor a mile from shore. From there you should be able to ferry the Madam Secretary to Dunsmouth. Good luck, Bude out."

Captain Davies spoke to his helmsmen, then turned to Madelyn. "We should reach the cove in about an hour," he said. "I'll take you ashore myself."

"Thank you, Captain," she said, also acknowledging the radioman and others. "I appreciate the entire crew's effort to get me here."

"An honor, ma'am," he said, then paused while he considered the question she was sure he'd been dying to ask since she'd first come aboard. "Can we fix it?" he asked.

She looked around the bridge at the sailors, all of them noticeably on edge. "I wish I could tell you all yes, but honestly I have no idea. There's a lot to figure out. But I do know one thing for sure."

"Yes, ma'am?"

"I'll be very happy to get the fuck off this boat."

The ship was steadier after rounding the tip of Britain. Madelyn packed her things and tucked the letter to her daughter inside her passport, hoping she could continue it later but not having any idea what later would bring. When she finished, she went to her berth and even managed to close her eyes for a while until the engines went noticeably quiet. She sat up when she heard the ship's anchor drop, and then Captain Davies was at her door.

A CRRC was poised at the edge of the ramp leading from the rear deck of the ship to the dark waters of the Celtic Sea. A sailor who looked barely old enough to babysit her daughter let alone be in the British Navy sat at the rear of the raft near the motor. Four other sailors stood ready to help launch the vessel once Madelyn and their captain were aboard. Davies helped Madelyn over the side and then gave his men a few last-minute orders before bounding over the side himself and settling next to her. They hit the water seconds later.

Madelyn watched the ship recede behind them, the lights of the vessel the only real brightness against the inky blackness. The moon's light was weak as they leapt across the tops of the waves. Madelyn looked up at the dark band of shadow cutting it in two, and was reminded of a *Tom and Jerry* cartoon she'd watched with her daughter, where Jerry the mouse cast a giant shadow against a wall, scaring Tom the cat out of his skin. If only their current problems were so overblown.

The sailor manning the motor saw the beacons first. He angled the raft toward a grassy landing zone that the delegation's crew had set up. The raft beached on what had previously been a goal line at the local university football field, and three men helped haul it onto dry land before another helped Madelyn out of the raft. He beckoned for her to follow him to a waiting SUV.

"Where are we going?" she asked.

"The university observatory, Madam Secretary," he said. "Everything east of the canal is underwater, including the communications center."

It was a short drive, and when they arrived, three large generators were thrumming in the quad out front, with thick cables snaking in through the main doors, which were guarded by armed men and women. The driver called ahead and then escorted Madelyn inside, where they were met by a young woman in a dark suit.

"Madam Secretary," she said, extending a hand. Madelyn noted the woman's holstered gun as they shook. "If you'll come with me, I'll take you to the others."

They walked to an elevator that was manned by two more guards. One of them turned a key on a pad next to the elevator, and the doors opened. They went up to the seventeenth floor and stepped out into the command-and-control center for Europe and the Americas—and soon, she'd discover, for the rest of the world.

As she approached the delegation, the German vice-chancellor was speaking into a conference phone. "No, Madam President. It's gone," he said. "No one has been able to detect it along its designated orbit since the event."

"What's gone?" Madelyn asked, drawing the attention of everyone in the room.

"Madam Secretary," the German vice-chancellor said, a broad smile breaking across his face. "I think I speak for us all when I say how happy we are that you've made it here safely."

A round of applause erupted from the group seated around the large oval table. Madelyn nodded to the Swiss president, an Irish cabinet official, the Spanish and Polish prime ministers, the Austrian president, and a handful of other BBC News and exposé regulars.

"Thank you. Good to see you again," she said. "I wish we were all together under happier circumstances."

"Is that her? Is she there?" Bonita Reyes's voice echoed through the room.

Madelyn answered, "I'm here, Madam President."

"Glad to hear your voice, Maddy," Reyes said.

Then General Tate chimed in. "Madam Secretary, we'd all love to hear about your journey, but we have very little time."

"Understood, General. Why don't you catch me up, starting with what you were just talking about when I came in?"

"The International Space Station," the German vice-chancellor said. "We hoped to reach the astronauts by radio to see if they have any information about the object, but we haven't been able to make contact."

"Like all of our satellites, the station probably became unmoored from its geosynchronous orbit when the event occurred," interjected a rail-thin young woman. She wore thick glasses and a dark blue turtleneck and was standing near a display of the globe. "I'm Dr. Isla Hoyt, Madam Secretary. I run this observatory."

"Dr. Hoyt, do you think perhaps the crew altered their orbit?" Madelyn asked. "Are we looking in the wrong spot?"

"No, I think they're dead, Madam Secretary, and we should turn our attention elsewhere."

The room went silent in response to Hoyt's bluntness.

Madelyn took her seat at the table and opened a folder that had been waiting for her near the tent card with her name.

"I hate to make you rehash anything on my account, but can we talk about the water?" she said, studying the information on the top sheet. "I got to see the flooding firsthand on my way here. What's going on?"

"That's not rehashing at all," said Hoyt. "I was about to get to that. All the water is migrating to the poles. Based on the information we've been able to gather in the last twenty-four hours, we've estimated the rate of sea level rise. If the current rate holds, this is what we will be looking at in the next ten days."

She advanced to another slide in her presentation—a map of the world, but not a world anyone had ever seen before. It showed a large landmass stretching the entire length of the equator, massive oceans at the caps, and completely remade Northern and Southern Hemispheres.

Hoyt set the clicker down, giving the room a chance to absorb the information. The room was so quiet that President Reyes asked if they'd lost communications.

"We're still here," Madelyn said.

"Ten days?" the German vice-chancellor asked. "Are you sure?"

"Our numbers match," said a small voice on the phone. "Uh, I mean, we concur with Dr. Hoyt's analysis. This is Eugenia Sang."

"We need to warn people," said the Swiss president.

"How? There's no power in most places," said the Polish prime minister. "Are we to knock door to door?"

"President Reyes, who else have you been able to reach on your side?"

"We got Columbia a few hours ago. They've been in touch with most of the South American governments."

"Yes, but they're in the safe zone," said the Spanish prime minister, whose country would be mostly submerged. "What do they care?"

"Let me be clear," said Hoyt. "No one is safe. This isn't a

problem only for the parts of the planet that will be swallowed by the oceans. The seismic stress will be enormous everywhere."

"Yeah, and it, um, it's going to start really soon too," Eugenia's voice rang out in the room.

"What do you mean?" the Swiss president asked, leaning toward the phone in the middle of the table. "Dr. Sang, please explain."

"It's like . . ." she stretched out the *like* by adding a sustained *umm*. ". . .when you're holding a water balloon. It's real wobbly, right? And when the water inside sloshes to one side, that side gets heavier. But it doesn't break because the balloon itself is flexible and we can adjust our grip so that we don't drop it. You see?"

Puzzlement united the people in the room in that instant more than the euro ever had. Luckily, Dr. Hoyt jumped in to help.

"The Earth is not flexible, and no one is holding it steady. So that means it's going to become very unstable as the water settles," she explained. "And since the waters are already on the move, we should expect the instability to increase in the coming days."

The Austrian president stood up and walked closer to the screen. He looked at his homeland, now erased by the waters of what had once been the Tyrrhenian and Mediterranean Seas. He touched the image as if doing so would make it more real.

"We must do something," he said. "We simply cannot allow this to happen."

The phone line clicked several times, and then a man's voice broke through. "Dr. Hoyt, we have Novorossiysk."

"Please merge the calls," she said. "That is exactly what we're going to discuss right now."

After a series of clicks, a deep voice said, "This is the Kremlin. To whom am I speaking?"

36

GASPS ERUPTED FROM THE AUDIENCE, choked cries of denial and fear, affirmations and halleluiahs. Midge let out a gut-wrenching sob, her knees buckling, and clung to Michael until Rose pried her loose and led her away. But Michael continued to stand tall before them, eyes squeezed shut and hand raised to the heavens. He let the moment build, the tension in the crowd rising, the silence washing over them once again.

And then he began his sermon.

"That thing in the sky didn't stop the world," he said, letting his arm fall to his side. "We did."

His head swept left to right as he tried to make eye contact with as many of these people as possible. Whether they were complete strangers or people he'd known his whole life, all of them were in need of salvation. Finally his gaze settled on his sister, who stood apart from the rest, worry etched across her sunburned forehead. He gave her the big brother's it's-okay smile, the one that used to make everything better. Then he continued.

"We stopped the world through our greed and selfishness. Through our pettiness and boastfulness. Through our blasphemy and lies and gluttony and sloth. For thousands of years, humans spun and spun through this universe, creating a maelstrom of sinfulness that echoed across the generations. We spun and spun in our sin just as the world spun, steady and constant and predictable."

He reeled them in as he spoke, scrubbing his hands through his hair, slapping his chest with each condemnation, ensnaring them through his rising and falling timbre and constant motion, back and forth like a tiger on the other side of thick glass at the zoo. And all the while, Noel watched them watching him. She watched as her brother disappeared and was replaced by someone utterly alien to her, a doppelganger she was afraid of and afraid for at the same time.

"God, you see, has finally had enough of his spoiled and sinful children. His holy judgment is upon us," he said, pointing to the object. "How will you be judged? How will you face your God and account for your sins on this Earth?

"Some will try to avoid His judgment. Right now, our so-called leaders are hiding inside a military base not very far from here, deep underground. The president and her generals and their scientists and mathematicians and scholars and all the rest of the godless men and women who helped drive this world to the brink of the abyss think they can hide inside their Mountain and avoid what is to come. But they are wrong! We are all facing the fires!"

He was whipping them into a frenzy. Shouts of disbelief and outrage popped like kernels in the tremendous heat all around. He let their anger build, his coda poised on his lips, ready to be a balm for the open wound he'd just exposed. And when the moment was right, he administered it and marshaled them in the same instant, mobilizing his new church on the broken steps of his old one.

"But we *can* still repent," he said. "We can beg Him for forgiveness and mercy. Damned, we certainly are. But if we have any hope of avoiding eternal damnation, we must repent! And we must start now! Who will join me?" Michael swept his arm above the enraptured crowd. "Who will supplicate themselves before God's messenger in these final hours?"

One by one, and then in multiples, people fell to their knees.

Michael set down his microphone and walked into their midst. He whispered to them and touched their heads as he passed. Noel lost sight of him as they surged around him, crying out thanks to him for sharing the truth, engulfing him in their fervor for penance.

Despite the oppressive heat, a shiver ran up Noel's spine. She fled the scene, tears running down her face. Jimmy saw her and followed, dodging people who wanted to pull him to themselves or toward Michael. He pushed them away, gently at first but then with greater urgency as Noel got farther from him. Once free of the crowd, he jogged to catch up to her.

"Noel, hold on!" he called, touching her shoulder.

"I can't watch this," she said, shrugging him off.

"Please, wait," he said, moving into her path. "Just wait a second."

Noel stopped and wiped her eyes. She looked at Jimmy, who appeared to be just as scared as she was by what he'd just seen. His best friend of thirty years becoming a totally different person right before their eyes. She pulled him close and clung to him. Later she'd wonder if she'd held on to him so tightly because it was him, or because he represented a past she was losing forever.

"He'll come back," Jimmy said. "He's just out of it because of what's happened. I'll fucking knock him out if I have to. But he'll come back."

"I don't think so," she said. "You heard him up there. This isn't exhaustion or some sort of mental break. He really believes what he just said. He's all in."

"He's a priest. Of course he means it."

"No, Jimmy, this is different. What he just did up there wasn't about faith or God's divine plan or whatever. It was zealotry, plain and simple. And I can't be a part of it."

"You can't give up on him. He's your brother!"

"Yes, he is. But right now, he belongs to *them*," she said, pointing back to the swarm of people around Michael, raising their arms to heaven and crying out for forgiveness. "The only way to get him back is to try and figure out what that fucking thing is up there. That means getting the astronaut and her data inside the Mountain."

"And if she doesn't make it?"

"She will," Noel said.

"How do you know?"

"I gotta believe in something."

He let out a deep sigh. "Yeah."

She grabbed his hand. "You need to watch him, Jimmy. Play along with his bullshit if that's what it takes to stay close, but watch him. Promise me."

He nodded, and then he leaned in and kissed her. He'd never done that in public before, but perhaps he figured there was no longer sense in keeping secrets. They held each other afterward, neither one wanting to let go. Then Noel kissed his forehead.

"Radio me if anything happens," she said.

"Be safe," he whispered, but she was already walking away.

Word of the service had created a surge of people toward the church, either to be a part of what was happening or just to see the circus. *Probably both,* Noel thought as she squeezed her way through the press of people and retrieved her bike. Even then it wasn't until she reached the edge of town that she really broke free of the throng, and as she finally accelerated, she reveled in the sense of freedom and the rush of air across her body, sweat drying and leaving salt stains on her shirt.

Michael's words echoed in her mind as she sped back to the radio tower. Even after he'd completed seminary and had taken his vows, it had always been hard for Noel to think of her brother as a man of the cloth. She knew this was a common reaction among the siblings of those who went into religious service. Eventually, though, she'd come to terms with Michael's faith—until now. What she'd just seen at the church, the look in his eyes as he addressed the crowd . . .

She didn't see faith there. Only mania.

She reached the bluff, but the service road was almost completely jammed with people making their way to the top. The place was nearly full at this point. As she weaved her Indian Chief back to the station, people waved or reached out for a high five. A few kids even ran alongside the bike, helping to keep people back, her own Secret Service guiding her to where they needed her to be —back at the controls of her tower.

Aster came bursting out of the station when she got word that Noel had returned. Noel pulled up next to her, killed the engine, and set the kickstand.

"This is nuts," she said, getting off the bike and handing Aster her helmet.

"You don't know the half of it," Aster said.

"What are you talking about?"

"There's something happening with the water."

"What water?" Noel asked.

"All of it."

MICHAEL HAD SUSPECTED it for a while, of course. All the little moments of weirdness between the three of them over the last couple of years, the subtle innuendos, awkward laughs, and hushed conversations. They now came flooding back as he watched them kiss. And when they embraced, the confirmation of their betrayal made his head swim and his vision blur.

He closed his eyes and staggered amid the heat and noise of the surging crowd, processing the idea of Noel and Jimmy. *Why?* he asked, silently at first and then aloud. He swayed back and forth in the simmering realization of their deception, made all the worse for being revealed to him during his moment of triumph.

Terrified shouts to give him space snapped him back from the brink. He opened his eyes and saw tear-streaked and stress-filled faces. They needed him to be their rock, and he was already failing them. He shot them a quick smile of reassurance, waving away his episode to quell their fear and confusion. And when he raised his hands to the sky and thanked the Lord for his mercy, their relief was palpable.

Still, even as he ministered to his flock, he tried to understand why he'd had such a strong reaction to this new revelation. It wasn't because he disapproved of whatever feelings they had for one another. That wasn't the damnable sin. The sin was the secret itself. *Why did they hide it from me? Was it fear of my anger? Of my imagined disgust, perhaps? Were they afraid that I couldn't handle a change in decades of status quo?* Whatever the reasons, their deceitfulness and sins would be just one more reckoning that would need to occur in the days to come.

He saw Jimmy wading through the crowd toward him. "Everyone, please let Sheriff Bell through!" Michael shouted.

They made a path for Jimmy to get to Michael. When he reached him, Michael threw his arm around Jimmy's shoulders.

"Everyone, please listen to me," Michael said. The crowd quieted down. "Many of you know this man. He has dedicated himself to the protection of this town and its people for his entire adult life. He is an honorable man, and someone we can all be proud to call our brother."

Michael released Jimmy and looked him dead in the eyes. "I know *I'm* proud to call you my brother."

Jimmy flushed with embarrassment and waved off affirmations from those around him.

"But like us all," Michael continued, addressing the crowd once more, "he is also a sinner, whose judgment will be spoken very soon."

Jimmy stared at Michael, seeing a stranger in his friend's watery, weary eyes. He didn't understand what Michael was saying and was unable to guess what this man he'd die for might do next.

"But it's okay," Michael went on. "It's okay, because when the time comes and Sheriff Bell, my best friend in this whole doomed and damned world, is faced with a choice, I know he'll make the right one."

Michael's smile was like a spear to Jimmy's heart. "I'd bet my very life on it."

38

NAVAL ACADEMY PILOTS share many of the same traits. For instance, they all have exceptional visual acuity and dexterity. They all excel at pattern recognition and mental agility. But maybe the thing they have most in common is the ocean of competitive juices flowing through their veins.

Despite what the movies want us to believe, flying isn't the best way to determine whose skills kick the most ass. In Uncle Sam's multi-million-dollar planes, pilots only get to do as they're told. So they have to find other ways to establish a pecking order. Speed chess, parkour, virtual reality games, darts, billiards—all of these have helped determine the only rankings that really matter to young naval aviators. During Yanez's years, Ping-Pong was the gauntlet of choice. Among her many distinctions and honors while at the academy, the one that she was proudest of was Paddler Supreme. Yanez had the fastest hands in the class of 2005, and all these years later, when some woman decided to aim a shotgun at her through Del's truck window, she proved she hadn't lost a single step.

She grabbed the barrel with her left hand and yanked it into the truck, toward the windshield and away from her and Del in case the woman managed to squeeze off a shot. The woman gasped and stumbled forward as she tried to keep hold of the gun, but only until the passenger side door smashed her nose when Yanez kicked it open. The woman lost her grip on the weapon, and Yanez leapt out of the truck with the shotgun in hand. As the blubbering woman stumbled backward, clutching her gushing nose, Yanez swept her leg out from under her, sending her to the dirt, and then aimed the gun at her.

Game, set, match.

Until she saw the little girl.

"Mommy!" the girl yelped.

Del dashed around the back of the truck and ran up beside Yanez, who lowered the gun to her side. The man who'd been working on the family's truck scrambled over and placed the girl behind him.

"Please don't hurt my wife!"

"Why did you do that?" Yanez screamed at the woman, who was using the collar of her shirt to stanch the blood seeping from her busted nose.

"I'm sorry," the woman said, her voice breaking.

"What if I had shot you?"

"I know," the woman said, looking over at her husband and daughter. "We've been stuck out here for two days and we're almost out of supplies."

"So you thought you'd steal our truck?" Del said.

"It was stupid. I'm sorry." The woman's collar was soaked in blood, which was freaking the little girl out. Del reached into his back pocket and tossed the woman his handkerchief.

"You could have just asked us for help," Yanez said. "That's why we stopped."

"We didn't know if we could trust you," the woman said, holding Del's handkerchief to her nose. "I was scared."

Yanez and Del took a few steps back and then waved the man and little girl over to the woman. The girl ran to her mother, threw her arms around her, and let out deep kid sobs.

The man moved more cautiously. "You're right," he said. "This was a terrible mistake, and we have no right to ask for anything from you. But if you could just let us go and be on your way, we'd really appreciate it."

"You'd still be stuck out here," Del said.

"That's our problem, not yours," the man said, standing above his family.

"How did you end up out here?" Del asked.

"We sat in a traffic jam for almost eighteen hours," the man said, scooping up his daughter. His wife got to her feet. "I thought maybe if we cut through the park, we'd be able to pick up the interstate on the other side. But a tree was down in the road, so we cut around a gate a few miles back, and then the engine died. I've been trying to fix it. I'm not very good with this sort of stuff though. I can't even see anything that's obviously busted."

Del paused, though Yanez already knew what he was going to say next. The man was a good Samaritan if ever there was one.

"How about I give you a hand?" Del said.

"We don't deserve your help," the man said, "but we would surely welcome it. My name's Ray."

Yanez put the shotgun in Del's truck, and then they all made introductions. The woman's name was Karen, and her daughter was Ellie. The girl wouldn't so much as look at Yanez, though; she was having no part of the reconciliation.

The adults made small talk for a little while, mainly to try and calm Ellie down and reset the whole situation, and then Del and Ray went to take a look at the dead engine. Yanez produced bottled water and a couple granola bars from the truck, and gave them to Karen and Ellie.

"Where were you heading?" she asked, watching Ellie gobble the bar down.

"My folks live in Tucson," Karen said. "We were hoping to ride this thing out with them."

The little girl was eyeing her mom's unwrapped granola bar. Karen noticed and faked being shocked before handing it over to her.

"How about you? Where are you going?" Karen asked.

Yanez decided against telling Karen too much. "Colorado Springs."

"Any news on what's happening?" Karen asked.

"Not really. Roads are packed with people, but you already know that."

Del and Ray reappeared. "I know what's wrong with the engine," Del said, "but we're gonna need a part to fix it. We're gonna head back to that outpost where we stopped to refuel, get what we need there. We should be back in a couple hours."

"You can fix it?" Karen asked.

"You bet. We'll get you going in no time."

Ellie let out a little "yippee" and did a happy stompy dance in the pine straw, clearly feeling better.

"Okay, just let me grab some stuff from the truck first," Yanez said. She pulled out food and water and camping gear, and handed them to Karen and Ellie, who'd come to help her. Then she grabbed her backpack—which she refused to be separated from—and the shotgun.

Karen gave Yanez a sideways look when she saw her walking back with the gun.

"Just in case we meet some crazies in the woods," Yanez said, smiling.

While Ray and Del were gone, the others made a small fire near the Airstream. Del's camping gear included an array of cooking paraphernalia, and Ellie was incredibly excited about the idea of cooking beans and franks in the little saucepan at the end of the telescoping handle. Once they got the fire going, Ellie set to work on dinner, and Yanez and Karen sat close by in case of any bean-related emergencies.

"What do you do?" Karen asked.

"I'm a pilot," Yanez said.

"Oh yeah? What airline?"

"Nothing commercial. I fly for the military," she said, feeling good about not straying too far from the truth.

"Ah, that explains the ass-kicking I got. What branch?"

"Navy," Yanez said.

"Fighter jets?"

"Some jets. But I fly all kinds of things," Yanez said. She quickly pivoted. "How about you?"

"Ray's a day trader and does pretty well. Mostly on the Nikkei. So I homeschool Ellie and we travel around a lot."

Ellie's beans and dogs were boiling, so Karen helped her get them into a bowl, avoiding any burns along the way. Ellie blew on her food with the sort of delight only a kid could have in a world teetering on the edge of chaos. Karen handed Ellie a juice box, and Ellie popped the straw off the little glue tab and tapped it on her thigh to free it from the plastic wrapping before handing the wrapper back to Karen, who snatched it without a thought. They moved with the familiarity of dance partners, performing a routine that'd probably played out hundreds if not thousands of times, the type of scene that hadn't yet found its way into Yanez's life. She thought back to all the arguments and fights with her ex-husband around starting a family. She didn't regret prioritizing her career back then. And she didn't regret it when the marriage ultimately ended as a result. But watching Karen and Ellie's dance made her wonder if a happy medium had been missed.

Once Ellie was slurping down her beanie weenie, Karen settled next to Yanez again. "So which way are you leaning? Rapture or little green men?"

"Those my only choices?"

"Unless you're gonna convince me the Matrix needs a reboot or that the government slipped something into the water. If not, feels like we're just talking about those two options, right? I mean, what else could it be?"

"Sounds like you've thought this through."

"Yeah, well, when you're stuck in the woods watching your

white-collar husband poke around under a hood he's never popped open before, you have lots of time to think."

The collapsible bowl snapped shut on Ellie's tongue as she licked the inside of it, trying to get every last bean. She gave a thumbs-up as she freed her tongue and sucked on the juice box to help the pinch go away.

"Which option have you settled on?" Yanez asked.

Karen shrugged. "After twelve years of all-girls Catholic school, I gotta go with the big man upstairs on this one."

"All those rulers on your knuckles worked, huh?"

Karen rubbed the backs of her hands as if they still ached. "Honestly, I just can't imagine anything else. I mean, seriously, how do you stop a whole planet? Sounds like God to me."

Yanez thought about all the times she'd looked down on the Earth from a vantage point that few had ever enjoyed, circling around and around in an instrument of man's genius above a planet that she couldn't fathom being the result of scientific or astrological chance. She'd always found comfort in that space between divinity and mankind. But now the presence of the object was daring her to pick a side.

"I don't know," she said. "If those are really my only two choices, I'm gonna straddle the line and say that maybe God decided to send us aliens instead of fire and brimstone. Just to defy expectations."

"That answer would get you a rap on the knuckles for sure," Karen said.

"I guess I'm just a vanilla-chocolate swirl kind of girl. And I'm not just talking about my skin tone."

At the mention of ice cream, Ellie looked up.

"What's for dessert?" she asked, patting her tummy.

39

THE BUNKER'S LONGEST TUNNEL, the main route between the north and south portals, was only two miles long, so the president had to run back and forth a few times to hit her daily miles total. Each trip took her past the bunker's fifteen buildings, all of them suspended on giant steel springs for stability in the event of a nuclear blast, the five lakes, one of which held a half million gallons of diesel in case the Mountain lost power and had to sustain itself on its generators alone, and the side tunnel that led to the famous twenty-three-ton blast door they always showed on TV and in the movies. It was a truly unique run in a truly unique place. What made it particularly special, however, was the fact that she was able to do it alone. It had been years since she'd been able to run solo—not counting the treadmill, of course, which was the devil. When she ran around the mall in DC, she always had to be accompanied by Secret Service. And while a run down a tunnel cut through millions of tons of granite didn't technically count as running outdoors, it felt damn good to be by herself. In fact, she felt so good when she hit her ten-mile mark that she decided to do one last loop, just to stretch out the moment.

Afterward, she went to the building that housed the fitness center. A quick stretch, cooldown, and shower, and she was on her way to the control center. As she approached, she saw Eugenia sitting on a bench near the front door, working on her laptop and blowing big pink bubbles. The computer lid was decorated with overlapping, colorful stickers of all shapes and sizes, including a unicorn farting out a rainbow.

"How's it going?" Reyes asked, catching Eugenia mid-blow.

Eugenia had been so engrossed in her screen, she must not have seen the president coming. She sucked in her bubble quickly and not entirely successfully, having to pull a strand away from her upper lip and nibble it off her fingertips. "Sorry, Madam President. I was, um, I mean, hi ma'am."

"Better watch out, Dr. Sang," Reyes said, pointing to the glob of pink gum stuck to the bricks next to Eugenia's bench. "You'll get detention if the teacher sees that."

Eugenia glanced at the wall and then swallowed hard. "That wasn't me, ma'am."

"Uh-huh," Reyes said, taking a seat beside her. "What are you working on?"

"I'm trying to figure out its shape," she said. She turned her computer screen so the president could see. "We've confirmed that the entirety of the viewable surface is reflective. We've been bouncing lasers off of it from the ground and high-orbit flights for the last twenty-four hours. We've also been using the big array at Peterson to send radio signals."

"Why radio?"

"You know," Eugenia said dismissively, waving off her answer before even giving it, "in case anyone's home up there."

"Not a fan of the alien theories?"

"I think any species with the ability to stop a planet's rotation would probably just get right down to business."

"And what if stopping the Earth *was* their business?"

"Then I'd have to ask why. If it was simply to destroy us, seems to me there are more efficient ways. If it's just to mess with us or see how we react, well then . . ." Eugenia trailed off.

"Well then what?"

"Then we got bigger problems than not spinning."

"Right," the president said, recalling a similar conversation with the NASA administrator when she'd first arrived at the airbase.

"Anyway, the beams and the radio signals have been returning to us at different angles, and that tells us the curvature of the object at each spot. I'm trying to put that together into an overall shape. This is what we've got so far."

She clicked a few times, and the display changed to a three-dimensional wireframe of a tube with a tapered end.

"The end narrows to a point almost like the tip of a dart," she said, tracing her finger along the screen. "But keep in mind we can only map the portions of the object we can see. We have to not only send the signal but be in position to receive the bounce-back as well. So we don't know how far out it stretches from the ionosphere, or if it changes shape farther out."

Eugenia closed her laptop and fished a pack of Bubblicious from her front jeans pocket. She took a piece and offered the pack to the president, who accepted.

"Sounds like you're making good progress," Reyes said, unwrapping the gum and popping it into her mouth.

"Not really. The shape is one of the easier questions. We still have no idea of its composition or velocity."

"Velocity? I thought it wasn't moving."

"Which implies velocity. Gravity doesn't seem to affect it. So if it ain't falling, it's gotta be moving away from us at some sort of speed. We just can't figure it out yet."

The two of them sat there, chewing for a while. Reyes blew a bubble, which popped and covered her chin. Eugenia did the same, and the two women let themselves be kids again for a brief moment, pulling gum from their faces and reveling in the sugar rush.

Until the Mountain shook.

The building behind them creaked on its heavy springs for the first time ever, and a fine dust sifted down on them from above. A siren sounded, and soldiers burst from the building, looking relieved to find the president right outside. She spit her gum into her hand and stuck it on the wall with a mischievous wink before following the soldiers inside. Eugenia stuck hers atop the president's and then ran in after her.

"What's happening?" Reyes said as soon as she reached the control room. "Is it starting?"

General Tate waved her over. "Seems so, ma'am," he said.

"How big?"

"Low impact here. Info from outside is coming in now," he said. "We were on the line with Brazil when it hit. Houston is trying to get them back."

"Any word from Maddy and the delegation?"

"They're over Russian airspace."

"What the hell is taking so long?"

General Dinesh jumped in. "We made them track south, ma'am, rather than fly over the North or Baltic Seas."

"Why?" she asked, taking her seat at the head of the table. "Time is certainly of the essence."

"A lot of Europe is dark. Only a few places have power, and the moonlight is obscured by the object's shadow. Without radar, the pilots have to use large landmasses as markers and rely on ground transmissions. But we got word from Minsk that they landed safely there and switched out to choppers for the rest of the journey."

The radio's crackle interrupted them. "Houston, do you read?" Tate asked, and was met with an "affirmative" from the operator in Texas. "Did you get them back?"

"Negative, General. All submerged lines through the gulf have gone silent," the operator said.

"So we've lost contact with South America?" Reyes asked.

"The gulf is being drained, Madam President," Dinesh said. "But we can try to reach them through overland lines crossing through Mexico and Central America."

"Son, how are things there?" Tate asked the operator.

"Power's down and we're running on backup, sir. Seems like the rest of the grid that wasn't impacted by the original event is now out. Early data shows a 7.0 on Richter."

"Thank you, Houston. Check in when you know more. Cheyenne out," Tate said. He took his seat next to the president. "Ma'am, we also have reports out of San Diego that the tide has risen more than twenty feet in the last twenty-four hours. And we lost all contact with Florida about an hour ago. There's massive flooding everywhere on the East Coast. Highways are completely jammed with people moving inland away from the shorelines."

"Recommendations?" Reyes asked.

"We're already connecting with as many locations as possible, getting updates on their readiness, and briefing them on what they can expect in the coming days," Tate said. "Other than that, we wait for the delegation to reach Moscow."

The president pushed back from the table and stood. She walked over to where Eugenia was once again pecking away at her computer.

"Got any more of that gum?"

40

A WOMAN from Rehoboth Beach sobbed as she described the ocean swallowing sand dunes, the boardwalk, and most of the town. A teenager related how his family had fought their way west out of South Carolina with thousands of others after their community was washed away. A chopper pilot reported on the rising Pacific and mounting devastation in Los Angeles. A Boston cop begged for backup as he tried to rescue elderly and disabled patients from a long-term care facility, but was forced to leave many behind. The airwaves were filled with stories like these, of towns and cities awash in flood waters, of people desperate to find safety inland.

After hours of listening, Aster had eventually dozed off on the couch, but Noel couldn't rest no matter how exhausted she was. She just kept turning the dial in disbelief—and wondering what to tell people. They needed to know what was happening at the coasts, but when she thought about Michael's doomsday rhetoric, she was afraid that this news would only feed the insanity—feed *his* insanity and make him dangerous to himself and anyone listening to him. Or anyone like him, for that matter, of whom there were many out there. If half the stories on the radio were of rising waters, the other half were of hellfire.

A knock sounded on the door, and Aster sat up and rubbed her eyes. The knock sounded again, urgently. Noel lowered the volume, then went to the door and opened it.

One of the telescope crew poked his head inside. Behind him, a hysterical woman was shrieking before a crowd.

"Noel, there's a woman out here from Portland. She's going on and on about how the city's gone. She's saying that Eugene and Seattle have been swept into the Pacific too. You should come listen to this."

"Be right out," she said. "Please shut the door."

He hesitated, but Aster was there to help him along. She closed the door on the guy and then turned back to Noel.

"Guess we can't keep this to ourselves anymore," Aster said, coming back over to the console. She took up her former seat and turned up the volume a bit. But Noel reached over and turned it down again, her mind made up.

"People need to hear the truth. As scary as it might be, the alternative is worse."

"What's the alternative?"

"They make up their own truth."

Aster nodded but stayed quiet. Noel forgot sometimes that Aster was still just a girl. She touched her on the arm.

"It's okay to be scared. I certainly am. Anyone who isn't probably has some major issues. But it's not going to stop me from trying to figure this out. How about you?"

Aster smiled. "So what do we do?"

Noel pointed to the dials on the console. "Which one do you think is best?"

Before Aster could answer, the same guy opened the door and poked his head in again. "Sorry, but you *really* need to get out here."

Aster spun the dial and raised the volume to confirm that it was the station out of Reno. The broadcaster was a professional, his tone even and clear as he talked to a trucker in California.

"This guy's good," Aster said. "He's been punching in people from all over the West Coast and shutting down anyone too crazy."

Noel listened for a few seconds. The guy at the door listened too, his cheeks reddening the more he heard.

"Wait a minute. You mean this woman out here is telling the truth?" he said, eyes darting between Noel and Aster. "She's not just some nut?"

"Put it outside," Noel said.

Aster reached for the switch that would broadcast the channel to the speakers they'd set up around the top of the bluff. "Are you sure?"

"I'm sure." Noel pushed past the guy at the door, who'd turned from red to ashen in seconds. Behind her, Aster flipped the switch, adjusted the volume for the outside speakers, and then followed, pulling the shell-shocked dude with her.

It took a moment for people to settle down and realize that something was coming through the speakers. They waved away conversations and shushed each other so they could hear. The woman from Portland was the hardest to corral. But eventually she quieted down too, and they all listened.

RENO STATION
Where did it come from?

CALLER
Basically everywhere. No matter where
you turned, you were in it.

RENO STATION
So you think McNear Channel overflowed?

CALLER
I mean, yeah, it definitely
was part of it, but I'm not talking
about a little bit of water, man.
This was a *lot* more than McNear.

RENO STATION
You mean San Pablo Bay?

CALLER
The bay and the ocean, for sure.
I told you, it was coming into the
city from all over.

RENO STATION
But Petaluma's gotta be over
twenty miles from both of those.

CALLER
Not anymore.

RENO STATION (after a beat)
Where are you now?

CALLER
Crawling up the 101. But I think
I'm gonna try and get east.

RENO STATION
Why?

CALLER
The vineyards to my left are flooding.
I think Santa Rosa's next.

Noel sent Aster back inside to lower the volume. When the broadcast had dropped to a murmur, she waved her hands to get everyone's attention.

"Listen up!" she shouted. "We'll put that back on in a minute, and we'll be sure to keep scanning the channels and broadcasting any information we pick up that seems credible. Everyone deserves to know what's happening out there. In the meantime, if anyone has any information from your time on the road before you got here, anything that can help us, please come talk to us."

Aster was watching from the door to the station. Noel gave her a thumbs-up, and the girl went back inside and raised the volume once again.

People broke off into clusters, many swarming near the poles with the speakers. A large group gathered around the vindicated woman from Portland. One young guy Noel thought she recognized but whose face she couldn't quite place was beelining toward her. As he got closer, he swiped the sweat off his brow and flicked it away.

"I know you," she said when he was within earshot. "You helped me with my bike. Right before you kicked me off the base."

"Yes, ma'am. Private Walsh," he reminded her. "Sorry about that. But I'm glad to see you're okay."

"Why are you here?"

"Once everyone moved over to the Mountain and the base was secured, command cut a bunch of us loose."

"I know how that feels," she said, chucking him on the shoulder to show no hard feelings.

"Just following orders," he said. "Listen, you said that if people had any information they should come forward?"

"What do you got?" she asked.

But before Private Walsh could answer, the ground heaved beneath their feet and the tower groaned.

41

MICHAEL WALKED down a road covered in branches. People were gathered on both sides. Men and women, young and old, wealthy and beggars, clothed and naked, black and brown and white as snow, mute and deaf and diseased. They all cheered and called out to him as he passed. He waved to them, the fronds crunching under his sandaled feet.

A woman ran to him and fell to her knees. She used the hem of her dress to wipe the dust and flecks of green from his feet. As she finished and bent to kiss the top of his foot, a wind rose up ahead of them. He watched as it ripped down the street toward him, a sickly yellow-brown blast that churned the branches from the ground into a great maelstrom, a cry of despair at its leading edge. It blasted the flesh from the people as it swept over them, leaving chunks of gristle and gore hanging from their white bones. Michael grabbed the woman's hand and pulled her to her feet so that they could meet the ill wind together. The howl kissed their faces.

And Michael was jolted awake.

Rose stood over him. How long had he slept? He remembered her helping him to his bed inside the St. Anne's rectory after he'd exhausted himself, speaking to his burgeoning flock for nearly three hours.

He wiped the afterimage of the dream from his eyes and looked up at Rose. Her red hair hung in loose strands around her fear-stricken face.

"What is it?" he said, sitting up in bed.

"Did you feel it?"

He stood up and hugged her close. As she trembled in his arms, he saw the crucifix on the wall hanging at an angle. He separated himself from Rose, righted the cross, then turned back to her. "Tell me what happened."

"A few minutes ago, a tremor shook the whole town."

"Is anyone hurt?"

"I don't think so. But people are scared. That's why I had to come wake you."

"You did the right thing," he said, walking to his dresser.

He stood before the mirror and smoothed his greasy hair. He picked up his white collar and tried to slide it into place, but missed on the first few attempts. Rose took the collar from his hands and threaded it through the opening near his Adam's apple. A small fleck of blood stood out against the white when she got it into place. She licked her thumb and tried to scrub it clean, but instead just smeared it. She was about to pull it free from his shirt and replace it with a spare, but Michael stopped her.

"We don't hide the truth anymore," he said. "Do we?"

"No, Father," she said, tears springing to her eyes.

Michael wiped them away, kissed his faithful servant on her forehead, and then strode out of the room.

The rectory was adjacent to the church, but had taken far less damage than he would have expected when the walls came down. The main water line had burst and had to be shut off at the street, and the kitchen was destroyed, but the rest was intact. He walked through the common area where he and Sister Harriet used to read to children during Sunday school, then stepped into the blazing sunlight. He shielded his eyes as they adjusted, then took in the crowd gathering in front of St. Anne's. He felt a jolt of energy race through him as he walked up the steps to the front of the ruined church.

There he waited and watched. He could see that the people came to him filled with fear and anguish and dread. They knelt before him and held their hands to the sky and hung their heads low.

A small group set up a gas-powered generator on the rectory porch, and under Rose's direction, they snaked an extension cord to the amplifier Michael had used the day before. After a few attempts, the generator coughed to life. One of the men fiddled with the controls on the amplifier, then shot Michael a thumbs-up.

Michael tapped the mic. The speakers popped, alerting the crowd that he was ready.

"Friends, the time draws near," he began. "But there is still time to repent for our sins. There is still time to beg God for his mercy for our villainy and evil in this garden that he granted us and that his only son died for, this paradise now standing still and waiting for his return and judgment."

The speaker crackled and chirped, the amplifier's volume pushed to its limits. But it wasn't enough. The amens and hallelujahs from the nearer part of the crowd were drowned out by the cries of dismay from those farther back. They couldn't hear his message. His flock was deaf to his ministrations at their time of greatest need. Rose's helper tried to adjust the knobs, but only elicited more squeals from the taxed speaker.

Michael gazed up at the sky and the object blazing above them. *Another challenge, my Lord*, he thought. *Another test of my obedience and strength.* He welcomed this test with a smile.

Rose appeared at his side. "Don't worry, Father. I'll get some guys to go out and find Jimmy. He'll know who has a better PA system."

All the while, people continued to come. They filled the space in front of the church. They stood on park benches and trash bins and parked cars. And still more were arriving, a steady stream from all around. Michael needed to reach them, to touch their hearts. And he knew he couldn't do it from here any longer. It was time to leave St. Anne's behind.

And he knew where to go.

He looked out over their heads and off into the distance, where the answer gleamed on a hilltop. God was showing him the way once again.

"This isn't all of them," he said to Rose. "Don't you see? Even if my voice reached every one of these people"—he waved an arm to encompass the crowd—"I still wouldn't be reaching all who need to hear the truth."

She twisted her hands, on the verge of tears for failing him. He saw her anguish and touched her cheek so she would know it was okay.

"But there's another way."

He walked down the steps and among his flock. He moved slowly, letting a path form before him, his people creating a road that pointed out of town. A road that would take him to his sister. And to her tower.

42

Ellie puzzled over the trinket. "Is it real?" she asked, squeezing the dull blue fur to feel the bones underneath.

"Sure is," Yanez said, unclipping the keychain from her backpack, the hard drive from the ISS tucked away in its main compartment. "I've had it since I was about your age."

"I can keep it?"

"It's all yours."

Yanez fastened the keychain to a loop on Ellie's jeans. The little girl spun in a circle so that the rabbit's foot flung out from her side, orbiting her as she twirled. When she stopped, Yanez held her by the shoulders to steady her, drinking in the flush on her face and the light in her eyes.

"You want to know a secret?" Yanez asked, immediately eliciting an emphatic nod. "Promise not to tell anyone?"

"I swear," Ellie said, leaning in toward Yanez so that their foreheads were almost touching.

"That rabbit's foot has been to outer space."

"Really?" Ellie said, a little too loudly. Yanez made a dramatic shushing sound, and the two of them giggled as they did a quick check to make sure the other adults hadn't heard Ellie's outburst. Del and Ray were back, although they'd had to go to two different ranger outposts to get the part they needed. The actual repair had taken very little time in comparison. Now Ray and Karen were anxious to get back on the road to Tucson.

"Really?" Ellie asked again in a whisper, looking down at the keychain hanging at her side.

"No kidding," Yanez said. She reached out and let the rabbit's foot lie in the palm of her hand one last time. "So it'll bring you and your mom and dad extra luck."

"What makes a dead rabbit's foot lucky?"

"No one knows," Yanez said. "It's a mystery."

Karen called over to them that it was time to go. Yanez let the rabbit's foot fall from her hand and into Ellie's, who gave it another quick squeeze. She twisted back and forth to admire how it hung at her side, then shot Yanez a satisfied smile. Yanez held up her hand for a high five, making Ellie leap to try and reach it. After a few jumps, they slapped palms and Ellie raced over to her parents, the blue trinket bumping against her thigh.

Yanez looked up through the canopy of trees at the object stuck in the sky. The sight drained some of the joy from the moment, sucking it into its gravity well of fear and disillusionment. *They're gonna need more than a rabbit's foot*, she thought. *We all are.*

She averted her gaze and made her way over to the family's truck, where Del had his forest service map spread out on the hood. He and Ray were discussing the best route to get to Tucson.

Del tore off the bottom third of the map and handed it to Ray. "Stick to those roads and you should be okay," he said.

"How about you guys?" Ray asked.

"We'll be fine," Yanez said, reaching out to shake Ray's and then Karen's hand. Karen held on a beat longer than normal, one last apology for the gun incident.

Del and Yanez stayed to watch the family pull away, Ellie in the back window waving to them with the blue rabbit's foot. Yanez placed her index finger on her lips and mimed a shush, which Ellie returned just before disappearing around the bend.

"What was that about?" Del asked.

"Can't tell you, man. It's a secret," she said, starting off toward Del's truck.

He settled in behind the wheel, and Yanez kicked off her shoes and buckled up next to him. He looked over at her and smiled.

"Other than threatening to blow your head off, they were pretty nice folks, huh?"

The road climbed along a steep and densely wooded ridgeline. Yanez dozed off in the thick, cool shade, dreaming of the carnival at Smuggler's Notch where she'd won the rabbit's foot in a water pistol game. It'd had cotton candy stuck to its fur for years until she trimmed it off in high school with her dad's mustache scissors.

When at last she awoke, harsh light and heat filled the cab. "Where are we?" she asked, the memory of caramel corn evaporating with the last vestiges of sleep.

"Just above Gunnison National," Del said.

Yanez looked up at the object and the corona of vaporized clouds around its edges. At this elevation, the object's iridescent surface threw light like a mirror ball.

Del pointed ahead of them. "Once we get down into that canyon, we'll be able to start making our way toward the Comanche Grasslands."

"How long do you think?" Yanez asked, blinking away the afterimage.

"There's not much between here and Franklin. With luck on our side, we can get there in about two hours."

Unfortunately, luck was not on their side. Things were fine at first, as they picked up Highway Two. But then they reached the bridge at Cottonwood Gulch—or what used to be the bridge. It had now collapsed. They had to backtrack all the way to the Gardner Byway, which shot them southwest and away from

Franklin. There, things looked up, as they found Interstate 21 mostly deserted except for some light traffic heading the opposite way toward Utah. But when they reached Cripple Creek, they understood why there was no traffic in that direction. The once-small waterway that wended through Colorado had overflowed its banks, completely washing out the road. There would be no travel in this direction.

An elderly couple was parked at the edge of the water, watching it churn past.

"Do you need any help?" Del asked. They got out of the truck and walked over to the couple.

"No, we're okay," the old man said. "We're just taking it in."

"Never seen anything like it," his wife said.

"Creek ever run this high?" Yanez asked.

"Not in about forty years. Took a month of rain back then."

"But that ain't even it," the wife jumped in. "Lord oh lord, I just can't believe what I'm seeing."

"I'm a park ranger down in New Mexico," Del said. "We deal with this sort of thing from time to time. It's amazing how much damage the water can do."

"No, honey, you don't understand," the woman said. "The creek don't flow this way. It goes the other way."

"Are you sure?" Yanez asked.

"I've been fishing Cripple Creek for almost sixty years," the man said. "Trust me. Water's going backward."

———

After chatting with the old couple for a bit, Del and Yanez back-tracked and picked up Gulf Road to County 88, where they stopped to refuel. Del swerved around a rockslide that sent them north to Phantom Creek Road, and they pushed through the Table Mountain Bypass and down through Beaver Creek Wildlife Preserve over to the logjammed 115, along which they crawled for three hours before they finally saw a sign for Franklin.

It was at about that time that the roadway suddenly rolled like a wave.

Everyone was instantly out of their cars and trucks. People scrambled to the woods adjacent to the highway with kids and pets in their arms. The few drivers who didn't flee the buckling road just ended up making matters worse. Cars ended up angled all over the highway and unable to move.

Del and Yanez stood in the unmown grass near the tree line and watched the sky with the others, everyone crippled by fear and waiting for what would certainly come next. But nothing did, and eventually everyone started heading back to their vehicles in a slow procession.

"We're never going get there in all this," Yanez said as they settled into the cab and looked at the madness on the roadway in front of them.

"You're right," Del said. "I think we'll be better off hoofing it. Hold on."

He put the truck into four-wheel drive and cut the wheel. The bank of the median was steep, but the truck managed to tear its way through the grass on the upslope and cross the highway to the other side. He rode the inside shoulder until there was a break in the vehicles that let him cross all the way to the other side of the highway, where there was a massive Walmart. He pulled into one of the few spots left along the edge of the parking lot.

"Well, I was off by about eight hours or so," he said, killing the engine and letting out a long sigh.

"You did great," said Yanez, placing a hand on his forearm and giving it a squeeze. "Your plan to use the forests is probably the only reason we're here. Thank you."

He waved off her praise while flushing a deep red. "Let me grab some stuff from the bed and throw it in back so we can lock it up. Then we can head into town."

Luckily it was only about a two-mile walk into the center of Franklin, and it felt freeing to actually be moving forward at a constant pace, rather than be at the mercy of the stop-and-go of highway traffic. Soon they found themselves on Franklin's main drag, between the wreckage of a church and the burned-out remains of what looked to have been a restaurant. People were everywhere; clearly this location was some kind of local epicenter. Probably because of the church.

Yanez spotted a woman with red hair who seemed to be in charge—or at least, she was directing some men who were fiddling with some kind of PA system. She grabbed Del by the arm and pulled him over to her.

"Excuse me, I'm looking for Noel Williams," Yanez said. "Do you know where I can find her?"

The woman smiled. "You may think she's who you want," she said, "but it's her brother you're really looking for. Come on, I'll show you."

PART V

43

"My God. Look at that," Madelyn said.

The chopper banked left over Saint Basil's Cathedral. Two of the church's colorful domes had collapsed in on themselves, leaving open wounds in the iconic structure. A deep crack cut through the central spire, its copper crucifix hanging at a precarious angle from the apex. Holes pocked the red brick walls, and one of the massive, tented roofs had crashed to the walkway that wrapped around the building's base. Thick smoke boiled through a gaping hole at the front of the cathedral, where a fire crew pumped in a steady stream of water.

The pilot broke in through their headsets to tell them to prepare for landing, and they touched down less than a minute later. As they unbuckled and gathered their gear, a Kremlin Regiment officer opened the chopper's main cabin door. Cold wind buffeted them as they were escorted to a waiting SUV. The helipad could only accommodate one helicopter at a time, so the rest of the delegation circled above, waiting for their turn.

"We'll begin with a discussion of the timeline," said Dr. Hoyt as soon as they had settled into the SUV and pulled away, their chopper already ascending to make way for the next. "Assuming the connection to America is intact, Dr. Sang and I will brief the

Russian team on our estimates for increased seismic activity as the oceans continue migrating to the poles. After that, we'll pivot to a discussion of Operation Skybound."

"I'd also like us to talk about other possibilities for what's happening," the Spanish prime minister said, turning to the German vice-chancellor. "There are religious implications that have been *ignored* thus far and must be discussed."

"Mr. Prime Minister, the time for debate has passed," the German vice-chancellor said, unable to contain his exasperation. "We must move forward—"

"I am sworn to represent the will of the Spanish people on this delegation. Our beliefs will not be pushed aside in this matter by any nation. I *will* be heard."

Madelyn jumped in, hoping to end the argument before they had a repeat of what had happened in Bude, and then again on the plane across the continent.

"Time is a factor, yes," she said, making sure to make eye contact with each of them, "but we will make sure there is enough of it to discuss a variety of options *after* we have briefed the Russians and hear from their team. And *only* after that. Agreed?"

The men grudgingly nodded and settled back into their seats. Madelyn and Dr. Hoyt exchanged nervous glances, anticipating the show to come once they all were assembled and had the rest of the world's representatives on the line. The debate would no doubt continue, but the fate of the planet depended on their agreement on a path forward. National interests had to be set aside for humanity's interests. And it had to happen in the next twenty-four to thirty-six hours or it would be too late.

When they arrived at their destination, they were met by another Regiment officer, who had to shout his greeting over the chanting of the crowd gathered in Red Square. Orange light filtered over the adjacent Kremlin Wall that separated them from the masses, mellowing the famous yellow bricks of the military building that had served as center stage for the spilling of so much red blood.

"Does anyone know what they're saying?" Madelyn shouted as they walked up the steps of the Kremlin Armory.

"God will be their light and night will be no more," said Dr. Hoyt. "It's from Revelation."

"Fitting," said the Spanish prime minister, eyes fixed on the German vice-chancellor, who refused to meet his gaze.

"You're full of surprises, Dr. Hoyt," said Madelyn as they entered the Armory.

"Please, call me Isla. My father was Russian, so I learned it growing up."

"And call me Madelyn. But my surprise isn't because you speak the language. I just didn't expect that a scientist who runs a deep-space observatory would be able to so quickly quote from the Bible."

Isla smiled as the Armory doors boomed shut behind them. "I study the heavens, Madelyn. Not just part of them. All of them."

A young soldier escorted them to a conference center where rows of seats descended toward a dimly lit stage. A large white screen occupied the center, displaying an equation so winding and complex that the screen couldn't have contained it if it had been twice its size. Behind the podium, positioned stage left, a thin, bald man dressed entirely in black with thick glasses too big for his face aimed a clicker at the screen, causing the equation to grow in density. When he saw Madelyn's group coming down the aisle, he set the clicker and his glasses on the podium and approached.

"I am Leonid Semenov, president of the Russian Ministry of Science," he said, extending his hand to Madelyn first and then the others. "Welcome to Moscow."

"Thank you for hosting us," Madelyn said, glancing around the empty space. "The rest of the delegation should be here momentarily. Will the others be joining soon?"

"Yes, Madam Secretary. Several members of my team will attend the session, along with the minister of defense, chief of the general staff, and several of the joint strategic commanders."

"And the president?" the German vice-chancellor asked.

"He has other business to attend to and will be briefed after we conclude," Semenov said, showing them to their seats near the stage. When the Spanish prime minister discovered his placard was next to the German vice-chancellor's, he swapped it with the French delegate's placard to put some distance between them.

Isla shook her head at this nonsense and turned to Semenov. "What about North America?" she asked. "Any trouble?"

"Cheyenne Mountain will be patched in as soon as we begin," he said. "The connection wavered during a recent quake, but we were able to reroute a few of the landlines and re-establish a strong signal."

Isla nodded her approval. "I'm sorry about your brother," she said in a softer voice so that it wouldn't travel up the aisle to where other members of the delegation were arriving.

Semenov gave her a quick nod of thanks, then went back to the podium to finish preparing his slides. Madelyn waited until he was out earshot before speaking to Isla.

"What happened to his brother?"

"I told you back at the observatory," she said, her head cocked at a side angle. "He's dead."

"I don't understand," Madelyn said. "Did we already speak about this?" She didn't recall any conversation of the sort.

"Sorry. His brother was Anatoly Semenov. He was one of the astronauts on the space station."

44

A DIRT DEVIL whirled in the blistering sun, kicking up red dust and bits of dry grass as it disappeared over the edge of the plateau. Jimmy squeezed his handlebars tight, twisting his wrists back and forth to test his grip. Unhappy, he spit into his palms and rubbed them together. This time they stuck to the rubber real good.

Michael was on his right, fastening the chin strap on his baseball helmet. He gave Jimmy a thumbs-up as he raised his kickstand. Next in line were Tucci the Mullet and Fitzy the Weasel. They high-fived and laughed like hyenas as Fitzy flipped them the bird, first aiming it at Michael and then Jimmy, but really putting his all into it for Mike's kid sister on Jimmy's left. He looked like he might bite off his lower lip as he waggled his fuck-you at Noel, who rested calmly on the banana seat of her new Huffy Strawberry Sizzler. She blew out a purplish bubble and returned a far less enthusiastic and utterly uninterested finger to the obnoxious douche, which only made him cackle louder.

Noel spit out her gum. "We gonna do this already?"

"Don't get your training bra all in a twist," Fitzy said. "We all know you're gonna bail before the big dip, like always."

"Leave her alone," Michael said.

"Settle down, Your Holiness. I'm just joking."

"Okay, you know the rules," Jimmy said, making eye contact with each of them. "No going until the first bong. And whoever passes the Drakes' mailbox first, wins."

They all inched their bikes to the edge and positioned their pedals to give them the best kick down the hill. Jimmy looked at his digital watch, which read 11:59.

"Get ready!" he shouted, twisting his ankle back and forth on the pedal, his heart pounding in his chest.

Michael sat with his eyes closed, his normal pre-race routine. Noel was bent forward, her chin jutting beyond the plane of her pink handlebars. The other two whooped and hollered to psych themselves up—and psyche the others out, or so they hoped. Jimmy wiped sweat from his eyes and glared down the dirt path in anticipation, his rock-hard thigh ready to uncoil like a spring when he hit the pedal.

The town clock rang out the first of its twelve chimes.

They shot forward as one. Jimmy was out in front, but only by a little bit as the road grew steeper. He cranked the pedals hard, trying to put some distance between him and the others before the road narrowed. He could tell Fitzy was right behind him by the high-pitched squeal of his rusty front tire.

Michael and Tucci nearly collided as the road pinched in toward the midpoint, neither of them willing to slow down and let the other by. As they brushed legs and recoiled away from one another, Tucci hit a rock and flipped over his handlebars in a cloud of dust and misery. Michael kept his seat, but he had to swerve and backpedal hard to engage his brakes, his tires fish-tailing wildly. Noel shot forward through the space between them and into third place behind Fitzy. But they were coming up on her nemesis: the big dip.

Jimmy stopped pedaling and leaned forward so that he could coast through the sharp drop in the road. Fitzy pulled past him, looking like he was going to keep pumping right over the edge of the dip, but then kicked his brakes and fell back alongside Jimmy.

Noel whipped past them on the right, her tires skirting the grassy edge of the road. When she was clear, she cut in front of them and stood up on the pedals, her Kinks T-shirt and the torn back pocket of her Jordaches flapping in the breeze. Dust and dirt kicked up into Jimmy's and Fitzy's faces.

Noel pedaled even faster as she neared the dip, faster and faster toward her doom. Fitzy howled with laughter, no doubt imagining a pink debris field, but Jimmy could only think about what Mr. Williams would say when they brought home the body of Mike's dead sister.

Noel didn't stop pedaling until the Strawberry Sizzler took flight. She pushed her butt back as far as it would go, resting her stomach on the banana seat and thrusting her arms out, locking her elbows. For a moment, she was truly flying, entirely at the mercy of gravity.

Jimmy hit the dip next, and she was still airborne. Fitzy was right on his heels, and still Noel flew. The ground rushed up to meet her front tire, and as it struck, she was nearly pitched over her handlebars, but then the back tire touched down too and she thumped down into her seat. Her feet slipped off the pedals, which whipped around madly, so she thrust her legs out on either side for balance and coasted past the Drakes' mailbox to victory.

Fitzy skidded hard and let his bike drop to the dirt short of the mailbox. He turned and looked back up the hill. Michael was walking his bike down. Tucci was nowhere to be found.

But Jimmy kept going. When Noel got her feet back under her and came to a stop, slapping the kickstand into place and hopping off her bike to stand there proudly, Jimmy pulled up right next to her.

"Great job!" he said, holding out his hand.

But she didn't shake it. Instead, she brushed it aside. The music swelled and flashbulbs burst as she grabbed both sides of his face and planted a kiss on his lips. They embraced for a long time under the bright sun, the camera panning around them.

Jimmy pulled back, and before him stood Noel as a teenager,

her sun-bleached hair highlighted with pink streaks. He'd always wondered if she did it in honor of the Sizzler. Then he blinked, and she was Noel as an adult. *His* Noel.

She was always mine, he thought. Always his girl, even if he didn't realize it and neither did she.

They kissed again, her lips soft and wet as he pulled her close. She knitted her hands through the back of his hair and pressed her body against his. Their lips parted, and she sighed and said . . .

"Someone's pounding on the door."

Noel and the bikes and Fitzy's tantrum dimmed and turned to black and white, then stretched and melted in the middle, like film burning up in the light and heat of the projector's bulb. Jimmy opened his eyes as the dream faded and the pounding came again. He squinted at his wristwatch, waiting for the numbers to become discernible. When his vision finally cooperated, he saw he'd only been asleep for a few hours.

He dragged himself out of bed, hollering to whoever was beating on his front door. He grabbed the shirt thrown over the desk chair and was about to put it on when he saw the bloodstain on the sleeve. He threw it into the corner with the others and took a fresh one from the closet, wincing as he shrugged it over his bum shoulder.

Looking through the window, he saw Ken Newsome pacing the porch, smoking a cigarette. Jimmy opened the door to find Ken spitting and coughing like an emphysema patient.

"When'd you start smoking?" Jimmy said.

Ken flicked the half-smoked lung dart into the shrub and pointed to the sky. "I know it's your time to get some sleep, boss, but we've got a real problem."

"What's up?" Jimmy asked, stepping out onto the porch.

"There's a big crowd heading up to Blue's Bluff."

"People have been going up there ever since Noel got the tower working again."

"I'm talking about different people."

"What people?"

"*Mike's* people," Ken said, rubbing the back of his neck and watching Jimmy, gauging his reaction. "A lot of 'em."

"Did anyone radio up there to let her know what's coming?" Jimmy asked as he went back inside and hurried around the living room, gathering his things.

Ken followed him in. "No, I mean—"

"Why the hell not, Kenny?" Jimmy asked, strapping on his belt and holster. "What're you waiting for?"

"It's Mike. I mean, Father Williams. He's her brother, after all."

Jimmy pulled on his boots and headed for the door. "Yeah, well, Father Williams hasn't been himself lately. Let's get some men up there pronto."

Ken nodded and stepped out onto the porch, already calling to a few others on duty with his shoulder mic.

Jimmy followed him out the door then had to duck back in and grab his car keys. As he reached into the bowl on the foyer table, he saw the framed photo next to it—Jimmy standing between Noel and Michael, arms out and pulling them both toward him as they stood astride their bikes, huge smiles on all their faces. He let the dream wash over him again, an imaginary hint of blueberry Bubblicious in his mouth.

Then he snatched his keys and walked out of the house to get between them one last time.

45

As the tremor rippled across Blue's Bluff like a rogue wave, a collective shriek went up from the crowd, and people scrambled for whatever cover they could find. But there was little cover to be had, and most just dropped to the dirt, covered their heads, and cowered as the rumble reverberated through the canyon's peaks and valleys.

Then, just as quickly and unexpectedly as it had come, the quake was gone.

For those among the gathered crowd, the damage was minimal. Two people were temporarily trapped under a camper that came off its jacks, and a woman got slightly barbecued when her grill toppled onto her. Most of the telescopes had fallen over and a few never got back up.

But there was significant damage to the tower. One of its top crossbeams broke loose during the shaking, and it clattered down through the uprights, cutting through the main line and killing the broadcast. It took Noel, Aster, and a team of helpers several hours of splicing severed wires and replacing a fried coupler before they were able to re-establish the connection to the rest of the world.

With the signal to the station restored and the power steady,

Aster and Noel scanned the high and low bands, hoping for an official broadcast that might shed light on what had just happened. In the end they settled for a local station out of Amarillo that was fielding calls about quakes from all over the Midwest. Aster flipped the switch to broadcast through the external speakers on the bluff, and when she ran out to ensure that everything was working, she nearly barreled into Private Walsh, who had to grab the door frame as she brushed by him.

"Walsh, there you are," Noel said. "I was gonna come looking for you. We got interrupted."

"Everything okay?"

"You tell me," she said, pointing to the co-pilot's chair just vacated by Aster. He sat down, thankful to be out of the sunlight and heat, wiping the sweat from his forehead with the shoulder of his shirt. The whole time they'd known each other, Noel had been watching him sweat.

"You used to work in communications, right?" he asked.

"Yep, sat control."

"Okay, good, so you'll understand. Two days after I left the base, I went back to grab some things from my locker. While I was there, I was talking with a friend of mine. He'd been reassigned to security for that building."

"Why does the comms building need security?"

"They're doing something with the array. Anyway, my buddy said there's a lot of chatter between there and the Mountain."

"I don't doubt it," said Noel. "With satellite comms down, makes sense they'd be using the array for long-range radio signals."

"Long-range for sure," Walsh said. "Anyway, he told me that earlier in the day he had been stationed outside the main control room, and he heard people talking in Russian."

"People in the room?"

"No, over the speakers."

"The array can't reach that far," Noel said. "They must have used a signal relay from somewhere Stateside. Probably Ohio or—"

Aster burst into the station at a full run. "Noel, you gotta come," she said, waving at them and pointing outside. "Right now!"

"What's going on?" Noel asked, kicking her chair back as she stood. She'd never seen Aster this frantic.

"They're almost at the top," she said, grabbing Noel's hand and pulling her toward the door.

They left the station to find the crowd pushing toward Scylla and Charybdis. Aster screamed for them to make way, then dragged Noel forward. Walsh trailed behind at first, but eventually got separated from them as people closed ranks, unwilling to lose their spots for whatever it was everyone was trying to see.

They arrived at the boulders, and as Noel looked down at the dirt road that led up the back of the bluff, she understood what was causing the commotion.

A huge crowd was approaching, winding up the series of switchbacks. The thick cloud of dust kicked up by their passing stretched all the way back to Franklin. And at their vanguard was her brother. She would recognize her brother's loping stride anywhere. But at the moment, it was the only thing she recognized about him.

Growing up, Michael liked to say he was *fastidious*. Noel preferred fussy or anal or neat freak, take your pick. But none of those descriptions matched the wild-eyed, disheveled, and filthy man now leading a horde up the path toward her, arms outstretched, dirt-and-sweat-streaked face luminous even in the intense sunlight beating down on them all. She could do no more than stand and watch dumbly as he gradually closed the gap between them.

And then he was right there in front of her, smiling widely through cracked, dry lips. The rest of his crowd stopped a few steps back from the siblings.

"Hey, sis."

"My God, Mike," she said, touching the blood splatter across his white collar and then his filthy cheek. "Are you okay?"

"I am," he said, gently grabbing her hand and lowering it from his face. "I really am." He looked at the people behind Noel, letting his eyes rest a moment on Aster. "Quite a group you've got up here."

"Nothing compared to yours," Noel said, searching the crowd for familiar faces, spotting Rose and Midge and then Zadie, who gave Noel a small wave. The rest of the crowd were strangers.

"Where's Jimmy?"

"I don't know. I assumed he was up here with you," Michael said, scanning her face.

"Why would he be here?"

He shook his head as if disappointed in her. "Denial of a sin is far worse than the sin itself." Then he looked her straight in the eye. "There isn't a lot of time left, Noel. I figured the two of you would be spending what little there is left together."

She'd always known that sooner or later Michael was going to find out. She and Jimmy had even talked about telling him at one point. They both knew he'd struggle with it, but they also figured he'd eventually get used to the idea of his lifelong best friend and sister messing around.

Neither of them had ever anticipated the clear contempt she saw in his face now.

"He's not here," she said. "In fact, he was supposed to be keeping an eye on you."

Michael leaned in close, his breath hot in her face. "It's okay. There's still time to ask for forgiveness."

She stared into his bloodshot eyes, not backing down from the judgment pouring off him in waves. "Whose, Mike?" she asked. "God's? Or yours?"

He stared at her for a few seconds, as if silently considering a response, then turned his head and looked back down the path at his flock, who were waiting patiently.

"I'm wasting time," he said, and he stepped around Noel and started walking onto the bluff.

"What are you doing here?" she asked, keeping pace with him, Aster a step behind her. "Why did you bring these people up here?"

Michael paused when he heard the broadcast over the speakers. A caller on the run from San Filipe was describing the flooding that had swallowed Baja California.

"What is this?" he asked, cocking his head to the side to listen.

"It's a transmission from Texas," Aster said. "This guy seems to have good information on what's happening, so we're sharing it with everyone."

"You didn't answer my question," Noel said, grabbing for Michael's arm. "Why are you here?"

He whipped his arm out of her grasp. "People don't need *this*." He pointed up at the speakers. "They need the truth!" he shouted.

People were pressing in around them now, a mixture of Michael's followers, who were flowing onto the bluff at a steady clip, and the people who had been camped out on the bluff for days now. In the distance were the sound of approaching sirens.

"Mike, listen, let's go inside," Noel said. She felt a tension in the air, as if all these people, bumping and elbowing for position, were a powder keg ready to explode. "Let's escape this heat for a little while and talk about it in the station."

"That's exactly where I'm going. But not to escape!" Michael shouted. He wasn't addressing Noel, but the gathered crowd. "There will be no escaping what's to come!"

He pushed through the crowd, and it was all Noel could do to keep up with him. At the jammed parking lot next to the station, he jumped onto the hood of an SUV as the sound of the sirens grew louder.

"I should command these people to tear down this tower of Babel," he said, pointing at the radio tower. "But I need it to do

God's work. So instead it will become my mouthpiece to spread the word far and wide."

"I can't let you do that," Noel shouted to him. Behind her, two police cruisers crested the service road. "Look, Jimmy's here now, okay? Let's go get him and talk about this and everything else. Just the three of us, like always."

Jimmy got out of the lead cruiser and jogged over to them. Noel gave him a tiny shake of her head and hoped the look on her face was enough to tell him that things were in a bad place.

"What's going on up here?" he asked, standing at the front of the SUV.

"Mike wants to use the tower," Noel said. "To broadcast."

The crowd pushed in on all sides, superheating the already crushingly hot air on the top of the bluff. Jimmy shifted to the side so that the light obscuring Michael's face was behind his head.

"Mikey, let's go talk. We can figure this thing out, for sure." He held out his hand. "Come on, man. Let's get gone from here."

Michael looked down on the two of them, standing side by side, united against him. A tear slid down his cheek as he let go of them both in his heart.

"The time for that is over," he said, wiping his eyes. He sucked in a huge breath and yelled at the top of his lungs, "It's God's time now!"

A wave of hallelujahs went up from Michael's flock, but for the first time since his first sermon on the steps of St. Anne's, the praise was peppered with dissenting voices. There were accusations of zealotry, ignorance, and fanaticism—and these were met by warnings of blasphemy and eternal damnation. Lines were being drawn, and if this kept up, things would soon get out of hand.

Yet Michael seemed ensorcelled by the deteriorating scene around him. He stared blankly at the crowd as it undulated and thrashed atop the bluff. The arguing was quickly escalating into screaming and pushing.

"Do something!" Noel yelled at him, hoping to break the spell.

When he didn't respond, she stepped onto the front bumper, ready to jump onto the hood and slap him out of his trance if she had to. But as soon as she took her first step, a rock thudded into her shoulder. She turned just in time to avoid a second one that would have hit her in the head.

And that's when the powder keg blew.

46

AWAC FLIGHT
Cheyenne command, do you copy?

CHEYENNE COMMAND
Reading you five by five.
What's your status?

AWAC FLIGHT
We're over Kiowa and have visual
on a storm coming out of the east.
Dark clouds maybe ten kilometers wide.

CHEYENNE COMMAND
Roger, flight. Maintain course.

AWAC FLIGHT
Check that, command. Storm looks to be growing.
Permission to return to base?

CHEYENNE COMMAND
Negative, flight. Adjust heading to 37 degrees
north and 105 degrees west. Climb to 20,000 feet.

AWAC FLIGHT
<static>

CHEYENNE COMMAND
AWAC flight, confirm.

AWAC FLIGHT
<static>

CHEYENNE COMMAND
AWAC flight, this is Cheyenne command.
Confirm new heading and altitude.

AWAC FLIGHT
Command, this isn't a storm.
It's something else.

CHEYENNE COMMAND
Flight, confirm heading and altitude.
Thirty-seven degrees north and—

AWAC FLIGHT
Bank hard right! Climb, climb!

CHEYENNE COMMAND
Say again, flight.

AWAC FLIGHT
Command, we are . . . go, go!
Take evasive—

CHEYENNE COMMAND
Flight, what is your status?

AWAC FLIGHT

CHEYENNE COMMAND
Flight, report. What is your status?

AWAC FLIGHT
Millions of birds! Everywhere!

CHEYENNE COMMAND
Flight, repeat your last transmission.

AWAC FLIGHT
<static>

CHEYENNE COMMAND
AWAC flight, this is Cheyenne command.
What is your status?

AWAC FLIGHT

"When was this?" President Reyes asked, looking at the projection screen showing a map of the Midwest. Dots highlighted two locations: Cheyenne Mountain and Kiowa, Kansas.

"At 14:33, ma'am," said General Tate, checking his wristwatch. "If that swarm stays on the same course, it should reach us within the hour."

"Well fuck you, Hitchcock," she said, turning to the group in the Mountain's main conference room. Present were the NASA administrator, the Canadian prime minister, and a number of other high-ranking officials in both the US and Canadian governments, but as Reyes looked around the room, she was met with stony faces. The only outlier was Eugenia Sang, who unsuccessfully tried to stifle a snort, spraying droplets of spittle onto the conference room table.

"Sorry, Madam President," she said, using her sleeve to wipe away the evidence.

"Is there anything else, Corporal?" Tate asked into the phone.

"No sir, that was the last contact with AWAC flight," said the young soldier who'd provided the report. "A ground unit is on its way to their last known coordinates."

None of the world leaders on this call—whether here in the Mountain, across the ocean in Russia, or holed up in Brazil—could see the young man, but by the sound of his voice they could imagine the brick he was shitting just by being on the line with them all. Tate thanked the corporal, then dropped him from the call.

"I've gotten similar reports from several members of the ministry," said Leonid Semenov, who had been leading the discussion from Moscow. "Nothing quite as dramatic, but stories of mass movement of wildlife."

His deep voice held up against the constant, low-level static coming through the line. Twice engineers had tried to clean up the signal, but it was being rerouted through a few of the older hubs. Ones that hadn't been damaged in the latest quakes.

"What does this mean for us?" Reyes asked.

"Magnetic fields have been disrupted everywhere," Isla replied. "It's clearly having an impact on birds' magnetoreception and probably also impacting other animals' migratory patterns."

"I'm sorry, Dr. Hoyt," Reyes said, squeezing her temples hard to try and keep her brains inside. "Give me the single bullet point, please."

Semenov jumped back in. "It means our timeline is accelerating," he said. "It means that we must stop this pointless debate and come to a decision immediately."

"I resent that, sir!" said the Spanish prime minister, whose voice was loud and clear even across thousands of miles of underwater and overland cable. The speakerphone immediately erupted into a chaotic swirl of accents and accusations.

The president air-stabbed her index finger at the phone, and Tate, with a nod, reached forward and pressed the mute button.

"Hell's bells," Tate said, flopping back in his chair.

"Indeed," agreed the Canadian prime minister. "That's exactly what our Spanish colleague is worried about."

Reyes turned back to the screen at the front of the room. "Eugenia, can you go back to the landmass projection?"

Eugenia flipped through slides filled with tables and equations and stopped on a planet-wide view with a massive red band around the equator indicating the location of the new megacontinent. The arguing from Moscow continued, but as Reyes rose from her seat and approached the screen, she did her best to shut it out.

She put her finger on Los Angeles. That was where she'd grown up; where her mother, sister, and nieces still lived. It was the home of her alma mater, and the city where she'd met her husband, back when he was a volunteer on her very first mayoral campaign. It was also the place where he was buried, after his death of an aneurysm four years ago. Los Angeles had been the site of her happiest and saddest moments, a cornerstone in her life.

And yet now, on this map, it was underwater.

"We can't let this happen," she said.

"Sorry, ma'am," Tate said. "Did you want me to unmute?"

Reyes walked back to her seat, snapping the bottom of her wrinkled vest to regain a sense of formality. She turned to Tate and air-stabbed the mute button again. When the lights on the phone switched from red to green, she called out to the squabbling parties.

"Colleagues," she began. She had to repeat herself a few times before they quieted down. "I'm going to suggest that the open period of our debate conclude and we move to an immediate vote."

"Madam President, if we could just—"

"The United States of America, Canada, and representatives from the South American governments in attendance vote to move forward with Operation Skybound," she said, cutting off the Spanish prime minister before he could launch his rebuttal.

"Germany votes yes," the German vice-chancellor said quickly, failing to mask his enthusiasm. The Swiss, Polish, and Austrian officials added their consent. Ireland and Spain voted against the plan. And then the line went silent as everyone waited on the president of the Russian Ministry of Science, the sole representative of the other nuclear power in attendance.

"Russia agrees to move forward with Skybound," Semenov said.

And with that, the vote was complete. Operation Skybound was a go.

And President Reyes spoke the words that changed the course of human history.

"Time to release some birds of our own."

47

FIGHTING BROKE out all across the bluff. Jimmy lunged at the man who had thrown the rock at Noel, leveling him with a right hook. Noel felt herself shoved from behind, and only the quick reflexes of a stranger who caught her kept her from taking a header onto one of the cement parking blocks. Aster was not so lucky; she found herself between two women who were throwing punches at each other, and took a hit that sent her sprawling. Private Walsh stepped in to protect her, and got an elbow to his kidney as he helped Aster back to her feet.

Noel looked back toward the SUV where her brother had made his proclamation, but he was already gone. She pushed her way over to Aster and Walsh. "We need to get inside the station!" she yelled.

Walsh gripped Aster's shoulders to help steer her through the crowd. But when they rounded the corner, they discovered a massive brawl at the station's front door. People were throwing rocks and punches in rapid succession. One woman rushed into the melee with a tire iron, which she brought down hard on a man's head. The man dropped to the dirt, and his attacker looked around for another victim.

"Can't go that way!" Walsh said.

Noel wasn't ready to give up. She thought maybe they could go around to the back and use the service ladder to the roof, but they found another large group brawling there. Noel was about to risk it anyway, but when she saw the fear in Aster's eyes, she changed her mind.

"Okay, come on!" she said. "Let's get out of here while we still can."

With Walsh and Aster at her side, she pushed toward the service road. But that proved to be nearly as challenging. The fighting had broken out all around them. They were about halfway to the police cruisers when one of Jimmy's men pulled out a canister of pepper spray and started blanketing the crowd with it. Whatever good that might have done, it didn't stop one bear of a man from barreling forward and tackling the officer to the ground.

For a brief moment Noel spotted Jimmy, but then the crowd swelled around him, and he was out of sight once more. Noel hoped he could get things under control, but she wasn't about to stay around to find out. Beckoning to Walsh and Aster, she pushed toward Scylla and Charybdis, leaving her station behind.

***

Yanez and Del kept a steady pace at the rear of Michael's group as they walked up the dirt road to Blue's Bluff.

"These people are intense," Del said in a low voice to Yanez, making sure that he wasn't overheard. "Did Noel ever mention anything about this brother of hers?"

"No, but we were going back and forth with Morse code," Yanez said. "There's only so much you can cover."

Suddenly, the people ahead of them started rushing forward. Yanez looked up to the top of the bluff, where a cloud of dust was billowing into the sky.

"What's going on?" Del said.

"I don't know," Yanez said, tightening the straps on her backpack. She grabbed his arm. "But let's go find out."

A bullet ricocheted off Scylla, sending shards of rock spraying across the path. Noel, Aster, and Walsh skidded to a halt, crouched down, and tried to protect their heads. The crowd grew quiet for a heartbeat as everyone scanned the bluff for the shooter. Then more shots rang out, and the mob shifted. Suddenly a mass of terrified people, many of whom had only just arrived, were rushing to get off the bluff.

But there was no clear path to escape, for the rest of Michael's flock was still trying to get to the top. As the two groups crashed headlong into one another, several people toppled into the jagged rocks and sharp scrub that flanked the road.

Noel tried to press forward down the path, but became pinned against the boulder next to Aster by a large man pushing past them in order to get onto the bluff. She elbowed the hulking man in the side, trying to get him to move, but it was Walsh, with two quick jabs to the man's face, who drew blood. The man stumbled off and was sucked into a maelstrom of bodies.

Noel seized the opening and quickly shoved Aster and Walsh onto the road. There were just as many people here, but now all of them were heading in the same direction: down. If any of Michael's stragglers were still thinking of going up to the bluff, the continued gunshots above dissuaded them.

Noel didn't stop running until she had reached the base of the slope. She grabbed Aster and Walsh and pulled them off the road to catch their breath.

"Are you okay?" Noel asked Aster, scanning her up and down for injuries.

"Holy shit," Aster said, sucking in huge gulps of air.

"Thanks for up there," Noel said to Walsh.

"You know that lunatic on the car?"

"Used to," Noel said.

She shielded her eyes and tried to see what was happening on top of the bluff. But from this angle, all she could see was a mushroom top of dust obscuring everything, including her tower.

"Hey!" Aster shouted. She started jumping up and down and waving her arms. "That's her! Over there!" She took off running.

"Aster! Wait!" Noel cried. She had no choice but to race after her.

Aster stopped in front of a man and woman who were standing in the shade of a rock outcropping just off the road. "Miss Prescott!" she said breathlessly, leading with an outstretched hand as she closed the last few feet. "I mean, Commander. Hi!"

The woman took Aster's hand and shook it. "You know me?" she said as Walsh and Noel joined them.

"I watched your launch on NASA TV. I'm so glad you're not dead. I mean, I'm glad you made it back. How the heck did you do that, by the way?"

Noel stepped forward and extended her hand. "I take it you're Yanez Prescott. We spoke . . . well, we signaled to each other a few days ago. I'm Noel."

"It's nice to hear your actual voice," Yanez said, clasping Noel's hand in both of hers. The others introduced themselves.

"What's happening up there?" Del asked.

"I lost my radio tower," Noel said, glancing back up at the bluff.

"Does this have something to do with your brother?"

Noel was stunned. "How do you know about that?"

"We heard a lot about him on our way from town."

Yanez and Del gave a brief recap of events after they'd reached town. Noel and Walsh then described the fighting up top, with Aster filling in wherever she thought they weren't doing justice. As they talked in the shade of the rocks, a steady stream of people passed them on the road back to town.

And then something caught Del's eye. He stepped out of the shade and looked at the darkening horizon.

"What the heck is that?"

The others joined him and peered at what looked like a dense cloud moving toward them from the east, stretching across the entire skyline. It cast a deep shadow, blackening the ground beneath it for the first time since the object appeared in the sky.

"That storm is massive," Yanez said, squinting.

"Storms don't normally come from that direction," Noel said, shielding her eyes.

"Shhh! Listen," said Aster, and they all fell silent.

A basso thrum filled the air, growing in intensity with each passing second. Then a higher-pitched chittering joined the wall of sound. And that was when realization set in, that what they were seeing wasn't a cloud at all, but rather a storm front of feathers, beaks, and claws.

They scrambled for safety, dropping low to make themselves as small as possible underneath the rock outcropping.

And the shadow overtook them.

48

SCREAMS OF ANGER and pain turned to wails of terror when the wavefront of sound reached the warring factions, and people dove into cars, vans, and tents as the birds approached. Once those options were exhausted, the mob ran for the only other shelter—the station. They tore the door from its hinges, broke out the windows, and clambered past shards of glass and jagged splinters of wood, creating a clown car of bodies inside the small building. The rest had no choice but to sprawl in the dirt and cry in fear as the massive flock ripped across Blue's Bluff.

Michael cowered at the base of the radio tower with his arms and legs wrapped around one of the uprights, his face pressed against the hot steel. The cacophony of beating wings and thundering caws masked the sound of birds crashing into the tower over his head, but he felt the vibration from the impacts and saw the bodies of those dead birds thumping down all around him. Oranges, yellows, blacks, browns, and even greens and blues speckled the red dirt, a grotesque rainbow of death. *Like light through stained glass*, Michael thought.

And that was when he understood his mistake.

God had shown him exactly what to do that day in St. Anne's

when he saw the unmolested window. But Michael hadn't been listening.

The vibrations gradually ceased, the flock passing by and continuing on its journey, the brightness of the object above returning with swift, hot vengeance. Michael let go of the slick steel and took in the aftermath.

The tower was a thing of nightmares, covered in blood and feathers and shit. People were huddled together crying or praying or looking for those they'd been separated from. But it was the people struggling and screaming to get out of the station that jumpstarted the terror once again.

A large man with a bloody nose was trying to hoist himself out through one of the smashed windows, smoke billowing around him. With a yelp and a shove from someone behind him, he popped free and landed atop Noel's fallen motorcycle. Flames rushed out behind him, and the others who had been sheltering inside came streaming out the door, coughing and hacking as the pungent smell of burning electronics filled the air.

Michael fell to his knees as the station burned. He remembered being up here with his father and sister. Noel would man the main board as he and his dad would play hearts.

So long ago, he thought. *And now that's gone too.*

"Father!" he heard someone calling. And then another and another, his flock looking for him. But he continued kneeling, watching the past burn, until he heard Rose yell, "Mike, come quick!"

He got to his feet and zeroed in on her voice. Spotting her near the police cruisers, he sprinted over, waving. When she saw him coming, she fell to her knees behind one of the cars and let out a shriek. And then he rounded the car and shrieked too.

Jimmy was lying on his back in a pool of blood. His light-blue police shirt had turned a deep indigo, darkest around the two bullet holes in his chest. One of the bullets had pierced the sheriff's badge over his heart.

Michael flew to his friend's side and screamed his name, his face just inches from Jimmy's. Rose stood over them and watched, racked with deep sobs as Michael tried everything to get Jimmy to wake up. He shook him and slapped his face and called him a fucker. He put his cheek on Jimmy's chest and listened for the breath that he knew would never come. He thrashed and pounded the blood-soaked dirt, making animal sounds and growls from a place deep and dark inside himself, sucked in spasmodic breaths as he hunched over Jimmy's body, and then finally flopped onto his back next to his best friend.

Michael looked up into the sky, the hovering object bearing witness to his penance. He stared at it until his eyes burned. And then he stared longer, until tears burst forth. He finally squeezed his eyes shut, the quavering afterimage of the object filling his vision, mind, and soul. And then he released a howl that shook the bluff.

Rose laid her calming hands on him. Then others came. His flock surrounded him and picked him up. They gave him water, praised God for his safety, and gave thanks for his deliverance from the darkness.

"Thank you," he said when his senses returned. He cleared his throat, still raw from his wailing, and thanked them once more.

Another group of people was now trying to contain the fire in the station. They were throwing dirt and bottled water in through the openings in an attempt to smother it, but were rebuffed by the flames and smoke. With Rose at his side, Michael walked over to the station and tried to wave off the people battling the blaze.

"But maybe we can save it!" one of the men shouted.

"Let it burn," Michael said.

"But Father," Rose said, quietly and just to him, "how will you reach everyone without it?"

Michael took her hands and kissed her fingers. Then he turned to face the group that had gathered around him.

"Friends, listen to me!" The group fell silent. "I was wrong."

Shouts of "no" and "never" went up around him. He held up a hand to quiet them.

"I was going to use this place as a tool to spread the truth about our final days. But that was a mistake. God showed me what I needed to do days ago, but I was too proud, or too stupid, to listen. That's why He shook the ground and filled the sky with messengers. To remind me. The mistake was mine, and I'm sorry. And I have paid for it in blood," he said, gesturing to where Jimmy's body lay.

A murmur swept through the crowd, their despair the unifying undertone. Michael gave it license to grow, his head hung low as he tried to scrub Jimmy's blood off his hands. And as the crowd's need was about to wash over the bluff, Michael raised his arms and face to the sky and cried out.

"Forgive my ignorance! I will spread your truth at the symbol and source of this world's damnation!" he screamed.

And he pointed in the direction of Cheyenne Mountain.

Despair was replaced by cries of joy. And Michael let the jubilation pour out of them, washing away the terror and replacing it with hope and purpose.

After another minute of chanting with arms raised to the heavens, Michael quieted the group and marshaled them into action one last time.

"My friends, let's go to the Mountain," he said. "It's time for me to deliver my sermon."

49

WHEN THE BIRDS HAD PASSED, Noel let go of Aster and crawled around the side of the outcropping. The flock was now disappearing toward the horizon, continuing on its westerly path of terror.

"They're gone," she called to the others.

The ground was littered with feathers and piebald splatters of shit. Injured birds flapped and twitched on the ground.

"That was insane," Del said, offering a hand to Aster to help her up. "I mean, why now? The thing's been up there for days."

"Could have to do with the tremors," Walsh said, sidestepping a bloody crow that hopped by him, dragging a broken wing.

"Maybe it's because of the water," Aster said.

"Yeah, we saw some of that too on our way out here," Del said. "Nature's all messed up."

As they talked, Noel drifted away from the group, her eyes on Blue's Bluff. Small groups of people were scrambling over the final turns in the switchback dirt road. Faint shouts filtered down from above. She strained to pick out words, but couldn't discern anything specific.

Then she smelled the smoke.

She took off running back toward the bluff and the dark cloud that rose from the top. She tried to weave around the detritus scattered everywhere, but eventually gave up and simply stomped through it. *Maybe the smoke's from a car or some other vehicle*, she thought. *Could be a propane tank on someone's camper got caught in the crossfire.* But she knew the truth in her heart as she looked up at the thick, oily cloud drifting into the Colorado sky.

When she encountered two men hobbling down the road, one of them leaning heavily on the other, his left leg limp and covered in blood, she stopped.

"What's going on up there?" she asked.

"It's fucking crazy," the guy with the injured leg said. "People beating the shit out each other. You can't believe the chaos!"

"And when those god damn birds started coming—" his friend said before Noel cut him off.

"Yeah, but what's on fire?"

"The radio building, I think. People broke in—"

Noel didn't need to hear any more. She took off running again, her worst fears confirmed. Her place of solace and last connection to her dad was burning.

"No, wait, please!" Aster screamed from just behind her.

"Maybe I can save it!"

Aster caught up and flung her arms around Noel. "Don't!" she yelled. "We need you here!"

Noel squirmed out of Aster's grip and made to run off again. But Aster grabbed the back of her shirt.

"It doesn't matter anymore!" the girl cried.

"It's *all* that matters!" Noel screamed, ripping her shirt away from Aster and immediately regretting it. She held up her hands and took a breath, stepping back to try to collect herself.

"Without that station, we're blind to what's happening," she said. "And . . . it was my dad's."

Aster took her hand. "I didn't mean it like that," she said. "And everything with your brother, too. It's gotta suck."

Noel squeezed Aster's hand and nodded. "It does."

She looked toward the top of the bluff, her eyes tracing the smoke upward until the harsh light bouncing off the object forced her to look away.

"But we've got Commander Prescott now," Aster said. "We can still fix this."

The girl was right. Of course she was right. This wasn't about the tower, or her dad, or her brother. She had a job to do. Something that might make an actual difference.

Noel gave Aster a hug. "Okay. You're right. Let's get going."

They walked back to the group. Yanez and the others met them halfway.

"Sorry about that," Noel said.

"Walsh filled me in on what happened up there," Yanez said. "I'm so sorry. It sounds terrible."

"Don't worry about it. Let's get you where you need to be," Noel said, eager to change the subject. She looked to Walsh. "What do you think?"

He flicked a bird's carcass aside with his boot. "There's no way we can get her into the Mountain by ourselves. Guys on the checkpoints are under orders to send anyone and everyone packing. It might be better to see if my friend at Peterson would help us send a message into the Mountain. But . . . it depends."

"On what?" Noel asked.

Walsh rubbed the back of his neck and looked uncertainly at Yanez. "Forgive me, Commander, but is there any way you can prove you are who you say you are?"

"Seriously?" Del asked with a snort.

"You wouldn't believe the stories, man," Walsh said. "Crazies have been coming out of the woodwork trying to weasel their way onto the base or into the Mountain. I hear one dude pretended he was the Pope."

"You think your buddy won't believe you?" Noel said.

"Oh, *he* will. But he's only step one."

"I don't have a NASA ID card or anything," Yanez said. "And I left my spacesuit back at the capsule."

"Well we're gonna need to show him something."

"I've got something that might work," Aster said. "But we need to go to my place to get it."

————

Walsh's truck was closest, so they walked the two miles to get to it and piled in. Aster sat up front with Del and Walsh to give directions, and Noel and Yanez rode in the truck bed. Riding in the back gave Noel a good view of the bluff. The smoke from the station fire had dissipated enough that she could see the tower.

"At least it's still standing," Yanez said.

"It won't do him any good, though. Without the station, it's as useless to him as the rest of us now."

"What did your brother want to do with it?"

"He's convinced that all of this is God's doing," Noel said, sweeping her arm around to encompass the sky and the whole upside-down world they now lived in. "He said he was going to use the radio tower to spread the truth. That this is the end and people should repent or something. They should be begging for forgiveness. I don't know exactly."

"What do you think he'll do now?" Yanez asked.

"Probably go back to Franklin. Where else is there?"

Noel picked a bit of dirt off the bed of Walsh's truck. She looked at the red clump and crumbled it between her fingers with a laugh.

"You know the crazy part," she continued, brushing the dirt off on her jeans. "Those birds are gonna make him worse."

"How?" Yanez asked.

"He's gonna see it as a sign. I know him. He's gonna believe that fucking flock of birds is some kind of confirmation of the Rapture. He's gonna be even more convinced that he's right."

Yanez measured her words carefully. She had just met Noel and needed her help. But she couldn't let the moment pass. This was her opportunity to ask the question she'd been asking herself since the moment she looked out the window of the ISS and saw the object.

"What if God *did* do this?"

"What?" Noel said.

"I'm just saying, what if God is responsible?" Yanez continued. "The object, the planet's rotation, the birds, the oceans. You have to admit it's possible."

Noel's face looked pained. She made a few false, sputtering starts before saying, "No, I don't have to admit anything. I can't."

Yanez shrugged and settled back against the truck's cab, her backpack resting between her drawn-up knees.

"Are you just asking as some sort of passing-the-time, intellectual exercise or something?" Noel asked.

"No, I'm seriously asking."

"But you've got the—" she said, pointing at the backpack. "You've got the thing, right there."

Yanez realized that she'd never actually shown Noel what was inside. So she unzipped the main compartment, removed the hard drive, and handed it to her.

"That's it. All the data collected from the space station's sensor arrays are on that drive."

Noel turned it over in her hands. She ran her finger across the NASA logo on its black metal case.

"Well then," she said, "there's no point in getting all mystical about it. Once we look at what's on here, we'll know what the real answer is."

"Will we though?" Yanez said. "I've been thinking about it for days now. Maybe the data will reveal the answer. *Or* . . . maybe the answer will come from the Bible or Talmud or Koran or some other holy text. Maybe it's a combination of all of it. I don't know. And honestly, I don't care where the answer comes from. As long as it comes."

Noel was surprised by Yanez's ambivalence. The woman was an astronaut, and the only reason she was even sitting here was that science and her own intellect had gotten her this far. Noel couldn't understand how a person like that could accept the supernatural so readily. She was considering pressing the point, but just then Aster knocked on the back window to let them know they'd arrived.

The truck stopped beside an old trailer, and Aster jumped out of the cab and ran inside. Del and Walsh came around to the back of the truck.

"Seems like a good kid," Walsh said, leaning against the truck. "How'd you guys hook up?"

"Her class was on a field trip at the base when shit hit the fan," Noel said. "And then I found out she'd been squatting in my radio station on the bluff to stargaze. The rest is history."

Aster came running back out with a magazine rolled into a tube in her fist.

"That it?" Del asked.

She unfurled the magazine and held up the cover for them all to see. Three female astronauts stood in their orange jumpsuits, Yanez in the middle holding a space helmet.

"Better than an ID card, right?"

"That should do it," Walsh said with a laugh.

"That must have been two years ago," Yanez said. "I'm honored you hung onto it."

Aster beamed with pride as she handed the magazine to Yanez. "It would rock if you signed it for me."

"Of course," Yanez said. "But let's wait 'til we see if it's enough to get us inside first."

Noel jumped out of the truck bed and pulled Aster aside. When they were out of earshot of the others, she put her hands on Aster's shoulders.

"Listen, Aster, maybe you should stay here."

Aster pushed away. "No chance! Are you kidding me?"

"We don't know what's gonna happen," Noel said. "What about your grandmother?"

"I left her a message inside. And she already knows I'm with you."

"Doesn't she need you?"

"She's got Mrs. Egan and the other ladies over at the rec center. Besides, ever since my mom died, Grandma's been waiting to die herself. So this shit is no big deal for her. But it is for me."

Tears budded at the corners of Aster's eyes. "Please don't make me stay," she pleaded. "I've got nothing to stay here for."

The truth was, Noel hadn't wanted to leave Aster behind. But she'd felt like she needed to offer her the option.

"Okay," she said, throwing her arm around Aster's shoulders and steering her toward the truck. "We kind of started this whole thing together anyway. Makes sense that we finish it together too."

50

"WILL IT BE ENOUGH?"

"Just a second, Madam President," Semenov said, looking to Isla for confirmation. She picked up a piece of chalk and finished scratching out the equation on the board. Semenov stared at the numbers, chewing on a jagged thumbnail. Then with a nod, he walked back to the conference table around which the European and Russian delegations were seated.

"Dr. Hoyt and I agree," he said into the speaker at the table's center, "even without launches from Irkutsk and Teykovo, we will be able to get enough missiles in the air to reach our planned yield."

There had been a few hiccups since the vote. The first had been the departure of the Spanish and Irish delegates, who refused to take part in the planning. Their show of defiance was short-lived, however, as they were met outside the installation by Russian military officers who took the two men into custody for their own safety.

The second and more troubling hiccup occurred when both the United States and Russian militaries finished readiness checks on their nuclear silos. Some of the missiles had been sitting untouched for decades and were deemed unsafe to fly by on-the-ground inspectors. Kitsap in Washington and Minot in North Dakota were the first to take their nukes off the board, followed by several from the Russian arsenal. This led to an hours-long conference between scientists on both sides. Based on the American team's estimates of the object's potential size, density, and composition, all of which were best guesses and confirmed by Semenov and his team at the Russian Ministry of Science, they determined that they would need to create a blast equivalent to nearly 22,000 petajoules to destroy the object. This was considerable, especially since the largest man-made explosion in history was just over 200 petajoules, created by Semenov's Soviet predecessors.

"Is Israel still an option?" President Reyes asked.

"Ma'am, I spoke with Prime Minister Eichelberg a short while ago," said Madelyn over the phone. "The Israelis refuse to participate until we give their scientists an opportunity to review all of the data and they have a chance to conduct readiness drills on their silos."

"Maddy, come on. They can't be serious," Reyes said, exasperated. "How long would that take?"

"Three days," Madelyn said.

"Madam President, we don't have that much time," said Semenov. "Coordination of the strike is key, and it would become impossible if we lose contact with any of our silos. Seismic activity will continue to increase, posing risks to our already delicate communications web. We need to maintain our current timeline."

The president, General Tate, and Dr. Sang were huddled around a speakerphone in the control booth that overlooked the cavernous operations center inside Cheyenne Mountain. Below them the room was abuzz with headphoned officers stationed at every available desk, speaking to silos across the country or tapping out Morse code instructions. At the front of the room, the massive bank of computer screens was blank, all except the one in the center that showed the countdown in red digital numbers. It had just broken the two-hour mark.

Reyes told Moscow to hold, then muted the line. "What do you think?" she asked her two trusted advisors, who looked haggard and in need of a stiff drink, bed, or both.

"I agree with Dr. Semenov," Eugenia said. "Stress on the continental plates is growing as the waters keep moving. Who knows what it'll be like in a few days?"

"We're only gonna get one shot at this," Reyes said. She looked to Tate, who was standing near the glass window, staring at the countdown. "Walter?"

Tate turned to face his commander-in-chief. "President Reyes, it seems we're looking at a literal now-or-never situation. I agree with Drs. Sang and Semenov. We lose the ability to talk to our people manning the silos, that could be the whole ball game. Same for the Russians. We have a plan in motion. I advise we stick to it."

Reyes walked over and put her hand on his shoulder. "Almost showtime, huh?" she said, drawing a wry smile from him. Behind them, Eugenia popped a pink bubble.

Reyes walked back to the table and unmuted the line.

"Okay, Leonid. Let's maintain—" she started to say before Tate cut her off.

"Hold on a second," he said, loud enough for the folks in Moscow to hear. He squinted down into the operations center where his assistant, Second Lieutenant Jill O'Neal, was jumping up and down and waving her hands like someone trying to get on a jumbotron. "What the hell is she doing?"

O'Neal spoke frantically to an officer at one of the desks and then made a mad dash up to the control booth. She burst into the room, the door slipping out of her sweat-slicked grip and crashing against the wall.

"General, sir," she sputtered, "we have Peterson on line seventeen. You need to punch them in."

"Whatever it is can wait," he said, turning to the president with an apology on his lips. But for the first time in her professional career, Jill O'Neal snapped at her boss.

"Listen to me, goddamnit! You need to put them through *right now*."

Tate was stunned into silence. Reyes had never seen him look so confused. "Leonid, please hold on," she said.

"No, ma'am," O'Neal said before the president could mute the line. "Dr. Semenov and the others will want to hear this too."

"Okay, O'Neal, you win." Reyes puzzled over the blinking buttons on the phone with no idea how to merge the calls. Eugenia leaned forward and punched a few keys, bringing in line seventeen.

"This is the president," Reyes said. "who am I speaking to?"

Through the speakers in the control booth at Cheyenne Mountain and in the conference room in Moscow, a voice spoke that no one had ever expected to hear again.

"This is Commander Yanez Prescott of the International Space Station."

Reyes looked to O'Neal for some sort of explanation.

"They showed up at Peterson's south gate," she said.

Several seconds passed before Semenov's voice, now sounding very distant, broke the silence. "Madam President, what is this? We do not have time for fantasies."

"Commander, this is quite a surprise," Reyes said. "Can you tell us how you made it back?"

"Our orbit was compromised and we had to do an emergency evac of the station," the commander reported.

Semenov broke in. "This woman is an impostor. The crew of the ISS was lost."

"The window was small and we had to initiate a modified ballistic re-entry," Prescott continued, undeterred. "Our capsule landed in New Mexico."

"What about the rest of the crew?" Reyes asked.

"We experienced problems with our main chute and retro rockets. Unfortunately, astronauts Susan Beck and Anatoly Semenov didn't make it."

The line went silent as both sides of the Atlantic absorbed this information. Reyes felt a pang of compassion for Leonid. He'd now learned of his brother's death twice.

"I'm sorry to hear it, Commander," she said. "Though I'm pleased you at least are still with us. However, we're in the middle of discussing a rather important matter, so unless you have some new information . . ."

"I do, Madam President. Before we left the station, I ejected the drive from the sensor array mainframe. I have it with me now."

Looks were exchanged around both rooms on both continents, no one sure what to do next.

Then Semenov broke the silence. "He had a tattoo on his left calf."

"Who am I speaking to?" Prescott asked.

"The tattoo! What was it?"

"It was a logo for his favorite band, Alice in Chains," she said without hesitation. "But it was on his right calf, not his left."

Silence.

And then, weakly, his voice heavy with emotion, Leonid Semenov said, "She's right."

"How do you know?" Prescott asked.

"Anatoly was my brother."

General Tate had been watching the digital countdown on the center screen down below, now at 1:43. But with the Russian's confirmation that Commander Prescott was who she claimed to be, he took action.

"Lieutenant O'Neal, coordinate with base security at Peterson and perimeter control. Get Commander Prescott in here now!"

51

Rose and Midge had tried their best to clean Bruce's old truck before they left town, but there were still splashes of bird shit and a stray feather or two near where Michael sat with his back against the cab. Jimmy's body was stretched out next to him, his head resting on a moldering sack of potatoes, the truck rattling beneath them both as Rose drove them slowly toward Cheyenne Mountain.

They were part of a convoy composed of nearly fifty cars, trucks, vans, and campers, many commandeered from the town, all filled with Michael's faithful traveling to witness his sermon on the Mountain. Anyone else who had tried this route had been turned away days ago, so the path was clear. Twin police cruisers trailed the truck carrying Michael, their bubblegums lit in honor of their fallen sheriff.

"Do you remember homecoming junior year, Jimmy?" Michael said aloud. "The theme was Camelot or King Arthur and his court or something. We spent three days decorating your dad's truck to look like a castle. We even made the tailgate a drawbridge. Your old man was so pissed when he realized we hot-glued some of the cardboard to the bumpers. But we took first place in the parade. You spent all night at the dance asking girls if they wanted to storm the castle with you. I found you the next day passed out in the back next to Tonya Arrington. She was curled up with a bunch of empty wine coolers against the back gate, so she didn't get it too bad. You were face down in the middle. Your back and bare ass were so sunburned, we called you Sir Purple Tush that whole summer. Man, you were in bad shape."

He looked up at the object, evanescent and ever watchful as his caravan of followers streamed toward Cheyenne Mountain, then looked over once more at his best friend's corpse. "I mean, not as bad as right now, obviously. But still, pretty bad."

A fly crawled up Jimmy's blood-speckled cheek and onto his eyelid. Michael waved it away then licked his thumb and tried to scrub off one of the larger drops of blood from Jimmy's chin, but only managed to smudge it. Jimmy's flesh was cold and rigid despite the sun beating down on them and the heat radiating off the scraped and dented truck bed.

"You idiot," Michael said, his eyes lingering on the bullet holes in his friend's chest. "You could have helped me. You could be helping me right now. Instead, you're just lying there. Dead! Dead as a doornail, you fucking idiot asshole!"

He thumped his head against the cab as he sat back. Midge jumped in the passenger's seat at the sound. Rose reached back and slid open the small window.

"Father, are you okay?"

"Please, Father, let me switch places with you," Midge pleaded. "It's nice and cool up here."

Michael waved them off. "Thank you, no. I need to be here with Jimmy."

Midge nodded and closed the window.

"Loyalty," Michael said, thumbing behind him to the two women. "Why couldn't you have been as loyal as them? But no, you chose my sister instead. Still storming the castle, huh, Jim?"

Up ahead, two jeeps were parked across the road with a set of wooden sawhorses, creating a poor barrier against the crush of vehicles bearing down on them. The four soldiers on duty scrambled as the caravan approached. One jumped inside his jeep and picked up the radio handset while two others grabbed rifles and took knees on opposite sides of the road. The fourth soldier addressed the convoy through a bullhorn.

"Stop!" he shouted, holding out his hand, palm facing the two trash trucks that led the parade. "This area is restricted! You must turn back now!"

The Franklin police squawked their sirens as they zipped up the shoulder on either side of the trash trucks. One of Jimmy's men got on his cruiser's PA and ordered the soldiers to get out of the way. The trash trucks blared their horns.

"We *will* open fire!" the bullhorn soldier screamed, but his voice was drowned out by the oncoming vehicles. He looked to the guys on either side of him and nodded.

Rifle fire rang out. The police cruisers fell back as bullets pinged off the hoods and radiators of the two massive trash trucks. One of them spewed steam, but both jumped forward as their drivers ducked low in their seats and put their feet to the pedals.

The soldier screaming into his jeep's radio handset reversed off the road. The two that had been firing on the caravan squeezed off a few more rounds before diving into the back of the jeep that the last soldier, bullhorn tossed aside, was frantically trying to crank to life. It started to move, but before it could get clear, the trash trucks barreled through the sawhorses and caught the front of it, spinning it off the road like a top. The convoy streamed through the wreckage and continued on toward the Mountain.

But just as their destination came into view, three armored personnel carriers appeared on the road ahead of them. The heavy-duty trucks' back gates banged open, and a flurry of soldiers jumped out hauling sandbags. They quickly piled the bags on the road as gunners took up the flanks.

Michael's caravan came to a stop about a hundred yards from the barricade, and everyone started piling out of their vehicles and moving forward on foot. Michael was about to jump over the side of the truck bed and join them, but then knelt down and whispered into Jimmy's ear.

"I know I should forgive you, but it's so hard," he said, tears sliding down his dust-crusted cheeks. "I just wish you could be here with me at the end of it all."

Michael turned his face to the sky. He shielded his eyes against the sun and held the object in his gaze. A chopper ripped across his line of sight.

Michael looked down on his best friend for the last time. He leaned over and kissed Jimmy's forehead.

"Time for me to get gone," he said, then leapt over the side of Bruce's truck and into the fray.

52

NOEL LOOKED out the chopper's window at the people pouring from the vehicles below. She thought she recognized a few of the cars, and when she saw the Franklin police cruisers and the trash trucks, she knew Michael was at the Mountain.

The helicopter circled the road twice and then came in for a landing halfway between the barricade holding off the crowd and the south portal to the Mountain complex. The side door slid open as soon as the skids touched down.

"There's a truck waiting to take you inside," the pilot said through their headsets. "Good luck, Commander."

Yanez slung her backpack over her shoulder and hopped out first, followed by Noel and the others. As soon as they were clear, the chopper lifted off, sending up a swirl of dirt and dust that momentarily blinded everyone. And when it cleared, Noel saw her brother.

He stood at the front of the crowd that had gathered across from the sandbags and soldiers. She took a few steps in his direction, but a soldier grabbed her arm and pulled her back.

"Ma'am, we have to go. My orders are to get you and yours into the Mountain, pronto."

"But I can help here," she said. "I know their leader."

"Don't worry, they aren't getting up this road. And they'll be sorry if they try."

"That's what I'm afraid of," she said. "Two minutes."

"Ma'am, I can't. General Tate'll have my ass."

But Noel was already jogging off toward the barrier. Behind her, she heard Walsh talking to the soldier, presumably convincing him to let her go. Apparently it worked, because the man didn't follow.

Unfortunately, the soldiers at the sandbags weren't as amenable. They wouldn't let her through.

Frustrated, Noel jumped and waved her arms to get Michael's attention. When he looked her way, she shouted to him.

"What in the hell are you doing here?"

Michael wiped tears from his grimy, smiling face. "My Lord, sister. You are as constant as the stars. Or at least as constant as they used to be."

"Mike, you can't be here."

"These soldiers don't get to decide that," he said. "God decides, and He's shown me that this is where I must deliver our message to our people."

"Listen to yourself! When did it become *our* people, Mike? When did you suddenly become so damn special?"

Her words must have struck a nerve, because Michael clenched his jaw and took a few steps toward her. The soldiers at the barrier screamed for him to hold his ground. If several of his followers hadn't grabbed him and pulled him back, the situation might have turned to violence.

"Go home," Noel said to him. "Or people are going to get hurt."

"People have already gotten hurt, Noel."

The way he said the words made fear shoot up her sweat-soaked back. She stepped up onto a short stack of sandbags and scanned the crowd, shading her eyes as her head swiveled back and forth. But the one person she was looking for . . . he wasn't there.

"Michael! Where's Jimmy?" she asked. Though somehow, she already knew the answer.

"He's gone, Noel," Michael said, never breaking eye contact. "He's dead."

Noel took the information like a snowball to the face—shock followed by rage. Jimmy was dead. It didn't feel real. But she knew Michael wasn't lying. She could see the truth in his eyes.

The blow delivered, Michael turned to his followers and addressed them. "I intend to put an end to all the treachery!" he shouted. "I will give the liars and deceivers and cowards a final chance at redemption before God's mighty hand strikes down upon this Earth and metes out His justice!"

The crowd roared hallelujahs and pressed forward toward Michael, which caused the soldiers to tense, guns at the ready. Noel screamed at him, but either he couldn't hear her over the cacophony that had erupted all around him, or he simply didn't care.

One of the soldiers grabbed Noel around the waist and hauled her back toward Yanez and the others. She struggled and fought against the soldier, desperate to get back to her brother, to spit at him and call him a liar. But just then a tremendous crack echoed across the valley, the sound pounding off the mountain walls and pulsing through her body, tossing everyone to the trembling ground. The road opened up, swallowing the entire barricade, one of the personnel carriers, and a few screaming soldiers. More screams sounded from farther away, and Noel looked on in horror as another fissure opened right in the middle of Michael's flock.

———

Michael could do nothing but watch as the ground swallowed his people. In barely more than the blink of an eye, the entire back half of the crowd that had caravanned from Franklin disappeared into the bowels of the Earth. Gone.

Michael tried to look for Noel, but hands were grabbing at

him, pulling him away from the barricade. He stumbled and fell to the ground, which sprang up to catch him, and his forehead connected with a jagged sliver of rock.

His vision went red. The ground continued to convulse around him, but his gaze was heavenward, directed at the messenger in the sky, seen now through a haze of blood.

I'm too late, he thought as his vision dimmed and the screaming faded to a soft hum. *I failed them.*

And then the ground dropped away.

Noel found herself on her back, looking up at the object burning in the sky above them. She hated it and thought it was magnificent, which made her hate it more. *It changed Michael into a monster and killed Jimmy. And now it wants to steal the rest.* She gazed at its awesome and terrible beauty and refused to let that happen.

The soldier who had dragged her away from the barricade helped her to her feet as Walsh, Yanez, Aster, and Del gathered around her.

"Are you okay?" Yanez asked.

"We need to get in there and end this *now*," Noel said.

They hurried toward the truck that would take them into the Mountain, but before they could reach it the ground fell before them, tearing the roadway in half. Walsh, in the lead, disappeared into the hole in an instant; Yanez, on his heels, reached for him, missed, and then scrambled for a handhold as she slid down the crumbling shoulder. A bit of sagebrush was the only thing that prevented her from following Walsh into the widening crevice.

Then a thrumming grew behind her, echoing from across the valley leading back to Franklin and Blue's Bluff. She clawed back up the rocks to the road above, scraping her hands raw. The sound intensified as the ground continued to crack and split. She reached the top, and one of her knees almost buckled as she tried to stand on the heaving ground.

"Yanez, hurry!" Noel yelled.

Yanez turned to see that Noel, Del, and Aster were already on the other side of the deep crevice that had swallowed Walsh. They stood on its edge, hands out and ready to catch her.

Yanez backed up a few steps and then ran at them, right to the edge, and jumped. Her foot touched down on the other side, but her damaged knee folded and she started to fall backward into the gaping hole. Noel reached out and grabbed her arm before she toppled backward, but Yanez's torso twisted and her backpack slid off her shoulders. It bounced once on the edge of the fissure, and then disappeared.

Noel yanked Yanez back from the precipice, and they both fell to the ground, which bucked beneath them like a rodeo bull. They held each other until the tremor passed, then Yanez skittered back to the edge of the fissure. She breathed a sigh of relief when she saw that her backpack had gotten hooked on a shard of asphalt. It was too far for her to reach, but it was there.

"I see it!" she screamed.

"Forget it. We need to get inside," said their soldier escort, now rising to his feet.

"No, we need it!" Aster yelled. She belly-crawled to the edge of the fissure and looked down. "Del, get over here! Grab my ankles and don't let me fall!"

Del didn't argue, just rushed over. "I got you!" he yelled over the rumbling, which was building again. Little pebbles toppled into the fissure as he grabbed Aster's feet and helped lower her down. Noel grabbed hold of Del's waist to make sure he didn't fall in as Aster became almost completely vertical in the hole.

"A little more," Aster yelled over her shoulder to Del. He passed the instruction to Noel, and they managed to lower the girl a few more inches.

"That's as far as we can go!" Noel shouted.

Aster reached for the backpack, stretching her fingers and brushing the canvas. She strained a bit further and was just about to wrap her hand around one of the shoulder straps when she saw a dark smear of blood on the rocks next to it. She looked past the backpack and found herself staring down into Walsh's dead eyes. One of his shoulders was wrenched up higher than his ear, and a booted foot was next to his jaw.

Her stomach rolled, as did the ground above her.

"Aster, hurry!" Del yelled, straining to keep his grip on her ankles.

She reached for the pack again, trying to avoid looking at Walsh's twisted corpse. The minute she had snagged the shoulder strap and pulled it free, she shouted, "I got it!"

Del pulled with everything he had while Noel supported him. When they had her waist over the edge, Del wrapped an arm around her and rolled her out of the hole on top of him. Noel flopped back onto the vibrating road. Yanez grabbed the pack, but instead of checking on the drive inside, she set it aside and flung herself atop Aster.

"That was crazy brave, kid."

"Crazy stupid," Aster said, squirming from between her and Del, who was sucking air hard.

"Okay, let's move!" the soldier shouted, grabbing Noel's hand and yanking her to her feet.

They all sprinted to the truck. One of its back wheels was already sinking into the leading edge of the fissure.

"Move, move, move!" the soldier hollered, leaping over a crack to get to the driver's side. Everyone else ran to the passenger's side and tumbled inside en masse.

The soldier cranked the engine and threw it into drive. The tires spun and kicked up gravel as the wheel that had sunk into the fissure popped up onto the roadway. Then they were accelerating toward the south portal.

Noel looked back to see more of the road disappearing behind them. The truck jumped as a shock wave rolled across the mountain.

"We're coming in hot! South side!" the soldier yelled into his radio handset.

"Any unwelcome guests?" a voice replied over the truck's speakers.

"Negative. But we lost a visitor."

"Roger that."

"Maybe Walsh is okay," Yanez said. "We'll tell them to go look for him as soon as we get inside."

"He's not," Aster said, not looking up from her lap. She leaned against Del, who threw his arm over her shoulder.

"We have a visual on you," said the voice on the radio. "When you get inside, head straight to the control center. POTUS is waiting."

53

THE CONTROL CENTER was a hive of activity. Rows of men and women wearing headsets were talking simultaneously to silos all over the country while flipping through spiral-bound binders and working on computer stations. Several soldiers were unspooling a thick cable from the front of the room and feeding it to a central console whose guts were spilled out everywhere, wires of all sizes and colors spaghettied onto the floor, while others stood at the ready with flashlights, screwdrivers, and rolls of electrical tape. At the front of the room was a wall of screens, though all were dark except for one showing a countdown in bright red numbers. Whatever it was counting down to would occur in just over half an hour. Directly beneath the glowing numbers, a small cluster of people were gathered around a general, who was speaking into a black plastic phone receiver from the 1980s.

All of it would have been mesmerizing to Yanez and her group if it weren't for the sight of the president of the United States jogging toward them, a hand already extended in greeting.

"Commander, I can't tell you how happy we are that you made it home," President Reyes said. "We'd feared the worst."

"Thank you, Madam President," Yanez said. She unzipped the main compartment of her backpack and took out the drive she'd risked her life to carry home from the International Space Station. "I hope our analysts can find something on this that will shed light on our situation."

"Me too. But right now, we just need the CliffsNotes version," Reyes said, taking the drive and turning it over in her hand. "Eugenia, I need you!"

A woman poked her head up from a console, looked like she was about to protest, then saw who the president was talking to and ran over.

"Wow, Ms. Prescott. I mean, Commander Prescott. You're really here and not dead."

Reyes made introductions, then handed the drive to Eugenia. "We need to know what's on this before that timer hits zero."

"Right!" Eugenia said. She moved down the aisles of consoles, pushing operators aside.

"Madam President, it's an honor," Noel said, coming up behind Yanez. Aster snuck in next to her, while Del hung back.

"Bonita Reyes," the president said, shaking Noel's and Aster's hands. "You're to thank for getting Commander Prescott here, I assume?"

"Yes, ma'am, in part. I'm Noel Williams, ma'am. I used to be on sat comms at Peterson. This is Aster Meekins. And back there is Del Curley."

"Private Walsh helped us too, but he didn't make it," Aster said, looking at her feet. "I never knew his first name. We just called him Walsh. I'm sorry, ma'am."

"No, I'm sorry to hear that," Reyes said, resting her hand on Aster's shoulder. "But thank you for what you've done. And just in the nick of time too."

"Madam President, if you don't mind me asking, what are we counting down to?" Yanez asked, nodding at the numbers ticking away on the central screen.

"A nuclear strike on the object," the president said. "We've coordinated with the Russians. We plan to hit it with everything we can muster from both our arsenals."

Before Yanez could ask for more details, Reyes turned to shout at Eugenia, who was in a frenzy running from console to console.

"Is there a problem, Dr. Sang?"

"Still looking!" Eugenia yelled, holding up the drive.

Just then, voices burst through the speakers in the room, and a small cheer went up from the technicians who had been working on the wiring in the open console.

"Leonid, can you hear us?" Reyes asked loudly.

"We hear you, Madam President," said a Russian voice. "Glad you are back."

"Likewise," she said. "While we were down, Commander Prescott joined us."

She turned to Yanez and gave her a silent okay to talk.

"Dr. Semenov," she said, "we brought the drive. I hope it helps us. I would not have gotten it here without Anatoly's help. He was a remarkable astronaut . . . and a very good friend."

"My brother was a hard man to impress, Commander Prescott," Semenov said. "But he was always impressed by you. I now understand why."

Eugenia's voice cut through the room. "None of these work!" she cried in frustration.

"What do you mean?" General Tate said, walking over to join her. "This facility is state-of-the-art."

"That's the problem," said Eugenia. "The space station runs on older tech. Well it did, until it went careening off into space."

"How old do you need?"

"We need something from like the WOPR era," she said, launching a droplet of spit onto his tie clip and then wiping at it with her sleeve.

"The what?" he asked, gently stopping her clean-up effort.

"You know, the computer that you guys used to use to practice blowing up the Russians and the rest of the world," she said, then clapped her hand over her mouth. "Umm, sorry, Dr. Semenov."

"Eugenia, that computer was from a movie. But if you need old equipment, I can show you where we store it."

Eugenia looked up at the countdown, which was ticking down to twenty-seven minutes. "We'd better hurry."

As the two of them took off at a run, Reyes followed, taking Yanez's hand and pulling her along.

"Let's go see what you brought us," she said.

"Yes, Madam President."

Reyes called back to Del, Aster, and Noel.

"Well? You guys coming?"

They caught up to Eugenia and Tate as he swiped his badge and placed his palm on a scanner beside a door down the hall. Once his clearance was verified, he led them inside. The lights flickered on automatically, illuminating ten-foot-high shelves filled with all sorts of equipment from the last five decades, including whole rows of old phones, dot-matrix printers, fax machines, typewriters, and even carousel slide projectors. Eugenia flew down the aisles, her head on a swivel, deep into the storeroom and out of sight. The others fanned out among the shelves.

"What should we be looking for?" Reyes asked.

"A modular server, blade or rack. Doesn't matter!" Eugenia shouted from somewhere in the room.

"In English!" Tate said.

"It's tall, not like a regular computer," she said. "With a bunch of the same-looking drives stacked on top of each other or side by side."

"Probably a black or gray metal case," Yanez added. "And the drives will have handles."

They shoved old equipment aside or pulled it off shelves and onto the ground as they hunted for anything that matched Eugenia's description. Aster was searching in an aisle filled with boxes of wires and circuit boards, much like she'd done days ago in the radio station. She was sad that the place she'd gone to to look at the stars—and where she and Noel had bonded after the world stopped—was now just ash and cinders. *But maybe we can fix it,* she thought. *We just have to fix the planet first.*

She shoved aside a heavy plastic tub, accidentally spilling a bunch of old punch cards from the dawn of the computer era. As she crouched down to start picking them up, she came face to face with an IBM blade mainframe.

"I think I got something here!" she said, pushing aside other boxes to get at the machine. She tried pulling it out, but it was much heavier than she expected. "Del, I need you!"

Del ran over and helped her pull the server free. Together they slid it across the floor to an open plug. Aster snaked the cord over to the wall just as Eugenia came around the corner.

"Eureka!" she shouted and slid in front of the machine like it was third base. "Find me a keyboard and monitor!" she yelled as she ejected one of the drives, confirming that the pins on the back matched the ISS drive.

A minute later, Tate and Reyes came around the shelf carrying an old RGB tube monitor. It was so clunky it took both of them to manage it. Del took it off their hands and set it on the ground next to the mainframe.

"Keyboard, keyboard," Eugenia said, and was surprised when Noel climbed down from a shelf right behind her and handed her a dull tan behemoth with cigarette burns and coffee stains dotting the keys.

Eugenia slid the ISS drive into the slot and turned on the machine. Everyone huddled around and peered over her shoulders as she sat, legs splayed out on either side of the monitor, keyboard on her lap. The fans sputtered and spun, kicking a decade or more of dust out the back of the machine, and a blinking green cursor appeared, which let Eugenia bypass the startup. Her fingers flew over the keys.

"Here we go!" she said.

54

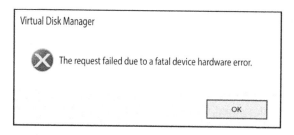

"WHAT DOES THAT MEAN?" Tate asked.

Eugenia pulled the drive out of the server and examined the pins on the back; all of them were fine. She flipped it around, checking the structure for damage. Finding nothing concerning, she leaned forward and blew into the slot, eliciting a tiny puff of dust from inside the computer's shell. Then she slid the drive back into position and repeated the startup sequence.

The result was the same.

"I'm sorry, Commander," Eugenia said, looking over her shoulder at Yanez and the others.

"Damn it," Reyes said. "That's too bad."

"We need to get back now, ma'am," Tate said.

The president gave Yanez's shoulder a small squeeze. "I'll go tell everyone," she said, then headed back to the control center followed by General Tate and Eugenia.

"It can't be," Yanez said, dropping down in front of the computer. She tried several ways to access the drive, but the dialog box remained. She pulled out the drive just as Eugenia had and ran her fingers across the pins. Reaching into the mainframe, she felt for obstructions, then slid the drive home again, her head right next to the slot to listen for the click. Then she restarted the machine, only to have the same dialog box come back.

"Noel, help me," she said, pointing to the plug.

Noel yanked the plug out, listening for the computer's fans to spool down. Then she plugged it back in again.

"Come on, baby," she said as she moved behind Yanez. "We need this to work."

Yanez didn't fire up the machine right away. Instead she closed her eyes in silent prayer. She thought of Anatoly and Susan in the canyon, Del's drone, Morse code, finding Noel, the family in the woods, her blue rabbit's foot, and the old couple by the river. All of it, every event from the very beginning to this moment, passed through her mind as she prayed. She ended with an "amen," opened her eyes, flipped the switch on the front of the server . . . and sighed when her prayers went unanswered.

"Maybe if we try another machine?" Noel said.

"The server and port are fine," Yanez said. "It's the drive itself."

"But we can't give up. We need that data!"

"It's over, Noel," Yanez said. "The drive's empty."

"It can't be. There has to be an answer, or this was all for nothing. People died for nothing!"

Yanez stood up and took Noel's hands. "Sometimes there are no answers. Just questions."

"You still got it here," Del said. "That's gotta count for something."

Yanez stood before these three strangers who had risked

everything to help her. And in that improbability, she found a tiny glimmer of hope.

"Not me. *We* got it here," she said, smiling. "Now let's go finish this journey."

When they got back to the control center, the countdown ticked past 6:33. But now the timer wasn't the only thing being displayed; it was surrounded by video feeds of the object, taken from various locations on the ground.

Eugenia was still arguing with the president about the drive. "If we had more time, I'm sure we could get in there and pull out some of the files," she was saying. "I know a data forensics guy who worked with me at the university. Dude's a whiz."

President Reyes stopped her. "We're *out* of time," she said. And then more loudly, "Leonid, do you agree?"

"Yes, Madam President," he said, the disappointment clear in his voice even over the thousands of miles that separated them. "We will proceed as planned. Startup sequence to commence momentarily."

The room fell quiet. There was nothing left to do but watch the numbers tick down to zero.

"Maddy, are you there?" Reyes asked.

"Yes, ma'am."

"Can the rest of the delegation hear me?"

"We hear you, Madam President."

"Secretary of State Frederick, none of us have any idea what's about to happen," President Reyes began. "But if we lose contact after launch, you are to work with the delegation and Leonid's team to figure out what the hell comes next. I grant you the authority to represent the United States and the contingency of nations from North and South America."

"Understood, ma'am," Madelyn said. "And, Bonita? Good luck."

The president joined Tate and Eugenia in front of the monitors. Yanez collapsed into an empty seat, all of the energy she'd mustered in the days since returning to Earth sapped from her. Aster stood off to one side at the back of the room, hugging herself as she watched the screens, and Noel walked over to her and took her hand.

"Remember what happened the last time you and I were in a control room?" Noel asked.

Aster smiled. "Do you think it'll work?"

Noel looked at the screens. One of the cameras corrected a lens flare and then zoomed in closer on the object, luminous in the clear sky, utterly unchanged since its arrival, its halo of blasted, vaporized atmosphere still encircling it.

"I hope so," she said, and hugged Aster to her side.

The countdown entered its final minute.

Waves of raw emotions crashed through Noel's mind. She thought about her brother and tried to remember him as he used to be, and not the person he'd become. She wondered where he was, and if he was alive or hurt. She wanted to let go of her anger and disappointment and just be worried about him, but she couldn't. Not after all he'd done. Not after what had happened to Jimmy, the man she'd grown to love.

They say time heals all wounds, she thought. *I hope they're right.*

The numbers ticked away. *It's all a matter of time now.*

"Here we go," General Tate said.

5 . . .

4 . . .

3 . . .

2 . . .

1 . . .

The screen flashed zeroes. Static crackled over the line. Operators on both sides of the planet confirmed launches, and everyone awaited visual confirmation.

A single streak angled up toward the object—the leading missile in Earth's assault, a vapor trail streaming out behind it.

Then others popped into view on various trajectories, an armada of rockets all heading for the same target, white lines from their exhausts crisscrossing the blue sky.

The lead missile climbed higher and higher. Seconds later, fire bloomed around the point of impact. The object quivered, its frozen halo shimmering in the blast. A second missile struck near the first, a wave of flame erupting from the side of the object. Dozens and dozens of others were right behind, on the verge of inflicting an unprecedented amount of damage on the mystery in the sky.

But before they could, it disappeared.

And the world went sideways.

Noel was the first in the control center to regain consciousness. Aster was lying on top of her, out cold, with a small trickle of blood on her lip where she appeared to have bitten through. Noel gently pushed herself out from underneath the girl and then leaned over her, calling her name and tapping her cheek. Aster came around, and grabbed at her lip.

"What happened?" she asked.

"I don't know," Noel said, getting to her feet. As she rose, she saw others were doing the same.

But not General Tate.

"Walter, are you okay?" Reyes asked, hovering over him.

"General," Eugenia said, kneeling at his side.

They turned him over onto his back, only to discover a deep dent in his forehead surrounded by dark, purpling skin. The rest of his face was ashen.

"We need help here!" Reyes called.

Del stumble-ran to them, a twisted ankle already starting to balloon. He knelt down next to Tate and felt for a pulse. Not finding one, he put his head to the general's chest. Jill O'Neal nearly fell on top of them as she came around a console, brushing past the president so fast she didn't have time to think about pushing aside her commander-in-chief. She watched helplessly as Del started chest compressions, then let out a sharp gasp when he eventually stopped.

"I'm sorry," Del said, shaking his head.

Reyes touched Tate's cheek then grabbed Jill's hand. "He was one of our best."

"Yes, ma'am," Jill said as the tears came.

The screens at the front of the room hung from their moorings. Some had come completely off the wall and lay broken on the floor. The ones that remained were either blank or showed static.

"Maddy, are you there?" the president said as she stood. "Moscow, are you with us?"

An operator scrambled over to the console where they'd patched in the feed from the subterranean cable that linked Europe and Russia to the States. He put one of the cans to his ear and listened.

"The line's dead, ma'am," he reported.

"Keep trying—"

"Look!" Aster yelled, pointing to one of the screens. It had come back online and was showing green startup code. Then the code vanished, replaced by an image of the bright Colorado sky.

And something else.

A black void hung where the object had been, its edges jagged and torn. The frozen clouds had been replaced by a shockingly clean and crisp cerulean blue. Static rippled across the image, affecting its overall clarity, but the most important thing was crystal clear.

"It's gone!"

"Are you sure?"

"What is that?"

"Did it change somehow?"

President Reyes slapped the console next to her to regain order. The room got quiet, but all eyes stayed fixed on the screen.

"Let's slow down," she said. "Could it be camera error?"

"I don't think so, ma'am," the operator said.

"Are you sure we're looking at the right spot?"

The operator grabbed the logbook at his station and compared the x- and y-axes displayed at the bottom of the feed to the last entry for the working camera.

"The astral coordinates on the screen match the object's location," he said. "The camera is off its previous horizontal tracking angle by maybe a half degree. But that's it."

"Wait, it's off?" Noel asked. She ran over to him, pulling Aster with her. "Show me."

"Yeah, but just by a little bit," the operator said, handing her the book.

"Every little bit matters," Aster said, looking at the book alongside Noel.

"Where is this feed coming from?" Noel asked, scanning the entries.

"It's from Peterson."

As Noel confirmed that the data in the log matched the display at the bottom of the screen, the horizontal tracking angle grew from 0.42 to 0.43 degrees.

"It's spinning!" Noel said, hugging Aster. "The Earth is spinning again!"

"Wait, how do you know that?" Reyes asked.

"I know this equipment, ma'am," Noel said.

"Satellites, right?"

"That's right. All of our on-the-ground cameras like this one are fixed on specific points in space. Those coordinates, the x and y you see up there on the screen, they don't change, ever."

"And why does that matter?" the president asked.

"In order for them to maintain their fix on a specific point up there, the camera tracking angle constantly shifts down here to compensate for the Earth's rotation."

"So, since the angle's changing, that means we're spinning?" Reyes asked, just as the horizontal angle grew again, this time to 0.44 degrees.

"Yes, ma'am, it does," Noel said, frisbeeing the logbook in the air and back into the hands of the operator.

Deep sighs came from all corners of the room, to mix with the soft sobs from Second Lieutenant Jill O'Neal as she knelt over her dead mentor.

And then, for the second time in as many minutes, someone pushed past the president. This time it was Eugenia. She pulled a chair over to the screen and climbed up on it for a closer look.

"What are you doing?" Reyes asked.

"Do you see these streaks?" Eugenia said, pointing to a spot just below the black void in the sky.

"They're just clouds, aren't they?"

"No . . . I mean, they look like it, wispy clouds stretched thin in a breeze, but there's a spiral pattern here, which doesn't make sense unless . . ." Then realization struck. "Oh, fuck," she said, cupping her hand to her mouth.

"What is it?" Reyes asked.

"I think it's the missiles."

Eugenia jumped off the chair, ran to the terminal near Noel, and started frantically typing. Then she struck a key and the image on the screen changed to a table of numbers.

"What are we looking at now?" Reyes asked.

"It's the camera log," Eugenia said. "It appears this camera has tracked its assigned point in space across the sky multiple times since we launched the assault on the object."

"Wait, how long were we unconscious?" Yanez asked.

The president looked at her watch. "A couple minutes, tops."

"How many times does it say the camera tracked back and forth?" Noel asked.

"Six," Eugenia said. "The exact number of days that the object was here."

Noel grabbed hold of Aster's arm to steady herself. Her vision swam as she looked at the forward monitor.

"That's impossible," she said. "There has to be a mistake."

"Ladies, what does all this mean?" Reyes asked.

Eugenia shook her head. "I don't know how, but it seems that in the time we were unconscious, the Earth compensated for all of its pent-up rotation." She hit a key, bringing the original image back up, and pointed. "I think those streaks are vapor trails from the rockets that didn't hit the object. It looks like they got caught in the super-accelerated atmosphere and were whipped around the planet multiple times when the Earth corrected itself."

"Where are they now?" Aster asked.

And that's when the most improbable guffaw of all time erupted from Yanez. "Son of a bitch!" she said. "It's just like the fucking tomato plant."

Everyone else was clearly confused. Eugenia did a double-take at the screen.

"Explain," said the president.

Yanez shook her head. "What I mean is, even though they're confused right now, those missiles will figure out which way is down soon enough."

And they did.

55

Five Years Later

"Hey, are you there?"

Noel's eyes fluttered open and her breath billowed out in the cold July air. The inside of the station was lit only by a faint orange glow from the dying embers in the wood stove and the red and green LEDs on the board. She pulled her thick blanket tighter around her shoulders and listened to the crackle of static from the speakers.

She'd spent most of yesterday helping get the new Tucson relay online. Snow and sleet had taken down the old radio tower there, and getting the new one at Wasson Peak up and running had required hours of walking a fairly green operator through the fundamentals.

We should just be happy we found anyone at all to man it, she thought as her eyes closed again. After the mass migrations south, there weren't a lot of people left in the Arizona safe zone, let alone tech-savvy ones.

"Noel, pick up. It's me."

She let out a long sigh, threw back the blanket, and sat up. Her back instantly protested, and her feet followed as soon as she set them down on the cold concrete. Form had definitely suffered at the hands of function when she and the army engineers rebuilt the station on Blue's Bluff. But at that moment, with the fire low, her feet frozen, and her back a shambles, her thoughts turned to maybe getting a better couch and a throw rug or two.

She stood up and walked to the board.

"I'm here. What's up?"

"Good morning to you too," Aster said over a baby's fussing, which quickly turned into a high-pitched wail. "Ah, shit. Hold on a sec."

Noel walked over and scrubbed at a spot on the frozen window so she could see the solar panels. Three of them were covered in snow and would have to be cleaned off first thing.

"Sorry about that," Aster said when she came back on.

"How's Izzy?" Noel asked.

Aster had named her daughter after the nickname for the old International Space Station.

"Teething, but otherwise awesome."

"Is Del back from his run?"

"Yeah, he got in yesterday afternoon. Izzy went nuts when she saw him."

Noel popped in a coffee pod and watched as her breakfast slowly filled the NASA mug that Yanez had given her on her last trip to Canaveral.

"What's the news?" she asked as she dumped in a few sugar cubes and stirred with her index finger.

"Salt Lake's about the same. Radiation levels are still over the limit, but he said they're better than last year."

"Lower's better than nothing, I guess."

"It'll still be a few years, they figure, before we can move anyone in."

Noel looked at the map she had tacked to a corkboard next to the main panel. She took a red pen and drew an X through Salt

Lake. "That's too bad," she said. "The Billings station will just have to hold out a little longer."

"I've got some good news, though."

"Good enough to wake me up three hours before my shift, I hope."

"General O'Neal just stopped by and said that Sat Launch Five is a go. She wants us in a meeting at ten this morning to go over the new orbital pattern with Eugenia and the others."

Noel took a sip of her quickly cooling coffee and looked through the window at her tower. The steel crossbeams were coated in ice, making the whole thing glow as dawn broke across the bluff, and the pearlescent sunlight reflecting off the steel was reminiscent of the light that had bounced off the object for those six remarkable days.

"Did you get that?" Aster asked, snapping Noel out of her trance. She set her coffee down and blew into her cupped hands.

"What makes them think this one will be any different than the other four?" she asked.

The previous launches hadn't gone well. The satellites had reached geosynchronous orbit and were able to maintain ground communications for a short time, but eventually every one of the satellites had been drawn into the void and disappeared.

"They think they can keep this one's apogee low enough to stay out of the void's pull," Aster said. "We'll get the whole story at the meeting. I'll see you when you get here."

"I'll be there," Noel said, then severed the connection.

The sat launches had only started eighteen months ago, once the atmosphere had cleared and temperatures had risen to the point where rocket launches were feasible. It was all part of the plan to re-establish a global communications network. Aster had joined the team right before Sat Launch One. It was unusual for someone her age and without an advanced degree to get such an assignment, but recommendations from the president and Yanez, the new head of NASA, carried some weight. Sometimes Noel and Aster would stand together in the control center and joke about the school trip where Aster broke the sky. In between the launches, they led a small team that monitored national radio communications, the tower at Blue's Bluff serving as a central hub for the country.

She rinsed her mug and set it in the strainer to dry. Then she put on her boots and heavy coat and left the station to clean the panels. As she rounded the corner, she saw someone walking up the path between Scylla and Charybdis.

Despite the heavy, fur-hooded parka, she could tell that he was rail-thin. Wind gusting up the canyon threatened to knock him over as he walked toward her across the open face of the bluff. His long hair and beard whipped around in the gale, obscuring his face.

"Hello," Noel called when he got closer.

"Hi, sis," he said, pushing back his hood.

Michael's eyes were sunken and dark. His sharp cheekbones protruded above his natty beard, shot through with gray. A jagged scar ran across his nose, which had taken on an odd angle.

"You're really here?" she said, half expecting him to say no and confirm her delusion. But he didn't.

"It's good to see you," he said, keeping some distance between them and struggling to maintain eye contact, his gaze darting back and forth between her and the snow-covered ground.

"Where have you been?" she asked.

He threw out his arms and shook his head back and forth as if searching for an explanation. "South," he said, "in Mexico for a while and down around Nicaragua near the continental rift. Lots of places, I guess. And really nowhere too."

"Why did you come back?"

"I got tired." He took a step toward her, and Noel reflexively took a few back.

Two months after the missile strikes, when they finally unsealed the Mountain, Noel had gone back to Franklin and found where Michael had buried Jimmy in St. Anne's Cemetery, a frozen pack of Marlboro Reds at the base of the makeshift cross, so she knew he was alive. But then the years passed, and she'd resigned herself to never seeing him again.

"Tired of what?" she asked.

"Thinking," he said, holding back a sob. "Believing. I don't know, all of it."

"What does that mean?"

"Please, Noel, don't."

"No, I need to know. Talk to me."

He almost let his gaze go to the sky, but then snapped it back to the ground. He pointed to the void without looking at it.

"I don't know what He wants from me," he said. "In five years of searching and praying, I still have nothing. I lost my church and my home. I lost my faith so many times, and every time I had to fight to get it back. I don't even know if I have it right now or if it's gone for good. I don't even know if I care. And I lost the people I cherished most. I lost you."

He fell to his knees in the snow, tears streaming down his face. "I believe in my heart that that thing is a message from God," he said. "But I still don't understand what it means. And I'm afraid I never will."

"You won't find those answers here," Noel said. "So tell me why you came back."

He hugged himself, rocking back and forth. Then he looked up into his sister's eyes and told her the truth.

"I'm scared, Noel."

"Of what?"

"That I'm the only one who feels this way. I'm scared that I'm all by myself. And I don't want to be alone anymore."

She stood apart from him and watched him shake with cold and grief. Then she felt something release inside her, something she'd held close to her heart for all the years since she'd last seen him at the Mountain. And it felt good to let it go.

"You're not alone," she said.

And she rushed to her brother.

She fell next to him and took him in her arms. They

embraced each other for a long time, letting years of angst and fear and rage and hope and sadness crash down on them and then evaporate. Noel felt wrung out and empty, but also fuller for the first time in a long while as she held her brother. But finally she pushed back from him so he could see her face.

"I don't know who it's a message from, or even if it is a message," she said. "I've tried to figure it out, too. A lot of us have. And none of us know what it means. None of us do, Mike. We don't know if that thing up there now, or the thing before it, is from God or the universe. But that's okay. At this point, it has to be okay."

"But which is right?" he asked, his dark, desperate eyes full of tears.

She took her big brother's hand, kissed the back of it, and held it to her cheek.

"Let's let it be both," she said. "You and me. We can let it be both now."

Michael nodded and sobbed as he clung to her. When he quieted down, she pulled his hood around his head and then helped him back to his feet.

"Come with me," she said.

He followed her to a tarp-covered vehicle parked next to the station. She pulled the heavy canvas off, revealing a strawberry-red snowmobile.

"Doesn't quite replace the bike," Noel said, "but it ain't too bad."

"Where are we going?" Michael asked.

"First, my place, so you can get cleaned up. You look like a hobo. Then we'll go check out what kind of pie Rose made today."

"She's here?" A smile broke across Michael's face for the first time in a long time.

"Yeah. She and Midge rebuilt the Biscuit."

Michael grabbed Noel's arm and turned her around so they

were facing one another. He wiped the leftover tears from her face before wiping away his own.

"I'm so sorry," he said.

"Me too."

She kissed his cheek and then hopped onto the snowmobile. As she started up the engine, she patted the seat behind her. Michael glanced up at the void and then climbed on behind his sister and knitted his arms around her waist.

"Let's go home," he said.

THE END

ACKNOWLEDGMENTS

This story swirled in my head for a long time. So I must begin with apologies to anyone whose ear I bent and patience I tried during its formative years. You know who you are.

In addition, I owe my deepest thanks:

To my first readers—Evan, Christine, Scott, Pete, Blair, Emily, Jim, Stephanie—who encouraged me and helped sand off the rough edges of this story;

To my remarkable editor, David Gatewood, whose genius made this book far better than it would have been otherwise;

To my parents and in-laws, for their love and unwavering belief in me;

To my brother and sister, for their friendship and laughter through the years;

To my sons, Ben and Charlie, for being the source of all my hope in this world;

And to my wife, Jill, for everything, always, forever.

ABOUT THE AUTHOR

Lou Iovino was born in Philadelphia, Pennsylvania. He splits his time between working in advertising, writing, and teaching. He lives in New Jersey with his wife and two sons.

Skybound is his first novel.

For more information, visit www.louiovino.com. You can also find him on the following social channels:

 facebook.com/louiovinobooks
twitter.com/LouIovino